Three Came Home
A Civil War Trilogy

Volume 2 – Sam

It was Spring and the bloodletting at Franklin was done. General Lee surrenders and only General Johnston and his small army of 21,000 stand in the way of complete victory by the Union Armies. After the battle of Bentonville, Johnston has 2,606 less men.

Sam Atkins and 18,000 ragged Confederates wait at Durham Station to see if they will have to again fight the well-armed and rested Federals. Seeing no way out, Johnston surrenders, and after giving up their rifles, Sam and his friend Leander, begin their long walk home through a devastated South.

In a Southern patriot's barn, they meet up with Alabamian, George Forrest, who, through a series of odd circumstances, fought with the North.

While cleaning his pistol, Leander accidentally wounds George. Sam reluctantly promises the mortally wounded George, the last man to die in the Civil War, that he will go to Alabama and tell his family what happened to him. On his way home to Florida, Sam encounters a fleeing Jefferson Davis, discovers a cache of Confederate gold, befriends a freed slave, and meets his first love in a series of events that will forever change his life.

If they break up, in God's name let the Union go... I love the Union as I love my wife. But if my wife should ask and insist upon a separation, she should have it, though it broke my heart.

—President John Quincy Adams

This book is dedicated to all the Confederate and Union Soldiers, then and now

Three Came Home

A CIVIL WAR TRILOGY

By

Edward Aronoff

Volume 2: Sam

SECOND EDITION

Three Came Home Publishing

There is no better soldier than a volunteer who fights for a cause.

—General, A.P. Hill

Printed in the United States of America

Three Came Home: Vol. 2 – Sam

ISBN: 978-14993715-6-7

Three Came Home Publishing Co.
Box 1253 Banner Elk, NC 28604

Other books by Edward Aronoff:

Betrayal at Gettysburg

Last Chance

The Pagliacci Affair

Three Came Home: Vol. I — Lorena

Three Came Home: Vol. II — Sam

Three Came Home: Vol. III — Rutherford

Toxic Food/Healthy Food

The Wartime Memoirs of Robert E. Lee

To order any book, contact:
edwardaronoff@yahoo.com

or write:
Dr. E.S. Aronoff
Box 1253, Banner Elk, NC 28604

Registered members of the Barstow County Yankee Killers, the Chitwood Brothers, Daniel, John and Pleasant, link arms and brandish their pistols and Bowie knives after enlisting.

Franklin was the blackest page in the history of the Lost Cause

Sam Atkins, Company H

Preface

At his map table, General Hood shifted his weight to his one good leg, looked up at the dark, pregnant layer of cumulus clouds and felt the cold drops of rain on his face. "Rain, rain, rain," he muttered. "This damned rain will not stop, and my army sloshes and stumbles through this downpour in a sea of mud." Hood turned his lamp up and lifted the waterproof tarp. He stared at the map of Tennessee.

There was a noise to his left. Hood turned. "Ah, General Cheatham, I see you're awake." Hood covered the map.

"Yes, General Hood, I am awake and eager to get at General Thomas."

Hood grimaced and shook his head. "It's not Thomas we face yet. First we must get past Schofield."

"Better yet," Cheatham replied. "Thomas is a Mississippian and can be stubborn. Schofield is made of less sterner stuff." Cheatham wrinkled his brow in thought. "Even though, surprisingly, Schofield fought well yesterday at the Spring Hill Crossroads."

Hood nodded his head and stroked his beard. "Schofield fighting well? That would be a surprise, General. No, it wasn't Schofield you faced, but General Stanley. It was Stanley who stopped us cold. Schofield is a pudgy fool. General Stanley is a fighter."

Hood put his good hand on the general's shoulder. "Cheatham, yesterday we went at Schofield's army piecemeal. Today you will charge all of your men at the same time with General Cleburne in the Van."

Hood fell silent and looked north as if he were searching for his wayward cavalry. "If only Forrest and his 6, 000 had stayed with us we could keep Schofield busy at his rear, while we attacked his line head on." Hood's face colored under his prophet's beard and his lips twisted into a snarl. "If we can do that today, then we will go after Thomas and avenge Atlanta."

"But, sir," Cheatham said, "you promised the men, no more headlong charges—"

Hood's face turned cold. "The men have become cowards, Cheatham. Haven't you noticed how laggard they are? A good headlong charge will make them heroes again."

Cheatham's face turned crimson and he shook his head in anger. He remembered the bitterness in the faces of the men returning from Hood's futile charges. "Cowards? General, I'll have you know these soldiers are the bravest—"

The sound of a large horse's hoof beats in the soft earth interrupted Cheatham and made the two men turn toward the sound. As the horse came closer they heard the sound of the rider's saber rattling against his leg.

+The newcomer pulled up before Hood. As he dismounted he spoke sharply to the aide following him. "Take my horse and have him fed and watered. Tell the men to rest but not to sleep. I think very soon we will have a good deal of business to do around here."

The man handed the reins to the aide, turned and saluted Hood. Hood's face reddened and he did not return the salute.

"General Forrest!" Hood said angrily to the newcomer, "where have you been? And you, of all people, should know better than to make such a commotion before a sleeping enemy."

Forrest glared at the commander, his eyes hooded, his pointed beard bristling. "General, the rain and mud were what slowed us down. And as for the noise, it's too bad someone didn't make some noise last night to tell you Schofield was walking by you in the dark."

"What?" Hood's face blanched. "He's not at Spring Hill?"

"No, General, he's not there," Cheatham said, his face coloring, "Apparently no pickets were placed to tell us Schofield was sneaking by us. My scouts tell me he had his men secure anything that would make a noise and stole away at one o'clock in the morning."

Hood bristled and banged his good hand on the map table. "My plans are ruined. When this battle is over we will convene a courts martial and punish the fools who let them escape."

Forrest turned and faced north. "Now you can be sure, Thomas will come down from Nashville and reinforce Schofield." He spun on his heel back to Hood. "With Thomas in charge we will have a hard day."

Hood eased himself down on a field chair at the map table. While they had been talking, the rain had stopped, the temperature started to drop and snow began to fall. Forcing himself to calm down, Hood looked up at the leaden sky and said softly, "Well, God's blessings. It's cold but at least the mud will freeze and we'll be able to move swiftly." He lifted the rubber tarp covering the maps and stared at the map of Tennessee on the table.

Hood pointed to Nashville and tapped it with his index finger. He then balled up his good fist and spoke through clenched teeth. "Cheatham!" Hood struggled to his feet and turned to the general. "If we can get a blocking force to Columbia before Schofield, we can defeat him there with our larger army. He reached over and tapped the city of Columbia on the map. "Then we can turn and take care of Thomas coming down from Nashville. Let us attack them at daybreak and break Schofield even if though his troops be led by Napoleon."

Cheatham shook his head. "Our men are brave, General, but the Yanks will be hard to move if Schofield digs in. I don't like the looks of this fight. Schofield and Stanley will have a good position and will be well fortified."

Ignoring Cheatham, Hood turned and addressed Forrest. "General Forrest, let's forget the past. I am relying on you to get to Columbia before Schofield and bar his way. We will then proceed to deal with him first, and then turn on Thomas." Hood pointed to his resting army. "This could turn out to not only be a local victory but a turning point for the entire Confederacy."

****

The Confederate Army of The Tennessee stood at parade rest waiting for its commander, General Johnston.

Sam Atkins, Company H, first platoon looked along the sparse line of men and whispered to his friend, Leander Huckaby. "After that battle at Franklin there aren't many of us left, Leander."

"Sure enough, Sam, an' if wuz up to that butcher Hood, they'd be even less."

"Too bad, Leander, for a while we had them by the scruff. But give credit when it's due. The cavalryman, Wilson led his smaller band of horsemen against our Forrest and beat him in detail. I don't know where them Yanks are getting their new cavalrymen, but they're sure enough better than the old ones. By the way, Leander, how many generals did we lose at Franklin?"

"Don't rightly know," Leander said, "but it sure was a passle."

Sam shook his head. "What a waste."

"I been in a lot of battles, Sam, an' seed a lotta men killed, but that Franklin takes the cake. The ditch closest to the Yankees was filled with our dead, all the way up to the top." Leander shook his fist at the sky. "That damned Hood sent us into a slaughter pen to be shot down like animals."

"Leander," Sam said sadly, "I hate to say something bad about an officer, but the wails and cries of widows and orphans made at Franklin will reach all the way to Richmond and beyond. It's a good thing we're now with Johnston. He knows how to fight."

****

At Franklin, Hood's officer class was devastated. He lost six generals, countless lesser officers and non-coms. In addition 7,000 Confederate soldiers were killed, wounded or taken prisoner. Instead of learning his lesson, Hood insisted his men charge into Nashville and defeat, Thomas. That wasn't to happen. As soon as the weather cleared, General Thomas attacked the freezing and starving Confederates first. The result was a forgone conclusion.

After losing another 6,400 men, Hood retreated and asked Richmond to be relieved. The army then scattered, most making their way home as best they could, while some, like Sam, joined General Johnston.

For four long years I have learned nothing but how to kill.

— SamAtkins

Chapter 1

Durham Station, North Carolina
5th April 1865
Dear Ma:
Please excuse my writing on the back of this wallpaper, but there ain't one piece of writing paper left in this whole dang army. When you send me a letter, please leave half of it empty space for me to write back on or else I'll have to write to you on the envelope. Writing paper here is now a dollar a sheet.
I got this wallpaper, for writing paper, when the boys tore down the porch of this ol' house for firewood. Don't worry Ma it was an abandoned place. The folks who

lived there were too smart to stay when they saw us coming. Anyway the boys said it was empty. Either way it was tear it down or freeze. I can tell you, they's a lot of homes 'round here that folks won't come back to no more.

I had a terrible duty yesterday. You remember Rowland, the Indian boy from Cherokee County? You know, the boy what helped us harvest the tobacco four years ago, when the work got too much for Dad and us boys. Well, anyway, 'afore the law was enacted that said, 'you're in for the duration', Rowland served his enlistment and got out.

I guess when he got home, he thought it over and decided his Chief, Stand Waitie, the Cherokee Nation, and the Confederacy was all wrong. Anyway, for whatever reason, he went north and joined up with the Union Army.

A few days ago, Colonel Anderson led us on a raid into the Union lines. Of all people, Rowland was one of the Yankees we captured. The colonel remembered him, and that was the end of that.

Most of the boys who knew him were real angry and wanted to shoot him down like a rabid dog right there, but Colonel Anderson wouldn't have none of that. So yesterday they had a Summary Court Martial. Of course Rowland was found guilty right away and sentenced to death.

After dark, some of the boys tied him up like a hog, cut all his hair off. Injuns must not like that 'cause, Rowland yowled about it for quite a while. Anyway, they left him out all night in the rain. I felt awful for him so I snuck out about midnight and gave him a blanket. It didn't help him much, but it sure made me feel better.

The next morning he was rudely yanked up off the ground by Sergeant McCord, and dragged in front of the men. I guess the generals were aiming to set an example for us.

Ol' Rowland showed some kind of courage though. He stood in front of the company, alone and naked, and stared down his captors.

I tried to hide as they were making up the shooting detail, but the Sergeant found me and 'afore I knew it I was standing at attention, my rifle at shoulder arms, with eleven other men.

Rowland was brave I'll give him that. Because of the rain, the grave they dug for him was half-full of water. Of his own accord, he went to the foot of the grave then turned and looked directly at us. 'Boys,' he said, looking over his shoulder at the water in the hole, 'Give me a drink of that would you. I hear water is scarce in Hell.'

But, the captain wasn't impressed by his heroics. He turned to us and said, 'Shoot the bastard!'

I fired over his head but some of the other boys didn't.

When the minié balls hit him, Rowland flew back as if someone had jerked him with a rope. His face became a bloody mask and he fell with a splash into his tomb.

The sight of him dropping lifeless into an unmarked grave was worse to me than all the other Yankees I've killed, and Momma, I've killed a bunch. God rest all their souls.

You know, if Rowland was an officer, they'd a given him a parole, and sent him on home. It doesn't seem quite fair. A General can resign, and that's okay. A private, that's another story. He can't quit. When he joins up, he can't even choose his branch of service. If he gets a letter from home telling him his family is starving and they need him, that's too bad. Then, if he leaves to help his folks, that's desertion. If you're a deserter, with General Bragg for instance, then it's certain you face the firing squad, jes like ol' Rowland. They's lots of times a boy wants to stay and fight, but his feet just won't let him and he gets executed too. It don't seem quite fair, does it, Ma?

Well, the army is stirring now and I gotta go. They's no food to eat, but someone in the squad up'd and got some green corn yesterday and we're gonna do something with it this morning. Even if they cook it I don't know how I'm gonna chew it 'cause all my teeth are loose. God, I'd give a year's pay in gold for a piece of your apple pie.

Rest easy about your first-born, my older brother, Dave. I saw him yesterday and he looked fit as a Texas steer. Say hello to Pa and tell your youngest son not to grow up too fast, and to definitely stay home on the farm with you. You sure don't want him to see the things I've seen.

One thing I can tell you, if I ever get outta this army, I swear to you and God, I'll never kill another living thing.

Love, your son, still alive and kicking.

Sam Atkins

Sam

All that's left of us are starved skeletons

Chapter 2

His pulse increased when he saw her at the top of the stairs. She looked over the crowd and then her eyes met his. The radiance of her smile warmed him.

She moved down the spiral staircase slowly and elegantly, while her family and the gathering of guests clapped politely.

Sam looked fondly at his beloved. Her raven hair was combed smooth from the part in the middle of her scalp down to her elfin ears. From there to her neck her hair hung down in a profusion of curls. One bright, white magnolia blossom was nestled above her right ear. Her bodice was cut low with a fall of lace against her creamy white bosom. She wore a scarlet wide-hooped gown, made of the finest velvet, with cream colored lace adorning the sleeves. Her dress, narrowed at a fashionable tightly laced waist, required two slaves to pull and tie. The hoops canopied over secrets that only Sam would soon know. Her matching red Parisian slippers pointed towards him, only him.

Their eyes locked, and she smilled so sweetly it made his heart beat faster.

He took a step on the scarlet colored carpeted stair toward his beloved.

Ho! What's this? A grimy man with an unkempt beard moved into Sam's way. Cadaverous men now appeared on the stairs, their bony, grasping hands pawed at her clothing. Hovering behind the men were dirty women with blackened and missing teeth. They shouted and asked for milk for the vacant-eyed children at their breasts.

Who let these people in? He had to get to her. He looked over the crowd for his beloved. They would run away together. *Oh God, she's being carried away by these people.*

There was fear on her face. Her plaintive voice called to him. "Help me, please, help me —"

He reached for his rifle but his arms were pinned to his sides. He couldn't move. He panicked and struggled to no avail. The lice-covered filthy-smelling crowd was pushing and pulling, separating the lovers. "Hang on darling, I'm coming… I'm coming…"

Someone grabbed Sam by the shoulder and was pulling him away from her… away from his beloved…

****

"Dammit, wake up Sam, and stop calling me darling."

Sam sat bolt upright on the hard ground. Damn these dreams. *In the daylight my imagination is a joy. At night it's a curse.*

He shook his head as he touched his face, felt his scratchy beard and laughed to himself. *This is not the face of the Sam in my dream.*

He shook his head at his silliness. *Here I am, dreaming of drawing rooms and society dances with women who are out of my reach. What a fool I am. That world was never mine, and anyway it's gone, even for the gentry. It exploded forever with the first shell at Fort Sumter.*

"Sam, you was movin' 'round somethin' fierce. What was you dreamin' 'bout?"

"A nightmare, Leander, just a nightmare."

Leander Huckaby spread his arms wide, taking in the entire encampment. "Ha! This whole bivouac is a nightmare."

Sam looked around at the ill-kept camp. Human debris littered the field. "More like a place everyone just collapsed with exhaustion," Sam said softly. "I guess that last fracas at Bentonville did our boys in; 60,000 well-equipped Yanks against 20,000 Rebs. Not quite an even battle I'd say. We bloodied their noses all right, but if it wasn't for General Hardee coming to our rescue at the last minute, we might be on our way to a prison camp right now. Or maybe, if he hadn't come on time, we'd all be pushing up daisies."

In the background, Sam heard the pleasant singing of a bubbling brook, the sound saccharine against the harshness of the two veteran armies.

Yesterday, all night long, stragglers kept coming in after falling out on the hard double-time march from Bentonville. During the long next day of waiting, Sam watched strong men turn weak in the burning sun, their parched bodies seeming to melt like wax figures in a hot fire.

Only the foolish and the brave kept up, and only us stupid doughbellies came back.

Sam laughed at himself realizing how absurd it was to keep running from the Yankees. "All that's left of us are starved skeletons our own mothers wouldn't recognize," he said aloud. "We're not much of an army any more, we're just ragged and naked Rebels. And, to top it off, our whole damned army is plagued with the scourge of diarrhea. I don't know what it is that keeps us going… keeps us fighting... Leander, this is a hell of a way to fight a war." Sam sat down on the wet ground shaking his head.

Leander reached into his shirt and picked off a few lice and crushed them with his fingers. "Damn graybacks," he muttered.

Sam looked at him fondly. Leander Huckaby was from the same county in Florida as Sam. His folks grew cotton and tobacco, farming just a few miles south of Sam's home near Lake City. The two boys had grown up together, gone to the same one room schoolhouse, and smoked their first corn silk cigarette in Sam's barn when they were ten. Sam smiled remembering his coughing fit after his first puff.

Leander was tall, rangy and used to be muscular. Now he was like the rest of this army of scarecrows, thin and hungry. He had wavy black hair and a thick, full beard. His face was usually in a scowl and his soldierly complaints were legendary in an army whose complaints would make a mule skinner blush. His dark brown eyes darted continually, looking for food. He also had a remarkable proclivity for staying alive. When he spoke, one could hear the cracker accent heavy on his tongue. Leander's family came from South Georgia and brought with them, to Florida, that deep South politeness, that quiet exterior that hid a violent passion underneath. *The south Georgians are so courteous one moment and so full of rage the next.*

Leander and Sam had joined up together and, except for the second and third days at Gettysburg, when Leander was in the hospital wounded, had been in the same company ever since. Being in combat together had made them closer than just childhood friends. They now had an unbroken, everlasting bond of brotherly communion.

Shorter by a head than Leander, Sam was thin and wiry even before he was starving. After four years of marching, fighting and Confederate commissary mischief, there was not an ounce of fat on his lithe body. Underneath his stretched skin his muscles were like ripples of steel. Though his ribs could be counted from a few feet away, his eyes sparkled with Confederate pride and his Enfield rifle was always clean and ready to fire.

He was clean-shaven when he could be, but just now, because of Yankee pressure, he had a five-day stubble. His somber blue eyes were made darker by his hair, the color of corn silk, bleached ever whiter by years in the sun. His finely chiseled features and patrician nose seemed fit more for a drawing room than a battlefield. His once gray uniform was in tatters, and only hinted at the proud Confederate costume he had first worn four years ago.

Sam had escaped adolescent skin problems and still had that look of youthful innocence, which belied the large number of enemy soldiers he'd killed. He escaped death so many times he thought his number might be up soon. Sam secretly despaired of still being alive when the war ended, although the latest talk of surrender around the camp gave him a glimmer of hope.

Sam looked up and squinted at the sun's ray poking through the pine trees that surrounded the field. *Gonna be a hot one*, he thought, as he got up and stretched. A southern wind blew across the field kicking up dust. Sam put his hand over his eyes and cursed as the dust particles got into them anyway. "Goddamn this war," he muttered.

"Better not cuss the war too hard, Sam. Them Yanks'll hear ya and think they won 'afore we have ter quit."

Sam feigned a look of annoyance. "I ain't quitting, you dumb doughface." Sam jumped up and leaned toward his friend his jaw jutting out. "Listen here, Huckaby. You and me been together since 'afore we went to school. We've been in this man's army since Bull Run, and you're my best friend. But, I suwannee, if you don't stay outta my business I'm gonna have to whup you."

The dark haired giant jumped up. "Whup me? Ha!" He danced around Sam with his fists raised pumping them in the air like a shadow boxer. "C'mon ya damn webfoot." Leander threw some punches into the air. "Whup me, will ya. Let's do a few bare-knuckle rounds. Let's just see if'n you kin whup me."

Slowly and deliberately, Sam dropped his jacket on the ground, made two fists, and at the same time flexed his shoulders. He eyed his large, ungainly adversary bouncing around like a drunken ballet dancer. "All right, Leander Boy, let's you n' me go a few—"

A thunderous voice bawled out behind them. "Hooookaby! Eeeekins! I see you two got some extry energy left fer fist-ee-cuffs."

Sam and Leander froze then braced to attention without being told.

"Maybe digging a few latrines might help to tire ya'll out a bit."

A bow-legged, grizzled Sergeant with a black beard speckled with gray, and a florid face with a large bulbous nose, loomed over Sam and evil-eyed the larger Leander. One fist was on his hip, the other shaking at the two soldiers. His black eyes blazed with authority. He had a foghorn voice that a soldier could hear above the din of battle, and eyes that pierced right into your soul.

The sergeant was a Texan, and regular army. He had spent all of his adult life in the United States Army, getting his schooling for the present war fighting with General Scott against the Mexicans. In a decisive battle he lost several fingers from his left hand at Cherubusco, which left him with a voice like a bull seeing red, and a disposition to match.

When the Confederacy seceded, he contemplated whether or not to remain loyal to Washington. However, when his brigadier, a Kentuckian named Hood joined the Rebellion, naturally the sergeant had to go with him.

Even with his spectacles off, the sergeant could take out a squirrel's eye at a hundred paces with his rifle. The men respected him not only because he knew how to fight on the battlefield, but more importantly, he knew how to keep a green soldier alive.

Despite that, Leander told Sam that since he had met the sergeant his life had changed from one of passive unhappiness to one of active misery.

More than once both men had received a blistering tongue-lashing from the Texan.

They both sheepishly looked at the ground.

"Sorry, Sarge, we didn't mean anything.

"Yeah, Sarge, we wuz only foolin'."

"Hookaby, let me see yer rifle."

"My name is, Huckaby."

"Hookaby, Hackaby, what's the difference. Let me see yer rifle."

"It's clean, Sarge."

"I'll be the judge of that, Hookababy."

Leander bristled but reached down, picked up the rifle and reluctantly handed the sergeant his Enfield.

The sergeant snatched the rifle, stared at Leander for a moment, then put the muzzle to his eye and looked down the barrel. The sergeant lowered the rifle slowly and gave Leander a withering stare. Without warning he flung the rifle back at Leander. "This rifle is filthy. Clean it 'afore you get in formation."

Leander reacted, his eyes flashing. "Clean it? What for? I ain't got no shoes, my ass is hangin' outta the rips in my pants an' I ain't et in two days. Why should I worry 'bout a few spots on this damn gun?"

In a flash the sergeant was on his toes, leaning in nose-to-nose with Leander. His face was purple rage, his eyes two bright pinpoints of hostility, and flecks of foam escaped from the sides of his mouth as he spat out the words in a gritty, menacing voice. "Cause this war ain't over yet, Hookaby. And, not only does your life depend on that rifle but also the lives of these men around you, *includin' me.* I don't give a damn 'bout your shoes or yer ass. You kin fight nekked if that's what it comes to. But one thing you kin count on is, yer rifle is gonna be clean and ready to shoot at all times."

With a sudden move the sergeant grabbed Leander's crotch.

Leander yelped and tried to push the sergeant's hand away from his delicate organ, but the sergeant's grip held him in place.

"And remember, you dumb Cracker, this is your *gun.* What you have in yer hand is *yer rifle.*" He grabbed Leander by the hair with his other hand, let his crotch go, and drew him down, face to face. "You got it?"

Leander's face went bright red and he trembled with fury. He struggled for words but his rage wouldn't let them out. He knocked the sergeant's hand away and, balling his fists, went back nose-to-nose with him.

Sam knew Leander, once aroused, was dangerous. He was sure his friend was about to attack the bandy-legged sergeant. Taking a quick deep breath, he quickly wedged himself between them and pushed Leander back. Over his shoulder he said, "We'll clean our rifles right now, Sarge. C'mon Leander let's go."

Sam half walked, half dragged his angry friend back to their tent. The sergeant watched them leave, hands on his hips, staring at their backs.

"Whew, that was a close one," Sam said when they got to the tent. "It's a shame that so much pain in this army is brought on by men with small minds."

Leander kicked the smoldering ashes of the fire in front of the small tent. "Small mind? That goddamn Mick! My ass is hangin' out in the breeze, an' I'm starvin to death an' all them sergeants is worried 'bout is groomin' horses and cleanin' guns. You shoulda let me be, Sam. That bow-legged son-of-a-bitch needs a lesson."

"And you'da been put under guard, maybe court-martialed. Do you know what you can get for striking an officer? Even a non-com sergeant?" Sam touched his friend's shoulder and lowered his voice. "Leander, be reasonable. It looks to me like this war's gonna end soon and I wanna go home. I don't wanna be waiting for you to get outta some damn jail, or worse, watching you get shot. 'Sides it's his job to be the assistant inquisitioner."

"Inquisa— what?"

Suddenly the sergeant was with them again. This time his face was tranquil and his manner easy. "Boys, ferget cleanin' them rifles. No time for it nohow. The lootenant jes tol' me to git y'all into formation." Now git, 'afore ah change mah mind," he growled good naturedly.

Sam grabbed his rifle and ran swiftly to line up with the rest of the company. Leander sullenly trailed behind him.

Leander got in line next to Sam and looked down the short line. "Not many of us here. There must still be a lot a stragglers."

"Must be, Leander." *Mostly the thinned ranks are due to deaths and desertions,* Sam thought, but he said nothing. He knew Leander was well aware of the state of things. He knew the Rebel Army was ill-clothed, ill-armed and starving; he didn't blame anyone for leaving.

The company captain came to the front of the troops, returned the sergeant's salute, then turned and nervously waited for the colonel.

"Dammit, Sam, the captain parades up there at the front and gets all the credit, when the whole brigade knows it's you that runs the platoon and sometimes the whole damn company."

"Quiet, Leander. You know a private occupies a social position roughly equal to that of a Hindu untouchable."

"Quiet, hell… A Hindu what? What the hell you talkin' 'bout? Anyway it's you that should be up there, not him. What the Devil do they teach them fellers up there at West Point?"

"It's not that, Leander. I been at this for four years and he's green as a spring stalk of corn—"

"Hoookabee! Eeekins! Cut the chatter and face front," the sergeant bellowed.

The captain stared at Sam, a frown across his face.

Sam's face colored. "Yes, Sergeant," he yelled back. *Damn Irishman, he pronounces our names as if he bit into a rotten apple and saw half a worm.*

There was sudden movement at the front and the diminutive bow-legged Colonel Fields appeared in front of the troops. Sam always laughed to himself when he saw Fields. *His legs are so bowed you could drive a horse right under the colonel without disturbing him. Don't matter how he looks though, he's a fighter. Good as Stonewall, some say. He's got a soft face, but when you look in those black eyes you know he's a dangerous man.*

Without fanfare, General Johnston appeared out of the woods on horseback and stopped behind the colonel. At the sight of him the army began to buzz like a newly disturbed beehive.

The general leaned down and said something to the colonel. Fields nodded, turned back to the men and shouted, "Battalionnnn!" The buzzing stopped.

The other officers echoed him all the way down to Company.

Fields waited an extra moment then yelled, "Attentionnnn!" In a split second the entire army brought its heels together as a unit, and stood ramrod straight. Sam felt proud of his army. *We may look like damaged goods, but we're always ready to fight.*

Colonel Fields looked over the men carefully, then shouted, "At ease." The men relaxed and stayed in place. Most of them put their rifle butts on the ground and leaned on the weapons. A murmuring buzz again rose among them.

Fields cleared his throat and began to speak, this time more softly. "Quiet men, General Johnston has somethin' to say."

Sam put his hands on his rifle muzzle then rested his chin on the back of his top hand. He studied the General, and then wondered how he would describe this moment in his next letter.

****

Durham Station, North Carolina.
26th April, 1865
Dear Ma:
I don't know what's going on but it looks like something important is about

to happen. General Johnston himself is just fixing to tell us something, and I hope he'll tell us we're going to fight Sherman to the last man.

I know you never seen General Johnston but picture this. He's a man, about fifty, small in stature, compactly built with black, restless eyes. It's strange but when he looks at you, it's like he's looking right through you. And if you speak to him you'd best be telling the truth.

I tell you, Ma, Ol' Joe Johnston has greater military insight than any general of the South not excepting even Jackson or General Lee. I know, I fought under all three of them.

He dresses like a perfect dandy, wearing the finest clothes that can be bought. Every article of clothing he has is prescribed by the war department in Richmond, even down to his horse, bridle and saddle. His light gray coat is tied with a bright red sash, and his black boots have large silver spurs that jingle and tell you-watch out-he's coming. His only deviation from a regulation uniform is his hat. That's decorated with a star and feather that he wears like the white plume of Navarre.

And he's tough make no mistake about that. He had seventeen men shot for cowardice at Tunnel Hill and executed a whole company that bolted at Rockyface Ridge. He also hung two spies at Ringgold Gap. But all of them were executed for crimes, not for spite, like that infernal Bragg. General Johnston is loved, respected, and admired by all the officers, and the men worship him.

Well Ma, one day this durn war'll be over, and then I hope you'll be seeing Dave n' me right soon. I saw my brother Dave only yesterday morning so I know he's okay. (Okay is soldier talk for alright)

I love you Ma, and Pa too.

Your loving son, Sam Atkins, still alive n' kicking.

P. S. Paper is still scarce. It costs one and a half dollars a sheet now. In fact, since I haven't got a dollar and a half,

I had to write a letter for a man to his wife, to get this sheet of paper I'm sending you. I borrowed the pen from another man, the ink from a third. Then I had to find a tree stump to write on. That was easy, our artillery shot down quite a few.

Tell Leander's Mom and Dad that he's okay, and that we'll both be home real soon. (I hope)

****

The murmuring died, and a stillness descended on the troops. In the background the wind kicked up and the company flags made flapping sounds.

General Johnston thanked the Colonel then turned to the men. He sat still in his saddle looking over the ranks for a full minute before he spoke.

Sam had the feeling that, although the General was looking at the troops, his mind was somewhere else.

"Generals, bah!" Leander whispered. "They get all the publicity but what are they? I'll tell you what they are. They're companies, brigades and armies. They're a whole bunch of us men. Sure, they get the glory; what private would be remembered? Not a one. Them generals sure will be remembered though, every one of them, good or bad." Leander kicked the ground making a small spray of dirt. "An' believe me, they's more bad than good."

General Johnston took off his hat and put it on the pommel of the saddle and absently brushed at his thinning gray hair. His slim, spare body was ramrod straight on his horse. It amazed Sam that he was always so clean and neat, and stayed so, even in the thick of battle.

After four months of fighting across 130 miles of rugged Georgia hills, Johnston and General Sherman had fought themselves to a bloody draw on the way to the battle of Atlanta. Only when President Davis replaced Johnston with Hood was Sherman able to drive the Confederate forces out of Atlanta. Johnston would never forget or forgive the humiliation caused by President Davis replacing him with General Hood.

The army quieted as Johnston began to speak. "I have received a communiqué from General Lee," he said, his voice quavering with emotion.

At the mention of Lee's name there began an audible buzzing of wonder from the troops.

Johnston adjusted his metal-rimmed glasses, fit them snugly on his ears, and looked down at the paper in his hands.

Sam noticed by the trembling of the paper that his hands were shaking.

"General Order Number Nine, from General Robert E. Lee, head of the Army of Northern

Virginia, and Overall Commander of Confederate forces," he began.

The men began to murmur again and Johnston looked sharply up and over the entire assembly as if he were a schoolmaster. He frowned and nodded his head as he saw stragglers come out of the woods and slip into the ranks.

Sam watched a man sheepishly take a place in front of him. *I thought all the missing troops had surrendered but it appears they had just been stragglers. Maybe, if there are enough of them there's still a chance— No, it's a fantasy. General Lee is too far away. And we wouldn't stand a chance without him against Sherman's hordes.*

The men quieted and Johnston began again. "General Lee's order says:

After four years of arduous service, marked by unsurpassed courage—

Sam tensed. Leander pulled at his sleeve. "What's he sayin', Sam? You think we're quittin'?"

—and fortitude, the Army of Northern Virginia has been compelled to yield to overwhelming numbers and resources—

In the rear men began shout, "No, no!" The shouting moved toward the front until all the ranks were shaking their fists and yelling, "NO!"

Leander took off his forage cap and, in a sudden fit of anger, slammed it to the ground. He turned his head and spit a long brown stream of tobacco juice. "Godammit, we are quittin', but I ain't. No sir, I'm goin' to the woods and fight."

Even though he knew surrender might be coming soon, Sam felt sick. *All the marching and all the dying, and for what! For nothing!* His mind flashed over some of the battles he had been in: *With Beauregard at Shiloh, fighting against Prentiss at the Hornet's Nest.* With pride he thought, *And I was with Jackson at Chancellorsville.*

In his minds eye he saw a picture of himself standing at attention, and in awe, when they brought the great Jackson in mortally wounded. *I am ashamed that I joined in calling him 'Fool Tom' when he made us march in the freezing cold to Romney. Most of us had no shoes, but that wasn't his fault. The locals told us later it was the coldest winter they had ever seen.*

It was after Romney that Sam went back to General Lee at Gettysburg.

On July third, 1863, a mighty blow hit the Confederacy when Sam, along with fifteen thousand men, charged the Union line at the Gettysburg. Pickett's men failed to pierce the Union line at the stone wall, while Jeb Stuart could not get past Custer, at Hanover Road, to attack the back of the Federal troops.

Disaster struck the Confederacy again the very next day when , on July Fourth, General Pemberton surrendered to Grant at Vicksburg. General Johnston was at Jackson, Mississippi, only a few miles from Vicksburg, but with too few troops. Hohnston had just got out of a sickbed and was already dispirited. When he saw the mgnitude of the defeat at Vicksburg, he decided not to risk further loss. He marched away, unable to assis the surrounded Rebel Troops, or the starving populous.

Reassigned, Sam was soon fighting with Johnston again, just in time for the brilliant retreat from Dalton to Atlanta. Finally Hood took over and led them to the disastrous battle of Franklin. Going full circle, Hood was decimated byThomas, Sam and the rest of the Tennessee boys made their way back to Johnston where they now stood hearing of the surrender of the Army of Northern Virginia.

There are seven of us left of the 120 men that signed up with me in Lake City. Sam shook his head. *Bragg and Hood were both butchers.* Despite his best effort, when he thought about his comrades, his eyes filled with tears. *Thank God they finally fired Hood and put Johnston back.*

It was evident the men were not ready to quit. Mutinous muttering rippled through the troops. Sam heard the word “Partisan” several times. He shook his head in admiration. Sam looked around at his fellow soldiers carefully. The few boys, recently conscripted, had stiff butternut colored uniforms. But most, like him, were dressed in a bewildering array of colors and features, their original gray uniforms long since gone. Cheeks were hollow and sunken in hunger, but their eyes were bright, and their rifles were clean and ready.

All the cowards are gone, Sam thought, *only the heroes remain.*

Suddenly the muttering turned to strangled cheers and then, just as if a giant hand had erased their voices, there was complete silence. General Johnston had stopped reading and gotten off his horse. He was moving among the men.

At first the soldiers fell back giving the diminutive General room. Sam, along with the other men stared at their leader with awe. It was not like him to mingle with the troops. There was quiet in the ranks anticipating Johnston's next words. But Johnston didn't speak he just moved among the men shaking hands.

Drifting over the silence Sam could hear the distant rattling of General Sherman's army waking. Less ominous, he heard the morning buzz of the crickets. Songbirds had long since fled the two armies.

General Johnston also heard Sherman's army, and looked sternly toward them, his face turning crimson and his eyes blazing fiercely. He continued walking among his men and with each step his face got redder until it looked like a ripe tomato, about to burst over his carefully trimmed white beard.

Bracing himself he pushed straight ahead through the ranks. The men, in adulation, began to yell and crowd in on the general reaching out to touch him. Those who could not touch the general patted the horse walking behind him. Suddenly Johnston stopped and remounted.

The horse, not used to being hemmed in, got wild-eyed and began to paw the ground. General Johnston calmed the horse, whispering to the animal and patting his neck. When the horse stopped moving, Johnston looked down at the men's faces and his own face softened and his eyes got moist. He lowered his head, oblivious to the noise and the crush of the men.

Sam, swept along with the others, felt compelled to touch his leader. But as he reached for the general's boot he was roughly pushed aside.

"You men, move away, let the General through." It was Colonel Fields. He reached the commander and took the reins of the hapless general's horse and led him to the front where his aides waited anxiously.

When General Johnston reached the other officers, he turned his horse around and again faced the troops. He looked over his army and wiped his eyes several times. Just then, as if on signal, the Confederate Flag over the headquarters tent stiffened and began to snap in the morning breeze.

Johnston took out his spectacles again and fumbled with them in an attempt to clean them. He put them on and then, looking over the eyeglasses, took the paper from General Lee out of his pocket and began to speak. The soldiers quieted.

"Men, I want to finish the order from General Lee." He looked down at the paper and began to read again.

I need not tell the brave survivors of so many hard fought battles, who have remained steadfast to the last, that I have consented to the result from no distrust of them. But feeling that valor and devotion could accomplish nothing that would compensate for the loss that must have attended the continuance of the contest, I determined to avoid the useless sacrifice of those whose past services have endeared them to their countrymen...

The scene around Sam began to swim as his eyes filled with tears.

Leander sat down on the ground and hung his head.

There were eyes growing moist, and noses being blown all around them. Johnston continued.

By the terms of the agreement officers and men can return to their homes and remain until exchanged.

There was an anxious shuffling of feet and shifting of eyes.

You will take with you the satisfaction that proceeds from the consciousness of duty faithfully performed, and I earnestly pray that a merciful God will extend to you his blessing and protection.'

The men looked at each other and then back at General Johnston. The talk of partisans, or going to the woods to fight, faded and died. The men now knew General Johnston meant to surrender his army completely.

I'm a prisoner in my own land, Sam thought.

The dejection and resignation of the soldiers was universal.

"Hold it boys, there's joy in just bein' alive," someone yelled, "an', we're goin' home."

Johnston stared the shouter down, and then finished the order.

With an increasing admiration of your constancy and devotion to your country, and a grateful remembrance of your kind and generous considerations for myself, I bid you all an affectionate farewell.

General Johnston put the paper down and stared at the men in broken ranks before him.

Even in this moment of defeat he makes a grand figure, Sam thought. He's small, but has a big heart. He's keen, and his restless eyes see everything. Was there ever another man so splendid? He loves his men and we love him. With Bragg and Hood we starved. With Joe

Johnston we got food and decent treatment. I believe I'd go to Hell and back for him. Sam smiled. *But I don't have to go anywhere anymore. I'm alive, and I'm going home.*

"Men," the general said with a tinge of sadness in his voice, "General Lee tried to join forces with us but couldn't break through General Grant's massive army. At the end, General Lee's army had no food and scant ammunition. As you can tell by his general order, he has therefore surrendered." Johnston's voice quavered at the word, surrendered.

"After reviewing our situation I asked for, and obtained a parlay with General Sherman. I have subsequently met with him and offered to stop the effusion of blood on both sides. General Sherman has offered us generous terms and I have accepted them. After you stack your arms, and receive your paroles, you can go home. The rebellion is over."

Colonel Fields turned and stood at attention. Without being told the men snapped up ramrod straight, and stiffly put their rifles at left shoulder arms, then fingers of the right hand across the barrel, every man saluting General Johnston.

The general stood in his stirrups and returned a stiff salute. Then, without looking back at the troops Johnston turned his horse. After taking a deep breath, he walked the animal past the headquarters tent through a copse of trees, and was gone. The soldiers kept their salute until he disappeared from sight.

With the general gone the soldiers began to mill about freely, some glad, some sad, and some completely lost. Leander sat down and put his head in his hands.

Sam wiped his eyes with the back of his hand, looked down at Leander and held his hand down to him. "C'mon, get up you slug. Let's get our paroles and go home."

Colonel Fields was back. He stood in his stirrups and yelled, "Atttennnnnshion." It was quickly echoed down by the junior officers, and the men stopped and quickly got back into formation. Leander stayed on the ground.

"According to the terms of the agreement, we have to surrender our weapons to the Yankees, so no one leaves yet." Fields turned his horse, hesitated and turned back. "General Sherman has generously offered to share his rations with us. I know..." his voice cracked. "I know," he repeated, "many of you have not eaten in days." His voice softened to a whisper. "Please stay here and you will be fed. Thank you. I will never forget you. That's all. Dismissed."

Sam grabbed Leander's hand and helped him up. Leander looked around at the other men, shook his head and said, "Wait hell, I'm ready to leave now."

A thought flashed through Sam's mind. Without a word he turned and ran, dodging men and equipment, toward the headquarters tent.

Scratching his head, an amazed Leander watched him disappear. He shrugged, took out a small pouch, spilled tobacco on a paper and began to roll a cigarette.

When Sam reached the headquarters tent he looked both ways before slipping inside. It was cool and dark in the tent and Sam waited a moment for his eyes to adjust to the dim light. Thank goodness, all the officers are gone.

Books and documents were strewn liberally on two tables. A lone field desk stood on one of the tables piled high with writing paper. Sam fingered the precious paper.

Hell, I gotta strip wallpaper to get something to write on, and just look at all this stationary.

Sam picked up a small packet of the paper, rolled it up and put it in his back pocket. As he turned away he saw official documents lying face up on the field desk.

Curious, Sam picked up the first paper. Across the top, in a bold hand, it said, COPY. Curious, Sam bent over and began to read the letter.

30, December, 1864

To Mr. Miles

Chairman of the Military Commission

Congress of the Confederate States:

Dear Mr. Miles:

It has come to my attention that the attrition of this Army of Northern Virginia, because of death and desertion, has made it ineffectual against the well-equipped, well-rested Army of the Potomac.

Because of this disparity, in arms and numbers, it becomes my solemn duty to propose what many will call traitorous.

My suggestion to you will be to advise congress to conscript, then free and arm, 200,000 slaves immediately.

I am aware that the president is against this and that he can only

be over-ridden by the Confederate Congress.
If the congress does not agree we will have no other choice but to fight on. But without new men to fill out our ranks we may be doomed to an early defeat—

Sam tore his eyes away, unable to continue. He looked at the bottom of the page to make sure whose signature it was. No mistake. Across the bottom was the familiar scrawl,

Your obedient servant,
Robert E. Lee

"Free 200,000 slaves among our population?" Sam muttered, shaking his head, unable to fully comprehend that unhappy event. At that moment Sam felt as if he were caught between hostile forces.

Sam looked at the next paper to forget the first.

Across the top was a large handwritten note. It began: *To General Grant...* He didn't bother reading the text but slid his eyes to the bottom of the page. ...*avoid useless effusion of blood*... It was again signed,

Your obedient servant,
Robert E. Lee.

Sam's face turned an angry color of red. This must be the original letter of Surrender. He angrily crumpled the paper and stuck it in his pocket. At least I'll have the back of this to write on. A nasty smile spread across his face. No, maybe I'll use it when I go to the latrine.

His eyes moved quickly around the tent and fell upon the regimental flag. This is what he had come for. It was hanging limply from a pole in a corner of the tent. *There it is. We can't let the Yankees have that flag. It's covered with the blood of too many good men.*

He stopped and listened. *Good, no one coming.* He quickly stripped the flag from its pole, folded it and slid it into his jacket pocket. *No, no good. The Bluebellies'll find it if they search me.* He quickly took the jacket off, took his knife out of his pocket and slit the lining. He carefully refolded the flag and slipped it inside.

Sam put the jacket back on and opened the tent flap to leave. He jumped back when suddenly confronted by an officer.

The officer stepped into the tent. Sam knew well the lean, tough face that was twisted into a permanent scowl. The scowl had a colonel's insignia on its collar.

Sam snapped to attention then tried to pass by the officer. "By your leave, Colonel Anderson."

As Sam reached the tent flap the colonel's face darkened and he barked, "Halt!"

Sam stopped dead in his tracks.

"What are you doing in here, Trooper?"

Sam's heart froze and his breath stopped. "I, er, was looking for my Sergeant, sir… to, er, find out where we need to uh, stack arms, sir."

Colonel Anderson's face softened and for a moment Sam thought he might smile. He didn't.

Anderson looked away, threw his gloves on the table, and spoke in a low, menacing voice. "General Johnston says we have to give up our guns to these damn Federals, and he's making me do the dirty work. Me, an adjutant in the Confederate Army, groveling before Yankees." He spoke the words as if there were bile on his tongue.

Anderson reached around Sam, opened the tent flap and stared at the men milling around the camp. "Johnston's gone to Durham to straighten out a misunderstanding with Sherman and maybe get us transportation home."

Sam's face turned hard. "I won't take their charity, Colonel."

Anderson smiled. "I won't either, Boy. But I got me a horse, you'll have to walk home. Where you from?" Anderson let the tent flap go.

“Florida, sir, with General Lane, attached to the Army of Tennessee.”

“Florida, huh. That’ll be a long walk home, Boy.” The colonel walked back to the desk and absently looked through the papers.

Sam followed him with his eyes, worrying about the document and the flag he had taken. He prayed Colonel Anderson wouldn’t spot the missing paper and the naked flagpole.

Anderson continued. “In the meantime, I’m ordered to surrender this army to Colonel Logan of the Union Army.” His face colored and his free hand squeezed into a fist. “I guess they think one of our Colonels is equal to a Yankee Colonel? Not in my book.”

Anderson let the papers go and turned back to Sam. His shoulders sagged. “No, that’s not fair.” He shook his head. “These Yankees put up a hell of a fight. But, if we’d a had a few more men, and a little more ammunition, we might have fought the good fight, and we might’ve even hooked back up with General Lee. But give the Devil his due. Sherman dogged us, and wouldn’t let us do any such thing.” Anderson nodded his head in admiration. “That damn Sherman, he’d flank the Devil right out of Hell.”

The colonel sat down on a camp chair next to the desk, slapped his knee and pointed to a chair opposite his.

Sam groaned inside, absently patted the hidden flag, and reluctantly sat down, one eye on the tent flap, and freedom.

"Boy, if Lee and Johnston could've tied up, them two would've given Grant and Sherman a few problems." He shook his head again and looked around as if making sure they were alone. "I heard, after they got trapped at Jetersville, Longstreet wanted to go on fighting, but Lee wouldn't have it. He said it was time to surrender. Sounds just like Lee, doesn't it? No excitement, no emotion, just clear thinking all the way through."

A ghost of a smile crossed Sam's lips as he touched the surrender document in his pocket.

"That damn Longstreet almost got us all killed several times, but old Bobby Lee knew what to do, and when to do it." Colonel Anderson shook his head and looked ruefully at Sam.

"What am I jawing with you for? You need to be back with your squad. The Yankees are sharing their vittles with us now, so get on back and eat hearty for a change."

Sam got up and began to leave.

"Hey, Boy!"

Sam's heart stopped.

"Where you from, Boy?"

Sam began to breathe again.

"I told you, sir, Florida."

"Oh, yes." The colonel shook his head and finally smiled. "It was the Florida delegation put our own General Breckinridge over the top when he ran for President in '60. There are lots of good men in Florida." Anderson shook his head and muttered, "Damned if that Breckinridge didn't get ten other states too." The colonel got up, walked to Sam and slapped him on the shoulder affectionately.

"Well enough of living in the past. You eat well and then rest, son. Like I said, you got a long walk home."

Colonel Anderson lifted the tent flap and let Sam walk out into the sun.

Sam saluted the colonel as he ducked under the flap. When he got outside, he patted the flag in his jacket and smiled broadly.

He ran back, dodging and twisting through the milling men, to his company. Leander was still sitting on the ground smoking.

Sam ran to Leander and squatted down beside him. In a few minutes he told him the whole story, all the while holding his hand over the hidden flag.

"And Leander," Sam said excitedly, best of all, Colonel Anderson said, 'Tomorrow y'all are going home.'"

Chapter 3

Durham Station, North Carolina.
April 27, 1865

Dear Ma:

Look, no more wallpaper, I have real fine headquarters paper to write on.

The first thing I'm gonna tell you is that the war is over. Better'n that I'm still in one piece.

Right now, as I write, General Johnston and General Sherman are meeting at a Mr. Bennett's home to finalize the surrender. Mr. Bennett is a local farmer.

Leander'n me are gonna wait 'til tomorrow afore we come on home. Seems we have to stack up our guns and give the Yankees our flags. I don't cotton to walking all the way home without my rifle but orders is orders. I ain't gonna give 'em our flag though, I got it hid.

Florida is a long way from North Carolina, so I don't know when I'll be back, but I'll come as soon as I can.

As I said before, Leander Huckaby is coming with me. He's alive and well. Tell his Ma.

Some of the boys didn't make it though. It hurts my heart to tell you this, Ma, but the death angel hovered over us boys, and gathered his best harvest in our last battle at Franklin, Tennessee. He took a bushel full of our boys across the River Styx with him.

You want a laugh, Ma? When I joined up I was afraid they'd get it over with 'afore I could get me a Yankee. Why, I was so patriotic I would have give a thousand greenbacks to have an arm shot off so I could come back with an empty sleeve. Glory, hah! Glory is at home with the ladies, at tea, not on the battlefield where we was all scared, and shells and bullets mutilate men. Ma, if you only knew what I have seen, and what I have done...

You remember Ollie Brown, from Gainesville? That was Orderly Sergeant Brown to us. Well he got killed at Franklin. He was sitting right next to me, eating supper, talking to me 'bout planting a crop of tobacco when we got home, when a minie ball came and— Well I don't want to say any more about that, 'cepting he was a good and God fearing man, and I'm sure he's sitting at the right hand of God in the vault of Heaven, where all good believing men go.

Sometimes I wake in the middle of the night wondering how the ball that got him missed me. As I was putting a piece of hardtack in my mouth, the bullet snatched the food right outta my hand and then struck Ollie.

I can't hardly believe it, but six Generals; Gist, Adams, Cleburne, Carter, Strahl, and Granberry, also got killed, along with 4,500 reg'lar soldiers. I tell you Ma, it was a feast day fer the Devil. My flesh creeps and crawls when I think of it now.

I know some lowly privates that would have planned and fought a better battle than that damn Pegleg Hood. You know, Ma, they call him Sam, same name as me. I'm thinking about changing mine.

They buried Sarge Brown under an old Oak tree. He's at rest now and at peace. The Generals are also at peace lying side-by-side, asleep in the officers section of Ashwood Cemetery. I don't know what they did with all the private soldiers. Prob'ly dug a trench and— Well never mind that.

Now we have to go and face the Yankees and surrender our guns to them. A lot of the boys are angry and want to go into the mountains and continue the fight. But General Johnston told us that, General Lee said we're to give up, go home, and live in peace. So we're going. But despite that order I hear lots of the men say they are going to Mexico rather than live under Yankee rule. Not me. I can't wait to see that ol' Florida sunshine.

The Yankee'll be coming south now to rule us for a while. Guess they kin do what they want. There's nuthin' to molest 'em but some womenfolk with broomsticks.

Your son, still alive, still kicking.

Sam Atkins

P.S. Your oldest son Dave is also alive and well. When I saw him last he told me he was going to Nashville to get a horse he hid from the Yanks. He'll be along right smart and probably get home long before me since he has a horse to ride.

You know Ma, it's been a long four years, but gosh, I'll miss these men, and camping out under the stars. What I won't miss is the killing. I swear to you and God, I'll never kill another living thing.

Sam

Why didn't they settle all this with a couple of hands of cards?

Chapter 4

Sam had a hard night. He tossed and turned, thinking of the night-long cries of wounded men as they died, burned and untended at the battle of The Wilderness. Thoughts of home and his family came next. When he finally fell asleep, a recurring dream he was to have for years visited him for the first time.

At the beginning he saw a line of ghosts in a graveyard. They beckoned to living men who would soon be as dead as they. As the men marched through headstones, toward the crypts, the line became shorter. When they reached the end only one man was left. It was Sam. He felt frightened and cold and empty as he looked back and saw the men getting into the graves. He stared at the headstones. On them were the names of all the battles he had fought in. The last stone was not a battle name. It simply said, SAM ATKINS.

When all the graves were filled except his, Sam turned to run. Before he could get started, his blood ran cold as he was confronted by a cadaverous figure, dressed in black, looming over him. It was Colonel Anderson facing him with a white, bloodless face, and no legs.

With a grinding noise, the ground opened up in front of Sam. Pointing with a phantom finger, Colonel Anderson looked down at the newly opened grave. In a booming, quavering voice the colonel said, "Get in, Sam, it's your turn."

Sam tried to run but was rooted to the ground. "No, no," he screamed.

****

Sam sat bolt upright, wide-awake, sweating and shaking. His heart pounded so hard he thought his chest would burst.

"Goddammit, Sam, pipe down! You'll wake the whole camp."

"Sorry, Leander," he wiped the sweat from his moist brow, "I just had a bad dream."

"You're not the only one who has nightmares. Keep it to yerself, an' let a man get some sleep."

"Yeah," Sam said softly, "let's both get some sleep." He lay back down on the hard ground. Sam tried to calm himself by listening to the brook bubbling nearby, but it only reminded him of the slowly moving Cub Run stream at Bull

Run, slick with soldier's blood. He had a difficult time getting back to sleep, and when he finally did, he spent the rest of the night being chased by legless men.

The next morning was a somber one, with many of the men speaking in whispers. Coffee pots began to boil even before the sun rose. Sam stretched and yawned. Most of the Rebels were boiling Southern Coffee made of parched corn and ground up yams, sweetened with sorghum. Not Leander. At the crack of dawn he had wandered over to the Union lines and traded his belt buckle to a Northern soldier for real coffee and was busy boiling the grounds. To Sam the smell of the genuine coffee was a treat beyond belief.

Sam heard another familiar sound, a rustling movement and the clanking of Sherman's men stirring. The Union Army was also coming awake.

Sam tapped Leander's shoulder and pointed to a gathering of blue and gray officers talking together. They looked almost spectral standing beneath a poplar tree with the morning sun streaming through the branches and surrrounding them.

"Look at them officers," Leander said, talkin' as if they been bosom buddies their whole lives. A day ago they were shooting at each other, or worse yet, making us shoot at each other."

Sam shook his head. "I know. Most of them knew each other before the war, but if they were such bosom buddies, why didn't they settle all this with a couple of hands of cards? Maybe all this killing was just a big game to them."

The thought made him remember his dead comrades. Heat and color came up in Sam's face. He tore his eyes away from the officers and pushed his feelings down with a will. *No sense getting riled up and court martialed when the war's over.*

After a solid breakfast, supplied by their former enemies, Sam and his mates lined up in formation. East of them waited the entire Federal Army, standing at ease. Union flags whipped about in the North Carolina morning breeze.

Sam looked along the line of the Federal Army. "Hey, Leander," he whispered, "would you look at the size of Sherman's Army. Even with our stragglers coming back, we look pathetic compared to them."

Suddenly General Johnston was in front of them on his horse, and the ragged, Confederate lines stirred. "Adjutant," the general said to his aide, "call the men to attention."

The General's aide stood in his stirrups and shouted, "Batallionnnnnnn!"

Back came the answering shouts, "Regiment!" "Company!" "Platoon!" The aide then yelled, "Attentionnnnnnn!"

Abruptly the men braced and stood perfectly still. Except for the snapping of the flags in the Carolina breeze, the world was deathly silent.

Each company sergeant looked down his line and yelled, "Dress right, dress!"

Lines of Rebel soldiers stuck out their left arms, touching the right shoulder of the man next to them and magically their lines straightened.

The color sergeants raised the company flags above the Confederate troops. Sam shook his head at the scant number of men, making the red flags crowd together, like a cocks crown.

Anger hate and frustration boiled up in Sam's chest, and he suddenly realized he wanted no part of this surrender. As the men stood to attention, Sam stepped back out of line and slipped behind a tent.

Leander whispered loudly, "Come back, Sam."

Sam ignored him. Expecting a body-shaking yell from the sergeant at any moment, he made it to a stand of pine trees without being seen.

When he was out of sight he stopped and looked back. General Johnston was telling the men something, but Sam couldn't hear him.

He wandered through the trees until he was fifteen yards from the Yankee army. He stopped by a large oak tree, sat down and waited. I'll just stay here 'til the surrender's over, and then Leander 'n me will start home.

Sam's tree was on the top of a rise and he had a good view of the proceedings. He watched the Confederate soldiers come to attention, make a smart left face, march over a small hill and disappear. Sam stared at the crest of the hill intently. As he expected, in a few moments the first troops appeared again at the top of the hill.

The Confederate troopers halted, dressed ranks and started down. To Sam the Confederate Army looked like a multicolored serpent stretching from the top of the hill along the undulating road.

The vivid memories of both armies drew them together. All the Union men were silent as if watching a sacrament. Some had moist eyes.

Sam was immediately sorry he was not marching with them as the Rebels came down the hill moving briskly on the dirt road in their old swinging route step. Above the troops their battle flags snapped in the mountain breeze. Sam stood up at attention, his eyes bright with pride. *It's not how we die, that's inevitable. It's how we live that counts.*

Colonel Fields, on horseback, led the column. Just behind him was Sam's brigade reduced to so few men he could count them in a flash. *God, the whole column is so small, it looks like there's more battle flags than men.*

Colonel Anderson, off to the side, was sitting erect in his saddle, but his head down, and his expression dark. The Confederate lines were evenly spaced, the men's faces grim. A Yankee trooper started a hurrah and sixty thousand angry eyes turned on him; he was instantly silenced.

The Federal Troops were at parade rest scrutinizing their former enemies. As the Confederates came abreast of the blue line, Sam heard an electric sound. Without being ordered, thousands of Federal muskets clattered to Union shoulders. To a man they braced to attention and saluted their former enemies. Led by Colonel Logan, in a huge gesture of respect, all the Union officers bared their heads.

At that moment, Sam saw Colonel Anderson come alive, lift his head and turn his horse toward the Union lines. The Confederate officer raised his sword, touched his forehead with the blade and brought it down to his boot in response to the Union salute. As they passed the American Flag, the Rebel troops, in unison, brought their rifles to right shoulder arms, company commanders saluted and shouted, "Eyes, right!" The Confederate officers saluted smartly and the Rebel soldiers sharply snapped their eyes right. Later, Sam would swear he heard their eyeballs click.

Honor answered honor; this was the proudest moment in the Civil War for both armies.

Sam's eyes watered and his brain turned numb. He stood up and saluted both armies, Blue and Gray.

Down on the dusty road there was not a cheer or a drum roll, but only the tramp of Confederate feet.

Sam shook his head. *It's like the passing of the dead in my dream.*

The Rebel soldiers halted, faced Colonel Anderson and reluctantly stacked their muskets.

Then slowly, almost in slow motion; with tears and agony on their faces, the color sergeants caressed and folded the blood stained, battle worn Rebel Flags and lay them on the ground.

Without being dismissed, the Southern men broke ranks, kneeled and touched the defeated flags. There were no dry eyes in the Confederate ranks.

Many of the Union Soldiers turned away, unable to bear the Southern grief.

Sam saw a few soldiers stuff small regimental flags in their jackets as he had done. He even saw a small group of men tearing up a Confederate battle flag and putting the pieces in their pockets. Sam shook his head. *They're defiant to the end.*

Sam's eyes went to another group of men gathering around one of the larger flags, the flag of St. Andrew. A lean, semi-starved mountain-man pushed through the ragged circle of men and stared down at the bloody and torn Southern flag, still attached to its pole.

The emaciated man was clad in a ragged homespun shirt, and had on pants with so many holes Sam wondered how his britches stayed up. He had a cone shaped black hat on his head with the front half of the brim missing. His graying beard seemed to burst forth from the bottom of a face burned black by a thousand suns. Slowly and reverently the mountain-man went to his knees.

He wiped his grimy hands on his pants, then picked up the stained flag of St. Andrew as if it were a sacrament. With reverence he pressed it to his breast. His eyes filled with tears that spilled down his cheeks only to get lost in his beard. He looked up at the others, one by one, as if he wanted thenm to share his grief. Another soldier, his eyes also moist put his hand on the scarecrow's shoulder and patted it several times. A few of the younger men looked down and scuffed the earth with their bare toes. After several heart-wrenching moments, the soldiers, singly and in pairs, began to move off. In a few minutes only the scarecrow and the torn flag were left.

The mountain man took a large Bowie knife out of his belt and gently separated the flag from the pole, folded the tattered and sacred flag and put it in his shirt over his heart. He looked at the backs of the departing men and slowly got to his feet. He began to move off, the flagpole still in his hand. He trailed it along in the dirt for a few feet, then let it drop to the ground. Shaking his head, tears still streaming down his face, this soldier, the last in his regiment, walked into the woods, out of the army, and into mythology.

After a long painful time, some of the Confederate soldiers drifted back, lined up and began to receive their paroles.

Realizing he would have to get a written parole to leave, Sam ran back, stacked his rifle, and slipped back into line.

"Bout time you got back," Leander said in a low voice. "Did you see them Bluebellies standin' at attention? I'da thought they would lord it over us, but they is bein' right respectful."

"Yeah, Leander. They've been fighting against us for four years and have come to have a high opinion of us. But I wonder how the Washington politicians will act when they come south. They'll be conquerors in our own country."

Sam grinned and pointed. "Look at that officer, Leander."

A Union general came up to Colonel Anderson on foot, and they both saluted. The Confederate colonel immediately slid down off his horse and shook hands with the Union general.

Sam looked down at his own worn shirt and pants, and then stared at the Yankee general. The general's uniform looked as if it had never been worn before. He had on a dark-blue jacket, a wool flannel shirt, light-blue trousers and a dark-blue single-breasted dress coat with a stand up collar. Only his black boots, showing he was cavalry, looked little scuffed.

In back of the two officers, with his reins completely slack, Anderson's stallion bent his neck and cropped the new grass shoots, a sure sign of spring.

"Who is that?"

"That Union feller's General Kilpatrick," Leander whispered. "He's their cavalry chief. Leander laughed. His jaw is so square he looks like his head oughtta be a lantern. I'll bet they call him ol' lantern jaw." They both stifled a laugh.

"Oh, yes. I've seen his picture in the papers." Sam turned thoughtful. "No, Leander, not Lantern jaw," Sam said in disgust. "I've heard his own troops call him, Kill Kilpatrick 'cause he got so many of his men killed needlessly in wild, unnecessary charges. Some of these generals are all show and no brains. Just like Hood!" Sam spat.

The two officers talked for a few minutes, shook hands, then stepped back and saluted each other again.

When Kilpatrick left, Colonel Anderson faced the Confederate Soldiers. "You men…" his voice cracked and he had to start again. "You men have done more than…" he stopped and had to strain to keep his composure. His face reddened and his eyes glistened. Finally, he turned away, shook his head, and said simply, "Dismissed. Get yer paroles an' go on home."

Anderson got on his horse, shook hands with a few Southern officers, and cantered toward the pine trees where Sam had watched the surrender.

As he disappeared from view, the men on both sides broke ranks and began to fraternize. Easily mixing with their former enemies, some traded

Southern tobacco for Northern coffee and some just walked about shaking hands, dazed and glad to be alive.

While walking among the Yankees, Sam was waved down by a New England Federal. He walked over to the soldier, dressed in blue wool, and eyed him cautiously.

The Union soldier had a ruddy face, a round belly and full cheeks. *No starving here*, Sam thought.

Sam suddenly realized his own face, with its sunken cheeks, reflected the gaunt, hollow-eyed look of all of his Confederate comrades.

He looked down at the Yankee's paunch and thought. He's as round as a pumpkin and not one of us weighs more'n a hundred thirty-five pounds soaking wet.

Sam's heart swelled. He took great pride in the starving men he fought with.

At first it was difficult for Sam to understand the New Englander, but with a lot of hand waving and gesturing they made a bargain. For his Confederate LeMat pistol, the Union soldier would give Sam a sack full of fresh vegetables.

At first Sam shook his head no. He loved his nine shot revolver. He took it out of its holster admiring it. The pistol had an upper cylinder with eight .44-caliber bullets and a lower barrel that fired a .60-caliber shot charge.

The revolver was so popular with Southern officers that Dr. Le Mat, the man the gun was named after, went to France on the ship *Trent*, with Southern diplomats, Mason and Slidell, to set up a factory for its manufacture.

On the high seas the *Trent*, was boarded by Union Sailors who arrested Mason and Slidell and took them off the ship. Only a vigorous protest by France allowed the emissaries to continue to reboard and continue to their destination.

Finally arriving in France, Dr. Le Mat, set up his factory and sent 5,000 pistols back to the Confederacy. Along with Sam and Leander, generals Beauregard, and Stuart also carried this unusual pistol.

Sam's stomach growled with pleasure at the sight of the fresh carrots and greens, and after a few more minutes, and a lot more vegetables, he made the trade. After concluding the bargain, Sam broke away from the milling soldiers, and stood alone admiring the vegetables.

After a few chews of the greens, with wobbly teeth, Sam carefully rolled up the sack of goods and stuck it next to the flag in his worn blouse.

Looking for Leander, one thought kept coursing through his mind: *I'm alive! I'm one of the unconscripted Rebels and I'm alive! For four years I've been in the big monkey show, and somehow I got through it. I'm but twenty years old; my feet are peeled like an onion, and every one of my joints ache like an old maid's. I'm burned black as an old nigger, and my uniform is in shreds. I've eaten Weevils, boiled beef, slush and hardtack. I've starved until my ribs ache and my teeth are loose, but I'm alive. And now, with God's grace, I'm going home and plant tobacco!*

Sam's heart leaped in his chest. He made a fist and shook it at the sky. *Nothing's gonna stop me, I'm going home!*

He fell to his knees, bowed his head, and unashamedly thanked God with all his heart. Then he stood up and shook his head in disbelief. "I'm going home," he mumbled aloud to no one in particular. Fearing his body heat would wilt the vegetables, Sam put the them in his knapsack. He took a deep breath, turned south, and took the first step on his long walk back to Florida.

Leander saw his friend start to move off, broke off a trade with the sharp-eyed Yankee, stuck his LeMat into his belt, and yelled to his friend, "Wait up, Sam, I'm comin' with ya."

Sam stopped and laughed heartily. "I wouldn't leave without you, Leander. Besides we gotta get our paroles."

Leander caught up with Sam and the two boy-men, an arm over each other's shoulders, went back to the company area.

"Sam," Leander said, "Look at those long parole lines. I'm sick of this army. I don't even want to wait fer a parole. Let's go home."

Sam thought for a moment. "Are you sure, Leander?"

"Absolutely."

Sam shrugged. “Okay, let’s go.” They gathered up their few belongings, struck their tent, and began their journey home.

Sam never looked back.

There's a monstrous mischief afoot in this land.

— Leander Huckaby

Chapter 5

Sam didn't realize it then, but the end of the war was a rite of passage, a crossing of the rubicon, going over that invisible line from boyhood to man.

Sam and Leander walked over hills and valleys, through towns and villages, along farmland overgrown and neglected. At first they talked volumes to each other. Soon they spoke only sporadically. Finally they went silent, just shaking their heads at the ruined countryside.

A deathly pall hung over the South. Sam felt it in his bones as he trudged along dusty roads. A few old men, women of all ages, and lots of small children, most of them gaunt with sunken eyes, and faces burned brown by the sun, stood in unkempt yards. They leaned on unpainted fences and stared at the two soldiers as they walked by. Their houses looked as forlorn and run-down as the people. It had taken four years without their men, but signs of decay had begun to show on almost all of the farms.

Some of the women gave them water. Most of them apologized for not having enough food to share. Anxiety on their faces, many of the women asked if they knew a Private Jones, a Sergeant Smith, or a hundred other men.

At the last place, where the people were so in need, Sam shared some of his precious vegetables. As they were leaving, Sam took a last look at the impoverished family. He stopped, turned back and gave the woman of the house the rest of his vegetables. The woman, with two children hanging on, one on each leg, broke down and cried as the boy left.

Walking down a dusty road, a thoughtful Leander turned to Sam. "Them folks look worser than we do, Sam." He shook his head sadly. "There's a monstrous mischief afoot in this land."

****

Finally, fortune smiled on the travelers. After weeks of walking, bathing in cold streams, and rubbing sore feet, they came to a two-story house that was spacious and full of enthusiastic, comfortable patriots. The home was a ramshackle affair, with a large porch circling the house. Apparently the people who lived there had added to the home as prosperity and children multiplied.

Off to the right of the house was a garden full of spring vegetables. In back of the garden there was a young peach-orchard with peach blossoms in full bloom, and a strawberry patch, the berries just turning red. After four years of blood and mud, to Sam, the modest home looked like paradise.

The patriarch of the farm was a South Carolina planter, a fussy old man with a wife that matched his disposition. He was pot bellied and irascible, with a pink face and silver hair; a little man with the excessive blustery dignity that small men often assume. His accent was Southern, but flat and nasal, nothing like the sweet rounded words of Sam's people from the Florida/Georgia border.

He had two daughters, in their late teens, still living at home, and one boy in the Army of Northern Virginia. The old man told the travellers that the last letter he got from the boy told of being in a nine-month siege at a place in Virginia called Petersburg.

With an exaggerated courtesy the farmer graciously invited the two ragged soldiers to dinner.

"The last I heered," the planter said when they sat down to eat, "was what I read in the newspapers. My boy's brigade attacked a place called Fort Steadman, led by his General, John B. Gordon. Never heered no more from him after that."

Sam didn't have the heart to tell him that the charge on Fort Steadman, initially a success, eventually was a complete failure, and that almost all the men attacking were either prisoners, or were now dead. It was Lee's last gamble at holding Grant.

If he is dead this boy will live in his Pa's mind shrouded in glory. I won't say a word. Another boy who died in the charge at Gettysburg flitted across his mind. The boy, Salem Jones was his name, was horribly mangled by a shell and died in Sam's arms. He was close to Salem, and Sam took it upon himself to write his mother:

July 15, 1863
Mrs. Mary Jones
Cowford, Florida

My Dear Mrs. Jones:

It becomes my duty to inform you of the death of your noble and gallant son, Salem.

Salem was a favorite of the whole company, and everyone concurs in saying that he was the best soldier in the regiment. The loss of one so brave and resolute cannot be replaced in our army, or in your heart.

There can be more said for him than can be said for one in ten thousand. He never missed a roll call, a drill, or a tour of duty. He had never been absent a day, or ever reported to a surgeon for sick leave.

May God keep Salem at his right hand in the vault of heaven. And may he always answer the long roll.

Your obedient servant,

Sam Atkins

Sam forced the thoughts of both men out of his mind.

The two scruffy soldiers, hats in hand, sat sheepishly at the sumptuous table while the daughters flitted around, serving first their father, and then the two travelers.

God, those girls smell good. Sam imagined how awful he must look in his shabby uniform. *But the girls don't seem to mind.*

One of them, a light haired sturdy young woman in her late teens, slim waisted with womanly hips and a large bosom, smiled at him a lot, repeatedly leaning on him when she bent over to serve the food. She was dressed in a flowered cotton dress that clearly showed her ample figure.

She was at that age where she was just beginning to understand the power of her womanhood. Feigning indifference for her mother's sake, it appeared she meant to use that power on Sam. The other girl, a bit older and more subtle, hovered around Leander.

Sam's pulse rose at every touch of the young woman. It was spring and the sap was rising in the trees, and also in Sam. He was intoxicated by even the thought of her.

Their mother sat at the foot of the table, eating sparingly, watching her girls and the two unwanted guests closely.

The white-bearded, tobacco-stained leader of the family was at the head of the table, gesturing with his fork as he leaned back on the kitchen chair re-living previous battles of the Indian wars.

Sam chuckled inwardly at the old man's ignorance to the flirting of the young people. When he told of killing Indians up close, his eyes flickered up at Sam as if he hoped he would be believed.

Sam had his doubts. When you do killing, you don't need to talk about it.

The girls began the meal by putting homemade bread and butter on the table. Sam couldn't believe his good fortune. After years of parched corn, green apples, weevil filled sloosh and hardtack, he was about to put real butter on bread. Forgetting his manners Sam slathered the butter on generously and ate it with obvious relish, ignoring his wobbly teeth. The sisters went back to the kitchen, whispering and giggling, and returned with trays of food, setting them down before the men.

Sam stared at the feast in front of him with wonder. *We died in the mud while they popped champagne corks.*

The long table had enough food for ten times their number, with a huge turkey in the middle straddled by a plate of duck, and another holding a large ham. The rest of the table was loaded with green peas, asparagus, spring lamb, and sweet potatoes, served in china and placed on a white damask tablecloth. Hunger overcame them and, without thought or manners, the two soldiers dug in.

To protect his teeth, Sam ate the softer foods until he felt he would burst if he ate another bite. Loosening his belt he sat back satisfied.

The old man stood up and raised a glass of Madeira. "To Jefferson Davis and the Confederacy."

"Hear, hear," Leander said with a wink at Sam.

The lady of the house got up, and Sam and Leander jumped to their feet, crumbs falling from their laps to the floor.

The old man laughed. "Sit down boys, the women'll clean up even if yer not perlite."

The old man got up, and Leander and Sam followed suit, excusing themselves as they trailed the patriot to the porch. All three men took their wine glasses, and made their way out the front door to smoke and chew.

The two girls and their mother cleared the table and Sam listened with a sad smile as he heard the old woman chide the girls.

"No, you can't go talk with the men." He heard a female whine, " Oh, Ma." and then the mother again. "Go on upstairs. Now!"

Ignoring the women the old man spit and said, "Things have been tough on us what with tea $18 to $20 a pound, butter $2 a pound, and worst of all, the coffee, if you kin get it, is now $4 a pound. We've had it tough alright, but even at that you boys are welcome to stay awhile." Between stuffing chews into his mouth and spitting over the porch railing, the old man sat back contented.

Sam thought about the lice and dirt and death he had been through. *Poor man*, Sam thought sarcastically, *butter, two dollars a pound. Never in the four years of war did I even see an ounce of butter at any price.*

The old man continued: "Food's not the only thing that's gone crazy. Our world has changed fer sure, boys. Jes last week I had a woman*, a woman*, mind you, come through here, on horseback, alone and hongry. Me an' the missus done give her a bed and some food, an' in return she done tol' us a story I *still* cain't hardly believe."

The old man combed his stained beard deep in thought. Then he spoke again. "Seems the Yankee general, Sherman, arrested her fer aidin' and abbetin' the Confederacy by workin' in an arms factory. Well, he ups and sends her on a train to the Canadian border, under guard, without a penny, and without tellin' anybody includin' her family." The old man leaned over the porch and spit again.

"Well, one of the guards on the train takes a fancy to her, and let me tell you I don't blame him fer that. She was a fine lookin' woman, flamin' red hair an' all. But he went past the admirin' stage an' tries to attack her, the damn Yankee. Well the woman tells us she turned the tables on the bluebelly an' stabbed him with his own bayonet. Then she high-tailed it fer parts unknown.

"After wanderin' around fer a while, she got a stake from a Southern gambler she met, on the Mississippi River, an' made her way down here. She left yestiday, jes one day afore you got here.

"I tell you, boys, if the rest of the Yankees behave that way, our women, an' us men, will be in a heap a trouble."

He shook his head sadly, then his eyes lit up as he remembered something important. "Lorena, that was her name, Lorena Oakburn, or Oakwood, somethin' like that. Anyway, Lorena said Sherman tol' her, '*any* woman who gives info or material help to the Rebs will be treated as a criminal.'"

Sam shook his head. "We've always put our women on a pedestal, someone to look up to, like a mother or a sister. I guess the Yanks don't see it that way."

The old man shook his head in agreement. He wrinkled his brow as if in deep thought. "By the way boys, my Nigras ran off a while back so if you boys want to stay here and work a bit..." He looked embarrassed. "I kin even pay you in greenbacks."

Leander shook his head.

Sam smiled as if he knew a secret. *I've heard it's thirty-five Confederate dollars for one of gold. And he has greenbacks backed by gold. What were these people doing while we slept in the mud and died for them?*

Sam cleared his throat and tried to warn the man. "There'll be a whole host of Reb soldiers coming, sir," he said earnestly. "If you're gonna help them, you'd best not be keeping guests."

Leander chimed in. "It won't be long 'til you're turnin' 'em away, sir. Johnston's whole army'll be comin' this way soon. You'll see. An' mebbe Grant's army'll be right behind 'em."

Sam smiled. *Leave it to Leander to embellish the truth with a little fiction.*

The old man looked indignant. He turned his head and spit a practiced stream of brown off the porch. "If they fit the Yanks, they'll be welcome at my table. And as fer the Yanks, well, they can go to—"

"Yes, sir," Sam and Leander said in unison. Then they turned and slyly winked at each other.

Meanwhile the old man sat back and chewed contentedly. "Yessir, I wish I coulda killed a few of them Yankees myself." He looked sheepishly at the boys. "But I had to stay here with the womenfolk... keep the place goin'..." He looked at both soldiers, his eyes pleading. "You understand, my age and all—"

Leander belched, excused himself, and leaned his chair back against the white pillar holding up the second story porch above.

Sam knew better than to say anything more, but anger was building up in him and he had to get it out. "We could have used a few more men like you, sir," he said as he looked at Leander with a feigned seriousness, "If we could have had men with more enthusiasm, maybe General Lee wouldn't have surrendered."

Not surprisingly, Sam's sarcasm went over the old man's head. Their host spit another long, looping brown stream, then sat back contentedly rocking his chair. "Damn right."

Suddenly he cocked his head and looked sharply at his visitors. "Are you sure Lee surrendered?" He shook his head sadly. "It sure sounds strange, Lee surrendering, that is. I cain't hardly believe it."

Leander shook his head. "Sometimes I cain't hardly believe it myself."

You'll find out how strange when the Yanks come and rifle your plantation, you old fool, Sam thought.

The old man's face got serious. "Well then, ifn' yer outta the army, how does it feel to be just an ordinary citizen again?"

Leander shook his head thoughtfully. It took him a few long moments to answer. "Like our nation, I am slowly splittin' apart. Half of me will miss the soldierin', the campfires with my companions, the singin', and most of all chasin' the Yanks over some hill. The other half of me will be glad to get home, away from the destruction and the killin', the noise and the lice, and always bein' hongry." Leander's face got somber. "Most hateful of all was the fear of knowin' you could die at any moment..." Leander's voice faded away and there was only silence. The three men stayed quiet, hearing only the night song of the crickets. After a few moments the old man looked at Sam expectantly. "I guess you'll both be glad to git outta the army." He smiled at Sam. "But answer me this. I allus wondered what my boy went through. How did you feel when you went into battle?"

Sam wondered what to say to his host. He thought back to his last battle and shook his head. He thought about the constant fear of things seen and unseen. *How can I tell about that insanity to someone who has never experienced this peculiar way men have of settling their differences?*

The captain brings us forward and I wait in the skirmish line, my pulse racing, my heart pounding and my mouth is dry. I try to swallow but I cannot.

The captain raises his sword and then drops it giving the signal to charge. Then all the other men, their anxiety, their fear, their rage, long pent up: *erupts. It rumbles and roars over the field; it is the rebel yell, making all hearts beat faster, even the Yank's.*

We are unleashed and catapult forward with one common thought; kill or be killed. The Gray Tide begins and rolls onward. The soldiers run and leap and shoot and stab. Suddenly the Yankees flee and we are alone. Some men jump and shout, some sink to the ground. Me, I stare at the blue and gray lumps that were men and now lie in grim repose. Then, because I've been so near death, I begin to tremble and shake. Sometimes I shake so bad I begin to cry.

Sam nods his head slowly and begins to answer. "How did I feel? I felt scared! I didn't realize death would be so near me all the time—"

Leander found his voice again and interrupted. "There were days of terrible rains, winds and snow, but they were nothin' to the storm tossed men. Day by day, week by week, and month by month, we had to endure life in never ending marchin' and boredom, punctuated by killin' and destruction, then back to boredom again." Leander lapsed into silence. Suddenly he made a start and blurted, "I remember clearly, after the first time I'd seen the elephant. I was tired, more tired than I'd ever been. I thought the Yankee rabble would run like chickens before us hawks. It weren't so. They were as brave as we—"

Sam spoke up. "The night after my first battle I tried to rest, but the din of war stayed in my ears. It was a roar I couldn't drive away. My head ached, my throat was parched, and my eyes would not close. Without cause I trembled with fear. Sleep was impossible." He shook his head. "I hear the guns now, and the great wounding cries of dying men." He shook his head as if clearing cobwebs. "And I still can't sleep."

Sam stopped smoking the cigar the old man had given him and looked at the trees and the peaceful fields surrounding him. Just at that moment a gaggle of fat geese, marching in line, passed the porch stairs. In the background he heard the gentle call of a whippoorwill, as the night shadows came on quickly.

Sam stood up and walked to the porch railing, still pondering the old man's question. He sat down on the railing but got up again and paced, too restless to remain still. What did the old man ask Leander? How does it feel to be an ordinary citizen again? The question is a fair one and needs an answer.

Sam stopped his pacing suddenly and pointed a finger at a distant field. "Sir, I look at your field of corn, your lovely family, and peaceful plantation, and I ask myself, am I the same man that a few days ago stood gazing down at the dead, bloated faces of my comrades on those awful fields of battle? After the bloodletting I walk among the dead of both armies, and they stare back up at me with their sightless eyes. And now I ask myself, am I in the same world, here and there?"

Sam stared out over the graceful grounds, and for a long while no one moved or spoke. The old man's eyes glistened for his son.

Finally Leander stood up, threw his cigar over the porch railing into the night. It hit the dirt and gave off a million sparks. Leander stretched and began to laugh. "And we did all that for four dollars a month." Sam smiled, but did not respond.

Leander shrugged. "You know, Sam, it wasn't all bad. You remember the Georgia sharpshooter? You know, the cornet player."

Sam smiled with pleasure.

"Mister, there was a sharpshooter who gave no more thought to killing a Yank than to plucking a chicken. But at night, he played the cornet so beautifully, the Yanks would forgive him, and both sides would completely stop what they was doin' and listen."

All of them were silent for a moment, contemplating the small bit of humanity brought by the cornet player.

Finally, Leander stretched again and yawned. "I gotta lay these old bones down somewhere. You think we could stay the night in your barn, sir?"

The old man wiped his eye with a quick brush of his gnarled hand and stood up. For a moment Sam thought he was going to salute.

"Of course you can." He looked sheepish again. "I'd love to give you a real bed in the house but the Missus... you know, with two daughters and all... you understand."

Sam smiled. "Of course, sir. We're used to sleeping in barns, and in the rain and mud. We'll be just fine."

The soldiers shook hands with their host, stepped lightly off the three steps of the porch, shouldered their knapsacks, and started walking to the barn.

Thinking about the abundance on the dinner table Sam turned to Leander. "I guess they didn't have any starvation parties in that house."

Leander laughed. "No, I guess we coulda fed a whole regiment of Lee's army with what we had tonight.

Sam mused about the worried look on the wife's face. *Is the lady concerned about her missing son, or the virtue of the girls?* He laughed to himself. *It better be the girls. There'll be a lot of sex-starved men coming through here in the next few weeks. She'd better be on her guard, or better still, lock them girls up. Or at least keep 'em outta sight. Those soldiers'll be wanting to dance with them girls all right.* He laughed at the naiveté of the old man.

"What you gigglin' 'bout, Sam?"

"Just thinking about all them boys what ain't been near a woman in two, maybe three years, pouring through here in the next few days."

Leander laughed. "I was thinkin' 'bout climbin' up a trellis and chargin' some breastworks myself tonight. Did you see that leetle dark haired one just astarin' at me?"

Sam punched Leander lightly on his arm. "She was staring at you 'cause you're as ugly as the backside of a mule. You'd best keep your private in your pants, boy." He pushed Leander away good-naturedly. "And stay on your own side of the hay, too. I want to stay a virgin. Leastways 'til I get home."

Leander laughed and Sam joined him.

The moon was bright and high in the heavens, and the barn was easy to find. When they got there, Leander opened the barn door and they stepped inside. Not wanting to bed down with a snake, Leander struck a match and looked for something to light. He found a kerosene lantern on a post, struck another lucifer and lit the lamp. Spectral shadows appeared on his face, as the light threw flickering shapes on the slatted walls of the barn.

Leander took off his hat and bowed to Sam like a cavalier. "Welcome to my humble home."

Sam looked at the pile of hay on the barn floor. He reached down and tapped the hay as if he were testing a feather bed. "After four years of sleeping in mud, rain and snow, I wouldn't know how to sleep in a bed nohow," he said.

Sam took the lamp from Leander and walked around the interior of the barn. There were several horses in their stalls, two cows chewing contentedly, and a large bucket of water next to a post in the middle of the floor.

"Yeah," Sam said, "just like down home." He kicked the mound of hay a few times, dropped his knapsack, and lay down.

Leander did the same a few feet from him.

Sam smiled at his friend and doused the light.

"Night, Sam."

"Night, Leander." Sam lay back and intertwined his fingers at the back of his head and stared above him at the hayloft. The barn was quiet except for the snuffling of the animals.

In the quiet, Sam's mind went back to the war as it did every night when his mind invited thousands of war ghosts into his bed. *Thank God I find it easier every night to tolerate the sounds of gunfire and bomb explosions as I go to sleep.*

"You know what the worst thing about the battles were, Leander? I mean besides the constant fear of being killed."

Leander mumbled something unintelligible.

"It was when the graybeards, the ones too old or infirm to fight, came on horseback or afoot to meet the ambulances. In so many cases they served as escorts taking dying, or dead sons, back to grief stricken mothers. Mothers just like your ma and mine." No reply. "What do you think, Leander?" Sam got up on one elbow and looked over at his friend. "Hey, Leander, you still awake?"

Sam snickered as he heard Leander's familiar, gentle snoring. "So much for interesting conversation." Sam lay back down again and pillowed his head in his hands.

The moon sent its rays through the separated slats giving the barn some natural light. Sam turned over, got on both elbows, put his chin on his hands and stared at the slatted openings. He could see slivers of the bright full moon.

Sam filtered the bright, yellow heavenly body through his memories. *How many times have I looked at the moon just before a battle? And after the carnage, watched it as the gloomy hours rolled by. Then, in the dark and the silence, the clouds would swallow the moon and bring on a dreary rain, almost as if God wanted to cleanse the earth of our damned foolishness. I guess I should be glad just to still be alive. He sat up and rubbed his temples. If only I could get the cannons to stop roaring in my head.*

Sam knew he had been lucky. Four different times, Yankee bullets killed men standing right next to him. That's not counting the artillery shells that almost got him a hundred times.

He felt a hot flush come over him as he remembered the first time a bullet struck him: Antietam!

He sat up and stared into the black space around him, reliving the battle. His blood was pounding through his body as he again peered over the ditch and saw the Yankees charging over Bursides Bridge. Hands shaking he drew his rifle to his shoulder and took aim. Before he could fire he heard a whiz by his ear and felt the iron missile graze his scalp. He put his hand to the sting and drew blood. Only a scalp wound, he thought. But the man next to him wasn't so lucky as the next bullet struck his head. Sam felt sick when he saw the man's brains and blood splatter on his shirt.

That sight, or something near it, occurred every night in his dreams. He shook his head to dispel the thoughts, but the visions kept coming.

In his mind he again saw the field at Franklin, heard the thud, and felt the searing pain as for a second time a bullet tore into him. *God help me, I could walk over the dead and dying for a mile and not come to the end of that damned trench.* His face got hard. *I was near the officers and heard General Cheatham say to General Hood, 'I don't like the looks of this fight as the enemy has a good position and is well fortified.' Cleburne and Forrest also knew the attack was suicidal but*

Hood ignored their advice. God Damn General Cleburne. I heard him say to Hood, 'We will take those works or fall in the attempt.' He was true to his word. He fell. Sam shook his head sadly. *And the Yanks, they kept shooting and shooting until most of my company was on the ground. The Enfield in my hands got hot from firing at them... Then they charged. What was left of us picked them off like flies... The foolish Yankee Generals spent men's lives almost as freely as Hood did.*

Sam absently felt the puckered scar on his arm where the ball had entered. *God, for a while I thought they'd have to take the arm off. Good thing I know how to beg.* He remembered the pile of severed arms and legs outside the surgeon's tent and shuddered. *Thank God that minié ball missed the bone.* After a while Sam's mind eased and he lay down again.

He was at that place between waking and sleeping when he heard a muffled cough. His eyes flew open and his heart froze. He sat bolt upright. *That wasn't Leander!*

He reached for his Enfield. It wasn't there. An annoying picture of him stacking his rifle in front of the Union army flashed across his mind. He felt naked without a weapon. "Leander" he whispered, "you hear that?"

In a flash Leander was at his side, his LeMat pistol in his hand. He put his finger on his lips for quiet and pulled back the gun's hammer. The click echoed in the barn, ominously.

Leander peered at the hayloft, his eyes fierce and resolute. "Who's up there?" he commanded with authority.

I hope it's an animal, Sam thought, *I've had enough of guns and killing.*

They heard a rustle and then a thud.

"Hey, don't shoot," a disembodied voice floated down from the loft, "it's only me, and I'm unarmed."

They heard more movement and the creak of a ladder.

The stranger spoke again. "The war's pretty much over, you know." The mysterious voice sounded anxious.

There was silence for a full minute. Then the hidden man spoke once more, this time his voice was subdued.

"You're not deserters, are you?"

Sam groped for the lamp and found it. He struck a match and lit the lamp. His hand shook and everything was shadows and movement.

Leander whispered forcefully, "Put that damn light out, Sam. It's blinding me. I can't see him."

Sam quickly snuffed out the flame.

"No, we're regulars," Sam answered. "Been with Johnston and Lee for four years."

"Put your hands up where I can see 'em," Leander said, his voice low and menacing. "You alone?"

Suddenly Sam could see the man's outline in the shafts of moonlight. His hands were over his head.

"My hands? Oh yes," he said dejectedly, "they're up. And yes, I'm alone."

"I see him! Now light the lamp, Sam."

Sam struck a match and lit the wick again. For a moment the light flared up bathing them all in an eerie glow then settled down and burned steadily.

One of the horses neighed as Sam put the lamp down on the edge of the stall and looked at the intruder with interest.

He appeared to be a young man, tall, erect and slender. He had a dignified, soldierly bearing with clear high-bred features. A dirty bandage was wrapped around his head, his blonde locks sticking out of it at odd angles. A dark bloody stain showed over the left temple. He had a Union kepi, with what looked like a horn on the top, gripped tightly in his right hand.

Even in this awkward situation Sam could see he had a ready smile and an air of self-confidence. In spite of their situation, Sam liked him instinctively.

"Leander, put that blunderbuss down. He ain't even got a gun. 'sides, he's got a southern accent, just like us."

"Yeah, maybe he ain't got no weapon, an' mebbe he sounds like us'n, but he sure as hell got on a Yankee uniform."

Sam looked at the man more closely. He saw the dark shirt and blue pants of the Union army with the broad red stripe of the artillery down the side. A flash of self dismay went through Sam. *How'd I miss that? One stinking day outta the army and I make a real dumb mistake.*

Sam's brow wrinkled and his eyes narrowed. "You got some explaining to do, mister. What's a Yankee doing so far away from his buddies? With that accent and them blue pants you must be a galvanizer?"

The man laughed easily. "Can I put my hands down?"

Leander hesitated for a moment, and eased the hammer down on the LeMat pistol slowly. "Okay, but keep yer hands where I kin see 'em."

The soldier made a show of keeping his hands out in front of him and sat down in the hay. Sam sat down opposite him. Leander remained standing, his gun holstered the LeMat, but his gun hand stayed hanging loosely at his side.

The newcomer looked directly at Sam. "You got the makin's?"

Sam reached over to his knapsack at his feet. "Got the makings right here," he said as he handed the soldier the pouch of tobacco and cigarette paper.

The new man began to speak as he opened the package of tobacco. "No, I'm not a galvanizer. I didn't switch sides. Let me explain about my Yankee uniform. My name is George Forrest. My family owns a plantation near Montgomery, Alabama." George took a deep whiff of the tobacco in the pouch and smiled with satisfaction. We got mebbe three hundred slaves on the spread. Prob'ly more by now."

Leander looked sharply at George. "Alabama?" he blurted out, his face in a scowl, "then what are you doin' dressed up like a monkey in them blue pants?"

George smiled indulgently. "I'll get to that."

Sam looked at Leander with impatience. "Damn it, Leander, let him talk." He turned back to George. "Go on."

Leander frowned and shook his head. He gripped the butt of his LeMat so tightly that his knuckles shown white.

Sam feared for the newcomer, knowing quite well that beneath the comely exterior of Leander, like many of his fellow Southerners, lurked a quick and deadly violence.

"Wait a minute," George said, and spilled the loose tobacco on the paper. He rolled it into a tube, twisted one end and tapped it down, making it firm, then put the open end in his mouth and wet it.

With a practiced move, Sam reached over and snapped his thumbnail over the head of a lucifer. The match flared, making all the faces of all three men grotesque, then settled down to a small flame. Sam held out the lucifer, and George leaned forward to light the end of the cigarette.

George took a deep drag, pulling the smoke down into his lungs, coughed once, then leaned back, a smug satisfaction written across his face. He expelled the blue smoke towards the roof and quickly took another drag. "Ain't had a smoke in two days. It sure feels good." He laughed. "This is just *one* of the vices I learned in the army."

"Stop yer dancin' around," Leander said, his eyes narrowing, "and keep talkin'." His gun hand twitched involuntarily.

George's smile faded. He put his forage cap on his knee and began to speak again.

"I don't get along real well with my father." He looked down and picked up a piece of straw, absently threw it off to the side, then took another drag on the half smoked cigarette. "He wanted me to boss his plantation, so he put me in the fields with his niggers and made me work with them all day long." He shook his head slowly. "I wanted to go on to school and maybe become a teacher, or a lawyer, but he wouldn't have none of that."

George's smile came back and he continued sarcastically, a hint of sarcasm in his voice. "He laid down with one of his nigger gals, 'bout twenty years ago, and made him a high yaller baby. The boy's just about a year or two younger'n me."

Leander's face remained stoic, while Sam leaned forward with interest.

George leaned back on his hands, the stub of the cigarette dangling on his lips. The smoke, coming up in a spiral, made him squint one eye. There was a look of admiration in his face when he spoke again. "That half-breed boy, name of Dakota, loves the plantation. Even when he was just a lad, he'd be out there bossin' the other niggers 'til after the sun went down. I told Daddy to let him run the place, but he said 'it wasn't fittin' for any half African to be the overseer. 'You're my son, he said, and it's your place to manage and inherit this plantation.'"

George gestured to Leander to let him get up.

Leander nodded warily and took a step back.

George stood up, stretched, and put his blue kepi over the bandage on his head. "I took it for a couple of years and then I had to leave. My ma paid my way an' I went off to Louisiana University and started school." He laughed. "You know who the chancellor of the school was?

Sam wrinkled his brow and shook his head, no.

"Sherman! Yes, our very own, General William Tecumseh Sherman." George laughed. "He was a bastard even back then. Always snoopin' around, fussin' with the buttons on his coat, or nervously brushin' back his hair a thousand times. He was always fiddlin' with somethin'. Anyway, my grades were good at the University, and when I finished I got a scholarship to a law college in Harrisburg, Pennsylvania."

He smiled wryly and shook his head. "That's when the fun started. They had a social and military club that was part of the school. I joined and went to parties and drilled with them. And after the drillin' we went to more parties."

George looked at the other two men sheepishly. "When you boys came from Richmond up to Gettysburg the first week in July of '63, the whole military club dropped their schoolbooks and picked up rifles."

A few of us, especially me, didn't want to go, but you know, no matter how absurd, ridiculous and preposterous some idea may be, there will always be followers. The trouble was the followers insisted we foot draggers come along. They preached at us about the South wantin' dis-union and all, and that it was up to us to save old glory. Then they led us on to Gettysburg, and like damned fools we followed."

His smile faded. "I thought it would be over by the time we got there. His face turned hard. "I soon learned better. It wasn't over by a durn sight."

Leander muttered, "I wasn't there at the finish of Gettysburg, I got wounded on the first day, at McPherson's Wood, a couple of days before Pickett charged. But, Sam was there. He told me the day of the charge was hot and nasty."

"More like ghastly," George whispered so quietly, Sam had to lean forward to hear him. "The first two days of the battle our brigade guarded wagons in the rear. On the third day they ordered us to the front line, next to a cemetery, behind a stone wall."

George laughed without mirth. "Funny thing: There was a sign at the entrance to the cemetery that said, *'Discharge of firearms on these premises are not allowed.'* What a laugh that turned out to be.

"Even before the sun came up it was real hot. Some of the boys along the Stone Wall were lucky enough to have some shade from a bunch of trees in the center. I wasn't. I lay there behind the wall swelterin', wishin' I was back in Alabama. By noon it must have been at least a hundred in the shade. The sergeant wouldn't let us take off our wool jackets either. He said it wasn't military to fight in shirt-sleeves." George laughed. "Not being in fancy uniform didn't seem to bother you boys none.

"About an hour later your artillery started shellin', then it really got hot. The guns were firin' high, hittin' everythin' in the rear, so a bunch of us got in front of the wall." He laughed with irony. "It was really safer there. In a short while, our General Hunt started answering your fire with our guns. With about three hundred of them cannons goin' off on both sides, the noise was deafenin'. God damned if I didn't think the world was gonna shake apart."

"Me too," Sam said quietly, remembering the noise, the dirt and the sweat. "It got so bad, some of our boys started holding their hand up over the breastworks, hoping to get wounded. Feeling for a furlough we called it."

"I know what you mean," George continued. "I sure got down deep into that dirt. Damn, I woulda dug a hole with my teeth to get away from that shellin'. Finally the bombin' stopped and it was like the world stopped too. Even the wind died down. Then I looked up over that stone wall saw y'all acomin'. I tell you, my heart started just apoundin'. From where I was, you looked like an irresistible gray wave, comin' up over the rise." George shook his head.

"Well, I'm not ashamed to tell you, when I saw y'all, and I realized y'all were comin' to kill me, I peed in my pants." He pointed to his crotch and laughed nervously as if he were still ashamed. "Looky here, you can still see the stain."

Leander and Sam both nodded. They didn't have to look; they knew.

"Well, I ain't never seen the like of it and never want to again. You boys came straight at us. On top of that y'all were bein' led by generals. Our generals, bless their souls, were never in front. Most of them were more comfortable suckin' on a bottle, safe in the rear." George got a bitter look on his face. "In my opinion generals are universally never to be trusted.

"Anyway, our long range cannons started firin' again and soon found the range. They cut a swath through y'all, but by God, what I saw then was hard to believe. Right in the middle of all that shellin' and killin' y'all stopped, dressed your ranks. After a minute or so, y'all started comin' again." George stopped speaking and shut his eyes. "I never seen the like of it afore, and I'll remember it 'til my last breath. Y'all stopped right in the middle of a damn bombin' to straighten y'alls lines."

For a moment there was complete silence except for the sounds of the insects, but in their minds the three soldiers could hear bayonets clicking, minies whizzing and men screaming.

Finally George continued. "About three quarters of the way up the hill you boys started runnin' at us, screechin' the Rebel yell. When y'all reached the wall it became bedlam. It looked to me like there were ten of you to every one of us. Colonel Cushing's battery, just in back of us, rolled up and started firing cannister. That slowed y'all down, and evened the score some." George's voice got lower. "That damned cannister oughtta be outlawed, don't ya think?

Sam nodded emphatically.

"When the cannister hit your boys comin' over the wall their bodies jes seemed to melt. And the Rebs who didn't get destroyed, fell back horribly mangled. To tell you the truth I woulda run, but they had file closers in back of us with big broad swords, and officers with pistols keepin' us in the line. I can hear the colonel now, yellin' to the file closers, 'Shoot any damn coward who runs.'"

George glanced at the two men guiltily.

"Then the cannister stopped and we stood up and started shootin'." He shook his head for emphasis. "But I swear, I never even looked when I fired. I was too scared." George leaned against the stall. His eyes were bright, his voice excited.

Leander had a look on his face, as if he had swallowed gall and wormwood.

George continued. "When y'all all came over the wall y'all were so close to us there wasn't no time to load and fire, so everybody stopped shootin' and started swingin' their rifles like clubs." He stopped and looked at Sam. "It was awful. Everone was shootin', slashin', an' cuttin'. Men with bashed heads fell by the dozen. There was blood everywhere." George closed his eyes and shuddered. "I pray I never see anythin' like it again."

Sam stared back with vacant eyes, his mind back at Gettysburg. Leander's mouth tightened to a thin, grim line.

George shook his head. "Later, and I can't tell you if it was a minute or an hour, you boys started to fall back. I stood up an' watched y'all leave. He laughed nervously, then cleared his throat and continued. "The next day they put me back on the wall, with a rifle in my hands. I was shakin' an' just aprayin' that y'all wouldn't come again. Thank God you didn't.

"For a while, after the charge, General Meade fussed and raged about goin' after you boys, but nobody wanted to." He laughed. "We sure dragged our feet. Down the incline, 'bout a mile away, we could see General Lee was preparin' a welcome committee for us if'n we did go after ya'll. The Yankee cavalry tried but were quickly driven off. Both armies stayed in place for a whole day and night. Then it began to rain. Thank heaven for the rain. The townspeople said they had never seen such a downpour. It rained as if the Almighty were trying to clean our stupidity off the battlefield. It didn't clean much, but at least the rain cooled you off. But," he shrugged, "on the other hand, when it stopped, the wet made our wool uniforms stink to high heaven." George's eyes were moist and distant, and his face was sad. "But the smell that came from the field was a whole lot worse."

George shook his head again. "Then came the most evil thing of all. After y'all left, we had to go out and get the dead and wounded; yours and ours. The dead were awful, but the wounded were indescribable! They kept cryin' for their mothers and for water. I guess the loss of blood dehydrated them and they desperately wanted some liquid. The surgeons told us not to give any to the ones with stomach wounds, but they were so pitiful we gave it to 'em anyway. Lots of men from both armies died before the next day." He shook his head his eyes mirroring the sadness from his soul.

Sam interjected quietly, "When the fighting started I thought the war would be glorious, but where's the glory in such carnage?"

George laughed sardonically. "Glory? I'll tell you what glory in this here war means. It means goin' hungry, or getting measles, pneumonia and dysentery. If you're fortunate enough to get past that, then it's two-to-one that you'll get mangled on the battlefield. If you're really lucky, you get a leg or arm shot off an' then maybe, just maybe, you can go home." He shook his head quickly. "It's like living through a pestilence. No one can tell if he'll be the next one to go."

For a few minutes all three men were silent. Finally George began to speak again. "You're right, there's no glory in war." Then as an afterthought he said quietly, "The dead were everywhere at Gettysburg. You could walk from one side of the field to the other and never set foot on the ground." He shuddered and touched the dirty bandage on his head. "I guess I was lucky after all."

For a while they were quiet, remembering. "At Appomattox it wasn't so bad," George said quietly. "Y'all were pooped and we outnumbered y'all ten to one. Gordon's troops charged us a few times but we pushed 'em back easy. After the last push, General Sheridan rode by the troops yellin' sarcastically, 'Run for your lives, men, *toward the enemy!*' But no one wanted to get killed when it was obvious that the bloodlettin' was almost over.

We mostly just ignored him when we could, and stayed put. Only when we were prodded by the file-closers did we half-heartedly charge y'all." George sighed deeply. "It was so hard to keep fightin' when Spring was in the air. All around us were aster and goldenrod, dried ironweed, sumach and wild onions, all trying to blossom. It was hard to think of dyin' when life was springin' up from the earth.

"After chargin', forward and back, I dropped into a ditch. I thought I would be safe there. My heart was just returnin' to normal when I felt a pain, like a hot poker, in my right arm. A sharpshooter got me, then fired again and grazed my head. I fell down hard and blacked out. The next thing I knowed, I was bein' dragged away from the line. After a while someone put a bandage 'round my skull." He pointed to the dirty bandage on his head. "And this one around my arm." George moved his upper arm and flexed his fingers.

"This wound made the arm stiff," he tapped his temple, "and this one sure made my head ache, but at least I was off the line. The next day our infantry beat y'all to Jetersville and that was it. General Lee surrendered all y'all at Appomattox."

George sat down, dropped his cap on the floor, wrapped his hands around his knees, and rocked gently back and forth. For a long while, no one spoke.

Finally, Sam broke the silence. "Seems to me that we'd best forget all that business. We fought for our state's rights, and to protect our homes, and the Yanks fought for the Union and power. Now the war is over and the Yankees won. The past is dead; let's let the past bury its dead. If we could go back and change it, I think we would. But we can't."

He looked at Leander. "I think it's time for all of us to forgive and forget." He patted his hip. "That's why I gave up my gun. Don't want it ever again. I'm through with killing. Let me tell you here and now, I've seen the elephant and I don't wanna see it no more."

George stared at Leander.

Leander glared back, his face intense, his eyes questioning.

Sam looked at first one man and then the other, his eyes narrowed to tiny slits, as if he were staring at the sun.

Leander's hand was on the butt of his pistol. His brow was furrowed with deep lines of thought and the bridge of his nose was wrinkled with indecision. Finally his face relaxed and he lifted his hand away from the gun. For the first time he smiled.

With a thankful sigh, George jumped up took Leander's hand, and shook it vigorously. Sam joined them and slapped them both on the back, laughing with relief. Leander joined in the fun and seemed good-natured. But deep in the recesses of his mind Sam could hear the constant voice of Leander whispering in his ear like Iago to Othello, 'Yankees are never to be trusted.'

Chapter 6

Sam woke abruptly from a troubled sleep and, bolted upright ready for intruders. He cocked his head, listening intently, but the only sounds he heard were the quiet snorting of the animals, the peaceful breathing of his compatriots, and the music of the ever-present crickets.

Going to the front of the barn, Sam opened the small door and quietly slipped outside. The moon was still full but the eastern sky was crowned with light. It was that time of day when the sun, just beneath the horizon, was about to show its full glory.

Sam felt more than heard the footsteps behind him and, by instinct, whirled and reached for his nonexistent pistol.

"Sorry, Sam, I didn't mean to scare you."

Breathing a long sigh of relief Sam exclaimed, "It's okay, I'm still a little jumpy."

George went around the corner of the barn and Sam heard the sound of him urinating. Sam moved off a few feet and did the same.

As George came back, he was slowly unwinding the bandage from around his head. As it came off, Sam could clearly see the burn wound on his temple. George threw the dirty bandage on the ground, bent over and splashed water on his face from the cow trough just outside the door. "Brrrr," he said, shaking his hair and making the water fly. He dabbed the water off his face with his sleeve. To get out of the cool air both men stepped back into the barn.

George stopped wiping and walked a few steps closer to Sam. "I'm glad you're up," he said in a low voice, "I wanted to ask you somethin' without Leander hearin'."

George looked over at the sleeping form of Leander. "I guess he don't like me much. He shook my hand yesterday, but I could tell he didn't mean it."

"It's not that." Sam was thoughtful for a moment. "It's more 'cause we lost so many friends… and your uniform—"

"Yeah, I've been thinkin' 'bout that. I guess it's time I got rid of these rags." He took off his cap and threw it on the ground. "I never wanted to fight nohow. It's just like I told you…" He shrugged his shoulders and couldn't finish.

"I understand," Sam said. He brightened as he thought of their host. "We can get you some new duds from the owner of the place. He's one of those people who've been buried for years but arises just before dinner."

George laughed.

"He's also an ardent Rebel and just loves us, but I don't think he'll care for you if he sees your uniform."

George nodded his understanding.

"Speaking of equipment, you know, Leander and me fought at Bristoe Station with Jackson against Pope. After the Yanks ran, they left a whole passel of Federal equipment. If I'da knowed you needed duds we coulda brought you a whole bunch."

Sam snickered. "That Yankee General Pope was really something. He had all kinds of strange clothing. He had men's undies made of silk, monogrammed hankies and lots of other delicate things. And foods; he had foods very strange to a bivouac, like canned ham and fish. He also had whiskey, lots and lots of whiskey. I was nearby when I heard Jackson say, 'I fear that Yankee whiskey more than I do General Pope.' That's when Jackson told his aides to destroy the kegs. Now that was a sight to behold. When the whiskey started flowing on the ground, I saw men on their hands and knees trying to lap up the spilled contents."

Sam laughed louder, remembering. "Later that afternoon I recall one of the Yankee wounded, I think a bullet had broken his leg. He asked to be helped to sit up so he could see the great Jackson. As the General walked by he had his kepi pulled down over his eyes and was all hunched over. He made some picture, being dusty, dark and scowling. Well the wounded man took one look at General Jackson, and said, 'Oh, my God! Lay me down.' And he laid right down. Well after that incident, any time any little thing would happen, the men would roll their eyes and say, 'Oh, my God! Lay me down.'"

George broke out in peals of laughter.

"And the men," Sam said, while snorting, trying to control his mirth, "they was all running around with Pope's elegant silk hankies applied to noses hitherto blown only by the thumb and forefinger."

With the sight of those men with silk hankies in their minds, Sam and George doubled over with hilarity and could hardly catch their breath. Sweet, gay laughter filled the old barn.

After a while they stopped and wiped their eyes. The memory of that hilarious event was still fresh to Sam and he could not stop grinning.

George's smile left him and his face got a serious look.

"Sam," George asked, a bit sheepishly, "I been wantin' to ask you somethin'." He hesitated for a moment then plunged ahead. "Would you mind if

I joined you fellows. It gets mighty lonely out here all by myself." He stopped and his face reddened. "If you don't think it's all right, I'll understand."

Sam nodded slowly, weighing the possibilities. "It's okay with me, and I'm sure Leander will come around."

"Thanks," George said energetically and shook hands with Sam.

"A man cain't get no sleep around here nohow with all this racket," Leander growled, sitting up and rubbing the sleep from his eyes.

"Mawning Leander. Sorry if we woke you," Sam said.

"Mawnin." Leander answered and stretched. "Outta the army a whole two days and y'all can't sleep past reveille?"

"Mornin', Leander."

Leander glanced at George, his face noncommittal. "Mawnin'."

Sam decided to get it all straightened out right now. "Hey, Leander, George here asked if he could team up with us. At least 'til we get near home."

George waited expectantly.

Leander eyed George as if he were taking his measure, and rubbed the stubble on his chin. "Okay with me." He pointed to George's pants. "But first he's gotta get rid of them Yankee britches."

Sam grinned, and George let out a whoop, ran over and pumped Leander's hand enthusiastically.

Leander broke away muttering to himself, "Youda thunk I made him the President of the Confederacy." But he was smiling as he went out the door and around the corner of the barn.

Sam put his hand on George's shoulder and thought to himself, *The invisible bonds of soldiering, even with this Yankee, bind us together in comradeship more tightly than the ties of family.*

The rim of the sun came over the horizon and by its meager light, Sam picked up stones that were lying around the yard, and made them into a fire-ring.

George went off to collect firewood, and they soon had a brisk fire going. The smell of Leander's coffee was thick in the air, and made their mouths water.

After a breakfast of eggs they got from the local hens, and the bitter, black coffee Leander had traded for, the three ex-soldiers went back into the barn to make plans.

Speaking first, Sam said, "I think if we head due south, through Georgia, we'll hit the Florida border in a few weeks." He turned to George. "Then me and Leander can continue south, and you can turn west, go through Tallahassee to the Alabama border and you're almost home."

"Suits me!" George exclaimed enthusiastically.

"Me too," Leander added laconically.

Sam got up and stretched. "Well let me say goodbye to the old codger-man in the house, beg some vittles, and we'll be on our way."

"That'll give me time to climb up the hay loft, gather up my gear and be ready," George said.

"Take yer time, Sam," Leander drawled, leaning his lanky, muscular body over and picking up his knapsack, "I need a little time to clean my gun. We might have to shoot a rabbit or two on the way home."

Leander took his LeMat out of its holster and twirled it. Then he laid it down on the ground and got his gun cleaner out of his knapsack. "I cain't believe I'm cleanin' this damn gun without some Sarge tellin' me to."

"That gun's a beauty," George said earnestly, "you mind if I sit here and watch you take it apart?"

"Sure George, have a seat."

Sam smiled. *Damn, Leander's loosening up.* He made a casual salute to the two men, walked out the door down a worn path to the main house. He touched his belt and muttered, "Sometimes I'm sorry I traded my LeMat. I almost feel naked without it."

Halfway to the house Sam took in the charm of the farm. An old brook with calm waters and willows growing on its banks trickled past the barn. In the distance he could see the two-story home bordered by roses, daises and yellow jessamine, delicately intermingling in a frozen splash of color. Sam breathed in their perfume.

As he walked toward the main house, his mind filled with thoughts of the younger sister. *Maybe she and I could take a walk—*

Sam's deep reverie was shattered by the blast of a gun. He froze.

The discharge was followed by a loud groan from the barn.

Sam stopped in his tracks unable to move. After a few moments he slowly turned toward the barn. The look on his face was one of extreme fright, almost as if he'd seen a glimpse of Hell.

Swallowing hard, he began to trot toward the barn. After another groan, he began to run wildly, feet churning, arms flailing. When he got there he flung the door open and his blood ran cold.

Leander, tears running down his face, was sitting on the floor cradling George in his arms. The smoking LeMat lay on the ground next to George's feet.

Leander looked up at Sam, his face a picture of agony. "I didn't mean it Sam, it was an accident."

George's face was white with shock. He shook involuntarily.

Sam looked at the spreading red stain on George's chest, and then at Leander.

Guilt ridden, Leander stared back at Sam, his eyes saucer round, filled with fear.

"The gun went off by itself. I was cleanin' it and the shotgun part just went off. I didn't even know there was a shell in it," he wailed.

Leander looked down at the man in his arms, and tears rolled down his cheeks and dropped on George's blue jacket. His voice was high and soft, like a small child's. "Please George, don't die, *don't* die."

Rushing to them, Sam knelt beside George.

George smiled wanly at Leander and spoke in short, sharp gasps. "It'll take more… than the likes of you… to kill me,… Reb." He turned his head to Sam and laughed sardonically. The laugh ended with a fit of coughing, small flecks of blood appearing on his lips.

"Damn, y'all," George sputtered, a tinge of bitterness in his voice, "I guess I'll have… the distinction of being… the last man killed in the Civil War."

Sam

He's as brave as any man

Chapter 7

Sam reached out and touched the wounded man's hand. "You hurt bad, George?"

"You… tell me… Sam," he gasped.

Sam stared at the crimson stain on his chest, then reached down and, with two fingers, carefully parted George's shirt.

The wounded man groaned, his face turning pale and pinched.

Sam took one look at the gaping wound, saw George's heart vainly trying to beat through the hole, and gently closed the garment.

"Is it… bad?" George asked, a touch of fear in his eyes.

"I've seen worse," Sam said with a weak smile.

Leander glared at Sam, a haunted look in his eyes. "He's gonna make it ain't he, Sam?"

Sam looked down at George, who now had his eyes closed, then looked at Leander, and shook his head slowly.

"Oh, God!" Leander said, and started sobbing.

George opened his eyes.

"Help me… sit up… Sam."

"Whaaaat? Are you sure, George?"

"Yeah, I'm sure… Give me a hand."

Both men started lifting George to a sitting position.

"OH, GOD!" George shrieked out in pain.

"Stop," Leander yelled.

"No," George said, gritting his teeth, "I… want to… sit up."

From deep in his chest, George gave another groan as they sat him up, and half lifted and half dragged him as gently as they could to the wall of the horse stall. They carefully leaned him back against the wooden planks. Gasping for breath, his white face turned red, and then a sickly gray. His breathing was now coming in short, painful intervals.

"Gimme… a pen and… paper. I want to write a note to my Father… before…."

Sam's eyes narrowed and he shook his head. He remembered what George had told him about being afraid on the battlefield. *It isn't true*, Sam thought, *he's as brave as any man I ever knew.*

The injured man pointed weakly to his gear. "I have a writin' tablet… in my knapsack."

Scooting over to it on his hands and knees, Sam rummaged through the knapsack, took out a pencil and a small notebook and handed them to George. The Alabaman's head was lolling but when the pencil touched his hand he straightened up.

A devastated and distraught Leander couldn't take any more. He stood up and wrung his hands. His eyes were bright as if he had a fever. His hands shook, and his body trembled. Suddenly, with a shriek that sounded as if it came from Bedlam, he bolted out of the barn. It was the last time Sam ever saw Leander.

****

Sam was torn between going after Lander and staying put with George. After a few distraut moments, he decided to stay with the wounded man.

With an enormous feat of will, George put the paper on his lap and started writing.

May 12, 1865

Dear Father,

This is my last letter to you. I am dying. I have a grievous wound made by the last shot fired in the rebellion.

At least it's a chest wound. You can rest easy since I was shot facing the enemy and not in the back like a coward.

A drop of blood landed on the paper and splayed out. Sam saw it and hung his head.

Gurgling sounds came from deep in George's chest. He closed his eyes and his hand fell to his lap. The pencil rolled off his leg and dropped to the dirt floor.

The abnormal sounds frightened Sam and he scooted back against the far wall and stared at the wounded man. He had seen dozens of men die, but never this way, never this close, never so agonizingly slow.

Like a knife in his heart, he felt the man's pain. He wanted to run away, to be free of watching another man die, to be a coward like Leander. Instead, he covered his ears and closed his eyes, praying to God to make the horrid scene go away.

When he opened his eyes, the gurgling had stopped and George was wheezing like a bellows. Sam felt the instant heat of shame on his face. Now the few yards back to George required an enormous effort. On hands and knees, Sam dragged himself back on this short but terrible journey. Finally he was beside George again and he looked down at him, his face full of pity.

George's cheeks, smooth a few moments ago, were furrowed now, as if the wound had made him suddenly older. He opened his eyes and where Sam expected to find utter terror, he saw peace.

"I need water."

Sam knew the loss of fluids from wounds made wounded men acutely thirsty. Sam also knew the water wasn't good for him, but he was sure George wouldn't last very long. *What difference will it make now?*

Sam got his canteen and held it to George's mouth. The injured soldier drank greedily. The water, tinged with red, spilled over both sides of his mouth, and ran down his chest to the gaping wound. As the water touched thew ound, George jerked spasmodically

When he'd had enough, George pushed the canteen away and gasped for air in short, rapid breaths. After a while his breathing slowed. He smiled gratefully at Sam and said, "Thanks."

As if the water gave him strength, George made a second extraordinary effort and straightened himself up.

Without being asked, Sam reached down, picked up the pencil and handed it to him.

George began to write again.

I was not always a good son to you and mother but I was always honest. So you will believe me when I tell you that I love you both.

I know that my death is inevitable, and that in a short while I'll be leaving this earth. Now that my inheritance is moot, the son that you claim is a half-breed can rightfully take over when you can't work any longer. Dakota's a good man, give him a chance.

The racking cough began again and more blood speckled the page. Sam stared at George's ashen face. *He has that look I know so well, that look of death that slowly, inexorably works from the inside out.*

Maybe if I just leave him. He's gonna die anyway. Sam gathered himself to flee, and his mind ran out the door, but his courageous feet wouldn't move and he stayed where he was, holding the hand of the dying man.

Finally the coughing stopped. "I'm... okay," George said between short, labored breaths.

George stared at Sam with a questioning, tormented look. A small dribble of blood escaped from the side of his mouth.

Sam reached in his pocket, took out one of General Pope's silk hankies. He hesitated for a moment, remembering he was saving the handkerchief for his mother, then dabbed the corners of George's mouth.

"You'll deliver... this letter for me... won't you.. Sam?"

Sam stared at George, his eyes became moist and he nodded. *Oh God. I don't want to deliver anything. I just want to go home. Maybe if he doesn't tell me his full name I can just throw the letter away. Then I can forget him and go on my way. But if he says it, if he says his name, it will be like a bayonet stabbed into me that will never come out until I fulfill his mission.*

"God bless you, Sam." His eyes rolled back into his skull and he went limp.

Sam stiffened and cringed. *His eyes are sunken. His cheeks protrude. His face is waxy yellow. It's the death mask.*

George's eyes came back down and he gave Sam a weak smile. "My father's… name is… George Forrest… same as mine. He's George Forrest Senior… of Folsom, Alabam…" He closed his eyes and dropped his head.

Sam moved closer to him and touched his arm gently.

George opened his eyes and smiled so sweetly it almost broke Sam's heart. Tears ran freely down Sam's cheeks.

George then looked down and began to write again, painfully and slowly.

I feel very weak and I'm sure I don't have much longer to live. I will die far from home, and the friends of my early youth. But I have a new friend here who is kind to me. I am going to give this letter to my new friend, Sam, and prevail upon him to deliver it to you. Of course I don't expect him to bring me to you, but I can assure you, even though you don't see me, I will be in a better place at the right hand of my Lord.

George stopped and began coughing. Frothy red bubbles appeared at his mouth. A bit of it trickled down his jaw.

Oh, God, the red bubbles, the precursor of death.

More spots of blood spilled on the paper. George reached up and weakly wiped his mouth with the back of his hand. Another smile at Sam and he began to write again, his handwriting becoming a scrawl.

I know you will be pleased that my friend, the messenger, is a Confederate. Don't hold it against him that he befriended a dying Yankee.

Tell Mother I love her

Sam could see the pencil was slipping. He gestured to George that he would help him. George shook his head no.

And tell my half brother I will pray for him, and for you too, from Heaven.
My strength is leaving, goodb

George's head lolled, he inspired deeply and his eyes rolled back out of sight. The bloody pencil smeared the last line, and fell to the earth.

Slowly, as if in a ghastly ballet, George slid in a quarter circle along the wall, leaving a gory trail of blood on the boards. He came to rest on the ground, his eyes open, staring at Sam, sightlessly.

Sam reached out and closed his eyes. He knew the look well. George was dead.

Sam

Damn the army and damn the war.

Chapter 8

Sam waited all morning for Leander to come back. He waited in vain.

When the sun began to sink toward the horizon, Sam took a shovel he found in the barn and went to the edge of the farmers land, into an uncultivated field.

A massive, bulging, white anvil, the precursor of a storm, appeared in the west and the wind began whipping along the open ground. Sam held on to his hat, walking about the large overgrown field looking for just the right place. Small bits of vegetation and dust whipped his body. He wondered if he should go and tell the farmer what had happened, then decided against it.

Finally he found a small copse of poplar trees that would give the grave shade for most of the day. Without ceremony he bent his back and began to dig. When he finally thought the crypt was deep enough he put his hand in the small of his aching spine and straightened up. He could feel his shirt plastered wet against his back. The wind whipping against the moisture in his shirt cooled him. Putting the shovel over his shoulder he made his way back to the barn.

There is an odor to death, a peculiar smell of decay that every Civil War soldier knows well. As he approached George, Sam could smell that abnormal aroma creeping out of the stall.

As Sam entered the stall he spied the note. He picked up the bloody letter. Although it had dried by now, he blew on it for good measure, folded it, and put it snugly into his pocket. He looked for the pencil and found it near the discarded pistol. He stared at the LeMat pistol, still on the floor where Leander had dropped it, and picked it up with two fingers. He turned it over and perused it as if it were some strange specie of fish, then sighed and shoved the LeMat into his belt.

Sam took a clean sheet of paper from the notebook and scribbled a note to Leander, telling him he was going south, and to catch up with him, then he pinned the note to the barn door on a splinter of wood.

Sam leaned over to pick George up when his eyes fell on George's almost new boots. He looked down at his own broken down brogans, sat down on the ground and quickly began to pull a boot off George's foot.

Suddenly he stopped. A wave of guilt came over him and he slowly let the dead man's leg down. "I can't do it, George," he muttered to the corpse. "Much as I'd like to have them, I just can't do it. I've done a lot of things in this war, things I never thought I would be capable of, but I ain't stooped to grave robbing. Not yet, anyway." Reluctantly he knelt and pushed George's boot back on his foot. He put his own worn shoes back on, stood up and stared at the slain boy. George's face was composed and peaceful. *Thank, God,* Sam thought, *I've seen so many boys dead with their faces twisted in agony.*

His eyes fell on George's jacket. *Gosh, his jacket is like new. It's still cold at night and I ain't got one. He won't mind if I use his.*

Suddenly the popular poem, *The Jacket Of Gray,* popped into his mind.

Fold it up carefully,
lay it aside,
Tenderly touch it,
look on it with pride,
For dear must it be
to our hearts evermore,
The jacket of gray
our soldier-boy wore...

Sam left the jacket where it was.

He started to lift his friend when George's forage cap fell to the ground. He let him back down, reached over, picked up the hat and stuck it in his back pocket. He bent over and grunted heavily as he lifted the corpse, putting it over his shoulder. Sam staggered when he started off.

"Damn, George, I guess the extra lead in you gave you some added weight." Sam grimaced at his own black joke.

Despite the cold wind, Sam was sweating profusely when he got to the grave. "Damn it!" he groaned, "it seems like a longer trip when you're carrying something heavy.

With great care he laid George down in the tomb as gently as he could. Sam cursed. The grave was deep enough, but he had dug the length too short. With a farm boy's practicality, Sam gritted his teeth and bent George's legs back double.

Picking up a few leaves lying on the ground Sam stood up. George's jacket was open and Sam's eyes went to the wound, the hole through which the young man's life had drained away.

"I've seen a lot of men die," he muttered, "but somehow this is different. He died for no purpose. What a waste." Sam thought of Leander running off and shook his head. *Accidents happen. He'll have to forgive himself.*

Absently he let the leaves go and they drifted down into the crypt and landed on George's wounded chest. Sam bowed his head. When he looked up the white anvil was directly over his head, with large, black cumulus clouds in back of it, darkening the sky. "I better get busy," he muttered.

Sam grabbed the shovel, bent his back, and with urgency, shoveled the dirt back into the hole. When he finished, he tamped the earth with his hands making a mound over the grave. Just as he finished the wind fell off and large, cold raindrops began to fall.

Searching the area, he found a few rocks and put them at the head of the tomb. He stood up and looked at the fresh earth, the raindrops making small divots on it. *At least the rocks'll keep the coyotes away.* Then he found an almost straight branch, stuck it in the ground and made a cross by tying a transverse branch with a piece of thread he got from his *housewife*, his soldier's sewing kit.

A squall was now sweeping along the plain and the dark, cumulus clouds boiled up over his head, blocking out what was left of the light. The wind picked up again and blew poplar leaves around Sam's lone figure. He stood at the foot of the grave, hat off, head bowed shielding his eyes from the dust being whipped along the ground. The blustering draft slapped his uniform pants against his legs and his hair whipped around wildly. The rain began to fall in earnest, and pelted his face, mixing with the sweat on his brow.

His face as dark as the clouds, Sam looked up at the sky, fell to his knees next to the freshly dug earth, and clasped his hands together. "Lord, I didn't know George very well, but he seemed like a good man. And I do know he loved you. Please accept him into Your Kingdom, where there is no North and South, and forgive him his sins. And while you're at it, forgive Leander too. I just know he didn't mean to kill George." Pictures of men he killed flitted across his mind. "And maybe you can stretch it a bit and forgive me also." He dropped his head. "In the name of Our Lord, Jesus Christ, Amen."

He got up, took George's cap out of his pocket and dropped it on the cross at the head of the grave.

Sam shook his head and muttered aloud, "George is dead. He won't know I broke the promise. I'm not going to Alabama, I'm going home." He took a few steps south, and stopped, his heart full of guilt. "Damn Leander and George, damn the army and damn the war, I just want to get home." Sam squared his shoulders, resolutely took another few steps south toward Florida, and stopped again. He turned and looked at the fresh grave, then raised his eyes to the boiling clouds, gritted his teeth and started walking southwest, toward Alabama.

As Sam walked away from the grave, a great gust of wind blew George's forage cap in a circle a few times, then lifted it off the cross and tossed it in the air. Then, just as if it always knew where it wanted to go, it started riding a gust of wind north, toward oblivion.

Forty acres and a mule

Chapter 9

Sam heard the squeak of the wagon but was too tired to look up.

"Hey, sojer, you needs a ride?"

Instantly Sam knew who it was by the accent. He forced himself to look up, squinting at the noon sun, but kept walking. "Ride with you, nigger? I'd rather walk."

After a flash of consternation crossed his face, the black man let his head fall back and he laughed, slapping his thigh. "I ain't no nigger no mo' Boss. Mister Linkum says I ain't. He says I is free, an' I gets forty acres an' a mule. I is a rich man."

Sam stopped, looked up again shielding his eyes, cocked his head and smiled.

"As you kin see, I already got dis here mule. Now all I needs is de forty acres." The Negro had a twinkle in his eyes, and laughed heartily, enjoying his own joke.

Sam took a closer look at him. He was at that age between youth and manhood. *Can't never tell how old they are.* He had faded blue work pants, a calico shirt with a worn collar, surrounding a thick neck, massive shoulders, and hands like two hams. He looks decent enough. The dark skinned man had an intelligent face with the flat nose characteristic of his race.

In spite of years of conditioning, Sam liked him immediately. *I'd best watch out, this is one smart nigger.*

"Damned if you ain't right, Boy. Well, since you're rich, I guess I will ride a ways with you." As he prepared to hoist himself on the wagon, Sam noticed the writing on the sideboard. *U. S. ARMY.*

Hmm, where did the likes of him get a Federal wagon? Sam threw his knapsack into the back of the well-worn wagon, stepped up on the wheel and slid onto the buckboard seat.

The wagon started up again and the Negro stuck his hand out. "Name's Pinkney, Lucius Pinkney, but all my friends call me Bo."

"Pleased to meetcha," Sam said ignoring his hand, and staring straight ahead.

Bo's smile faded slowly and he reluctantly drew his hand back. In a few moments he shrugged and was grinning again. “Where you goin’ Boss?”

“A place called Folsom. Know it?” He stole a glance at Bo. The black man shifted a great wad of tobacco from one side of his cheek to the other, leaned over and spit a long brown stream. Sam noticed he had the muscular body of a field hand and handled the mule with ease.

With muscles like that, he must be a farm boy. But he doesn’t look away when he talks to me. He’s an uppity nigger besides being smart. I better watch my step. No, he better watch his step. Sam patted the LeMat.

Bo leaned over and spit another stream of brown fluid over the side and shifted the wad again. His face got serious. “Sure, bin dere many times with de Massa. If’n dis here mangy mule will make it, I’ll get you dere.” His face turned darker. “Last time I was dere dat bastard Massa beat me in front of de whole damn town,” he threw up one hand in a questioning gesture, “jes ’cause I was a few minutes late. I’m sho glad he daid now. Yankee bullet got him.”

He recovered and his face split into a huge smile again. “It was worth it though. The gal I was with was de best lookin’ whore woman in town. Dey say she serviced all de town niggers but I never believed it. She was only half nigger, the other half bein’ pure injun. Much too good fer field hands.” Bo leaned back and smiled enjoying the remembering.

"Her skin was a light tan with a touch of pink. I tell you man she was soft and sweet. And she smelled real good, not like dem field women on the plantation. Dey is hard and mostly smell like skunks." He laughed and wrinkled up his nose. "I heered the whore up and got sick 'cause I had to leave. Dat's why I'm goin' back, so's I kin cure her."

Despite himself, Sam slapped his thigh and let out a whoop. "Bo, you're the biggest liar in the South, but a real good 'un."

Bo's grin got bigger. His teeth gleamed against his black skin. "No, Boss, I swear. She's still in town, waitin' for me. Waitin' for the cure. You'll see."

They both broke out in peals of laughter until Sam had to hold his sides.

That night they camped by a stream, Sam in the back of the wagon, using his knapsack for a pillow, while Bo slept on the ground, by the fire, with Sam's blanket roll for a cover.

Sam tossed and turned. He had difficulty sleeping, haunted by the frequent, hateful dreams of the men he'd killed. Finally, giving up any thought of sleeping, he got up and sat by the dying embers of the fire. He rubbed his sore feet half wishing he had taken George's boots.

The large shadow that came up at his back caused him to start. He reached for his absent gun, and felt his stomach drop when he realized it was in his saddlebag. His hands gripped into fists, and he turned to meet his adversary. With a great sigh of relief he recognized Bo in the reflected moonlight. *I got to get a holster and keep my gun on.*

"Cain't sleep, Boss?

"Too many bad dreams, Bo. Can't forget the men I killed in the war." At the memory of it, even this far from the battlefield, he shuddered.

Bo shook his head and sat down on the other side of the fire. "I done killed a few sojers too. At a place called Get-ees-burg.

Sam's head snapped up. "What? Gettysburg? What the devil were you doing there?"

Bo nodded his head slowly, a wry smile on his face. "After two days in dat place, I learned to hate killin' real quick."

A broad grin stole across his face until he was beaming ear to ear. "But dat's how come I is free."

Sam

The world was full of sound and fury.

Chapter 10

Gettysburg, the second day

"Bo, you lazy nigger, get up."

Bo woke with a start. It wasn't a dream that he was lying on the hard ground. He heard his name again.

"Goddammit Bo, get your lazy black ass goin' and get some coffee brewin' or I'll lay a whip on you somethin' fierce."

Bo sat up and stretched, undisturbed by his master's impatient instructions.

"All dem other sojers do for themselves," Bo said under his breath, "maybe you don't 'cause you got a lazy white ass under them fancy zooave britches you wear."

Bo's master stopped pouring water out of his canteen and stared at his slave. "What'd you say, Boy?"

"I said I'll get the water goin' right smart."

"You better. An' mor'n that, you better 'member yore place. I seen you lookin' down on these small farmer boys what ain't got no slaves. Even though they is po' white trash, they is still a heap better'n you."

Bo was going to ask how come one of the po' white trash had been voted in as an officer higher than him, but thought better of it. "I'll go get de water, Boss."

Bo walked through the waking camp like an unseen shadow muttering. "Some boss man. He riots aroun' de country attendin' every cockfight, hoss-race an' fox hunt, layin' wit any woman he kin get his hands on, black or white, an' he ain't never done a days work in his life. An' he says I'm lazy. He gots a pimply face an' caint grow a decent beard. An' he goes round dese cracker boys lordin' it over dem 'cause he gots a slave wit him. Mebbe one of dese cracker boys'll shoot him durin' a battle an' den we'd all be rid of him. Good riddance!"

Most of the soldiers never spoke to Bo, except to give him an order, and there were only a few other Negroes in camp. General Lee's cook, George, was friendly to him, and they usually shared Sunday leftovers together, even on the march.

When Bo got to the river he laid his bucket on the bank, looked around for cotton mouths, then dipped his hands in the water. The cool liquid felt good as he splashed his face and washed it several times. After rinsing the cotton taste out of his mouth, he filled the bucket and started the half-mile walk back.

Suddenly the ground started to rumble and the world began to shake. Clods of dirt erupted around Bo, hot iron whizzed by his head and his heart began to pound. Without thinking he let the bucket go, fell to the ground and hugged the earth. This was Bo's baptism under fire.

After a few moments the shelling let up and he raised his head. Men were running everywhere knocking over tents and grabbing stacked rifles. It looked to Bo like some giant foot had stepped on an anthill.

A passing soldier tapped him with the butt of his rifle and yelled down at him. "Better get where yer goin', Boy, It's gonna be hot 'roun' here fer a while."

Bo jumped up and ran back toward his tent.

When he got there, his master was fixing his cartridge belt. Bo ran up breathing hard, his hands shaking, and his shirt soaked with sweat.

His master's face was beet-red. "Where the goddamn hell you been, you lazy nigger. We got Yankees comin' at us. Get my extra rifle an' stay right behind me. And hold on to this." He threw his canteen to Bo.

Fightened, but also angry Bo gnashed his teeth but did as he was told. He shouldered the extra rifle and trailed along in back of his master until they reached the firing line just at the edge of a large wheat field. He hung back ten paces as his master slipped into position. Looking up he saw the rock strewn high ground blue with Federal soldiers. Bo yelled to his master. "You be careful Marse. Dem rocks be in de Debbil's mouth; an' dem Yanks up dere is thicker dan weevils in a cotton field."

The artillery of both sides started firing again and the world was full of sound and fury.

His master turned and yelled back to him. Bo screwed up his face and cupped his ear, but couldn't hear what he was saying.

Bo stared at the wheat field. A strong breeze came up leaning on the wheat making rippling waves, like seaweed in a storm tossed sea. His gaze moved to a point where the wheat field ended, then up to the heights the Confederate soldiers were going to charge. He could see men in blue uniforms with gleaming rifles facing them at the foot of the rise and in the rocks above.

At least the wheat will hide them a bit and give them some protection. But after that it's an open field and uphill all the way through the rocks.

Bo shook his head. It seemed to him that there were blue uniforms behind every boulder. He got a sinking feeling in the pit of his stomach when he looked at the wheat stalks bending in the summer breeze.

Suddenly the firing ceased. An uneasy stillness enveloped the field. Bo began to feel queasy. The breeze slowed and then stopped, leaving both sides in a blistering oven.

A picture of his master's mother flitted across his mind. She was shaking her bony finger at him, her white hair hanging in strings around her face. "Don't you let anything happen to my boy. If'n he don't come back, don't you dare come back neither." Bo shook his head and the apparition left.

The sun came up strong over the hills in a cloudless sky making it even hotter. Bo shaded his eyes and looked up at the bright orange globe beginning its daily trek across the sky. He felt a trickle of sweat down his neck. *It must be a hundred in the shade already.*

Bo trembled as he watched the captain get the troops ready. Realizing he had to get his master's rifle prepared, he reached into the leather belt wrapped around his waist, took out a cartridge, bit off the end and poured the powder into the barrel. Bo then slid the minié ball down the barrel on top of the powder. Swiftly taking the ramrod out of the Enfield, he packed the bullet on the powder with a few swift strokes. Stopping for a moment to wipe the sweat from his brow, Bo finished the job by putting the percussion cap in place.

Cradling the rifle on his knees, he crouched down and made sure he knew where his master was.

General Hood and Colonel Rice rode up and dismounted. General Hood was to lose the use of one of his arms that day, the first of two wounds that would make him a cripple for the rest of his life.

Hood raised his arm in a beckoning motion and the company captain halted the troops and double-timed to the general.

The three officers spoke quietly with Hood pointing directly to the top of Devil's Den. When they were finished the colonel and the general mounted, saluted and left.

From the Devil's Den, Union skirmishers began a desultory firing of rifles. Without being told, the Confederate troops got down on one knee.

With a deliberate show of courage, the bearded company captain stood up in front of his men, his back to the enemy. His high-pitched voice broke the stillness. "You men of Virginia, General Hood and Colonel Rice are counting on you to take that hill. And remember this, General Lee himself will be watching you. I know it looks like a rough job, but I also know if anybody can take the high ground, you can. They call it Devil's Den, so let's make it a Hell for the Yankees inside it."

The men roared their approval.

The captain turned around and looked at the blue line forming on both sides of the wheat field, then threw back his head and laughed. When he finished he turned back to the men. His normally florid face was even more flushed. "Would you look at that. The commanding idiot of the enemy has moved too far forward of the main Federal line. Now his flanks are up in the air. I want the furthest squads on the right and left to go through that wheat field and encircle the Yankee bastards. The rest of you will go at them at the oblique this way." With his arm, the captain angled a line in the air toward the enemy.

The captain's mouth corners pulled down sharply and his face darkened. "I have detailed the sergeants and lieutenants as file-closers. They will drop back when you charge. If any one of you fails in his duty, they are ordered to shoot you down like the dog you are. You will be dumped into a common grave and your family will receive a letter from me telling them of your cowardice." His eyes flashed as he looked up and down the line. "Any questions?"

He pointed off to his right at the Colonel on a small rise. "You men keep your eyes on Colonel Rice over there. He'll give the signal."

Bo riveted his eyes on the officer. The colonel, dressed in a zouave uniform like the men, stood apart from the troops. The make-up of the Zoave uniform was baggy white pants, tan colored gaiters, reaching from mid-calf to his ankle, and a form fitting bright red jacket that ended at the waist.

The colonel's once puffy pantaloons hung limp in the heat. He raised his sword, but before he had a chance to drop it, the world began to explode again. Shells from both sides filled the air.

Colonel Rice fell to the ground and the troops took cover as best they could. Bo hunched over, dropped the rifle, and for protection from flying metal, put his arms over his head. Great holes were gouged out in the earth by the Yankee shells, and sizzling pieces of hot metal flew about like angry hornets.

After a few minutes the Union artillery fire slackened, then stopped. Bo looked toward the Confederate guns. Colonel Alexander was still firing furiously at the Yankees. When he realized the Yankees had stopped firing, Bo heard Alexander yell, "Cease fire! Cease fire!" Colonel Alexander's call was echoed by his captains, and one by one, the Rebel guns fell silent.

In the ensuing quiet, the men tensed and all eyes again went to Colonel Rice. He got up off the ground, dusted the front of his pantaloons, picked his sword up, and again raised it above his head. For a moment he seemed like a statue in stone, immovable and deathly still. Suddenly the colonel's arm dropped. At his signal the Confederate troops rose up as one and with a shrill, piercing Rebel yell, charged through the wheat field toward the Devil's home.

Bo ran along with the second wave keeping his eyes glued to the back of his master. As the second line of soldiers got into the wheat field, Bo hesitated, hating to get into the maelstrom he knew was coming. A backward, scowling look from his master got him moving again and this time he stayed right with the others, his master's canteen banging against his ribs and the butt of the extra rifle bumping against his hip.

As the men pounded through the stalks of wheat, a storm of lead came back at them from the Union soldiers at the edge of the field and from the rocks above.

To Bo, the continual firing sounded like a sheet tearing. He saw the Confederate men bent over leaning forward into the hail of lead as if they were bending against a slanting rain. Within moments of getting into the wheat field, men started falling all around Bo. Soldiers near him, some groaning, some screaming, and others, eerily silent, began to die.

He heard the minié balls hum, whiz whistle and shriek by his ears and he desperately wanted to run away from this madness. Only the thought of the file-closers with their orders to shoot deserters kept him in place. *I wonder if dey would shoot a slave?* Bo thought. "You bet dey would!" he grunted aloud, answering his own question.

The withering fire had its effect. It made the men around him stop running and, either lay down prone, or get down on one knee. They began to load and fire as rapidly as they could at the Federals.

A sudden gasp in back of him made Bo turn. He was just in time to see the sad-eyed blonde giant, General Hood, reel in his saddle and sprawl to the ground with a thud.

Bo's eyes widened when he saw the wound in his arm stain the general's sleeve bright red.

An aide ran to him while the general struggled up on his good elbow. "Never mind me," he shouted at the aide, "right now we need men with guns in their hands."

Bo marveled at his courage. He watched intently as a brigadier galloped up, dismounted and raced to the wounded general. Just at that moment several of the general's aides also converged on him. All of the officers gathered around the fallen general.

One of the aides tried to sit the general up against a tree. Hood groaned and shook. The aide gave up, let him down easy and stood up.

He addressed the brigadier. "General Law, it appears that General Hood is indisposed. I believe it will be incumbent upon you and your South Carolinians to carry on in his stead."

General Law's finely chiseled features and firm mouth hardened. He nodded his understanding and the aide braced and saluted again.

General Law casually returned the salute and watched as the aides carried Hood off in search of a surgeon.

For a while General Law watched the battle, smoothing his mustache with a finger while he thought. Suddenly his eyes lit up and smoldered with fire. "Captain," he said to his aide, "go and make sure General Hood has my brigade surgeon tend to his wounds." Law addressed General Hood's colonel without taking his eyes off the battle developing in front of him. "And you, Colonel, I want you personally to go to your brigade officer and tell him to advance straight, instead of obliquely, toward the base of that small mountain."

"But General Law, General Longstreet himself said to charge at that angle—"

"Things have changed here. I refuse to expose my men to enfilade fire at their backs. I will take full responsibility. Now, follow my order."

The colonel braced and threw his shoulders back. "Sir, General Longstreet gave me a specific command to charge obliquely. I will change those instructions only upon a written order from you, General Law."

The general's face reddened. "Very well, Colonel." A small notebook appeared in Law's hand and he quickly wrote a few lines and handed it to the colonel. "Now, go quickly before I lose my temper and my brigade." The colonel saluted, Law barely answered, and the colonel left. "Damn Philistine," Law muttered.

Bo watched the colonel run off toward the major in charge of the brigade. General Law nodded once, convinced he had done the right thing and turned his attention back to the field.

Bo watched the Rebels charge, his eyes full of concern. *General Law, it's too late. We've been licked. Our men are running back, lickity split.* When the Rebels came dashing out of the wheat field, Bo had to laugh. The retreating Confederates were being led by the speedy file-closers.

Bo looked back at the wheat field and shook his head. He was amazed that the minié balls and artillery from both sides had scythed the stalks of wheat almost to the ground. Brown, blue and gray clad bodies littered the field, and the few stalks left standing were red with their blood.

Along with the other exhausted men, Bo's master sat on the ground at the Rebel starting point, unhurt, but shaken and winded from the ordeal of battle, and the inglorious retreat. He was breathing hard, his face covered with grime and sweat, his mouth slack with fatigue.

Crouching low, Bo ran to him and knelt at his side. The master looked at his slave plaintively. "I wish you could shoot, Bo. We need more men up on the line."

"You knows I kin shoot, Boss." He handed the canteen to his master.

Bo's master drank greedily, the precious liquid spilling out both sides of his mouth.

When he had slaked his thirst he lowered the canteen, breathing heavily. "I know you can shoot, Bo, but they won't let the likes of you fight."

The man sitting on the ground next to them laughed and looked balefully at Bo. "He's right, no chance they'll let a nigra on the line."

Another soldier, a farm boy from the flat coast of South Carolina, pointed a bony finger at Bo. "Yore boy kin take mah place any time he wants." The others laughed but not the farm boy.

Bo also did not see the humor, and looked from one soldier to the other, his face grave.

The major, brandishing his sword, moved among the men shouting, "Get up and get ready boys, we're goin' in again."

There was a collective groan from the troops. But they all got up on one knee, keeping their heads down to avoid the bullets still whizzing around them.

Forming the men into a semblance of a line, the major prepared them for the charge. "Instead of at an angle this time, General Law wants you men to go straight toward that small mountain, and don't stop for nuthin'—"

"Ceptin' maybe to kill a few Yanks," someone joked. No one laughed.

The major raised his sword and shouted, "It'll be easier this time, they won't be able to fire on your backs and you'll be supported on your right by the Fifteenth Alabama. The Fifteenth is led by Colonel Oates. And he never retreats. Y'all ready?" The major raised his sword and waited for the signal from the colonel. When he saw the colonel drop his blade the major dropped his own sword and yelled, "Charrrrrge!"

Bo got up on both knees and watched his master stand up, get into an infantry crouch, and move forward with the others. Bo reached for the bayonet on his belt and snapped it on the spare Enfield.

Stepping into the bitterly contested wheat field, Bo's master took a few steps then suddenly his head jerked back and his blood stained hat flew off. He stopped in place and seemed to just throw his rifle away. For a moment he stood there, then slowly turned around and faced Bo. He opened his mouth to scream but nothing came out. Then his eyes rolled up in his head and he crumpled to the ground.

Bo uttered a cry and raced to him in a crouch. When he got there he knelt down and stared at his master's face.

His blond locks were parted showing dark blue eyes that were open, staring sightless at the sky. A small hole in the forehead had expanded and taken part of the back of his head off. A scarlet stain, deeper colored than his red vest, flowed from the wound on his forehead down his face and neck, joined the rivulet from the back of his head, and dripped into the earth.

Bo cringed. *Lawd-a-mighty what am I gonna tell his ma. She'll take my hide off sure.*

A bullet whizzed by and caught the tip of Bo's ear. He yelped in pain as he felt the sting and put his hand to his ear. It felt warm and sticky. He looked at his hand. The pink part was tinged red with his blood. Bo's heart began to pound. Then a great rage boiled up in him and he put both hands on the extra Enfield and stood up.

"God damn you all," he yelled at the Federals, who were at that moment cautiously entering the decimated wheat field, and began running toward them. Other Confederate soldiers, skulking back, saw him, and by twos and fours stopped, and turned around watching the black man race forward. For a few moments they hesitated, then, feeling ashamed, they gripped their rifles tightly and started running after Bo. Soon the whole Confederate line had turned and were charging the Federals.

In a few moments they were among the blue coats shooting, cutting, and slashing.

The soldiers of both sides, with their anxieties, their fears, their rages so long pent up, erupted. They shouted and roared throughout the wheat field.

The Rebel Yell, bursting from the throats of the Confederates, made all hearts beat faster.

The Yankees tried to out-shout them with a gutteral roar.

The unleashed Rebels catapulted forward with one common thought, kill or be killed. And so the gray tide rolled on. The soldiers fired until both sides were so close they had to use their muskets as clubs to brain the nearest enemy. Suddenly the Yankees gave a little, and then without warning, the bluecoats turned and began to run.

Just as quickly as it started, it stopped, It appeared that the Rebels were in sole possession of the wheat field.

Some of the Confederates jumped and shouted and others sank to the ground glad to still be alive. Some of the more thoughtful soldiers stared at the blue and gray lumps that were once men.

Unexpectedly, and with a yell that could be heard for miles, the Yankees were back. Rebel soldiers, caught off guard, stumbled back. Bo was among them.

From the time he had a memory Bo had been bullied, first by his mother, and later, because he was a scrawny child, by other children. When he became of age, he was put in the cotton fields. Although the work made him strong, he was used to being bullied by the other field hands. The few times he fought back, he was caught and beaten by the overseer. When the scion of the family was old enough, Bo was given to him. He was not a kind master.

Now on the battlefield, with a gun in his hands and no one to stop him, all of the repressed rage stuffed into Bo by his family and his owners erupted. He became a madman. He rushed wildly toward the charging Yanks. Amazed at his courage, the retreating Confederates stopped, reformed and ran to his side.

Bo dropped to one knee, pulled the trigger of the Enfield, and a blue coat fell. Then, because he had no time to reload, he jumped in among the Yanks, stabbing and cutting with his bayonet. Union men ran from his fury. Though he couldn't understand what they were yelling, Bo heard soldiers shouting strange, unrecognizable sounds. All around him were cries of the wounded mingled with shouts, curses and the screams of men dying, and men in peril. All of it came together to Bo's ears as a detached, muted roar.

After a while the fighting became a blur. Bo lost count of the men he had cut down. He was among the bluecoats, braining and slashing, when suddenly a burly, red-faced man with a full black beard, seemed to pop up in front of him. The man raised his rifle like a club, and stopped in mid arc when he saw Bo's black face. He growled, "Fighting to stay a slave, huh!"

He took another step toward Bo, and again began the swing of his rifle, aiming the stock for the black man's head.

With the desperation of a man about to die, Bo brought the Enfield up to block the blow. The

Yankee gun splintered but knocked Bo to the ground. The Union soldier, his weapon destroyed, pulled a bowie knife and left his feet, leaping for Bo's throat.

Instinctively Bo thrust his rifle up and the Yankee landed on his bayonet. Instantly his portly abdomen showed a dark, red stain. The Union soldier bellowed in pain, went to his knees, his eyes, big as saucers staring at Bo's black face. For a few moments he stayed there with a puzzled look, then his face darkened and he went to the ground. He sprawled on his back like an obese rag doll, Bo's bayonet still sticking in his abdomen, the Enfield rifle tilted at an obscene angle.

Bo got up on one elbow and stared at the dead man. Suddenly Bo again became aware of the bedlam around him and quickly got to his feet. He grabbed the stock of his rifle, put his foot on the man's chest and yanked the bayonet out. He stared at the dead man for a moment longer, felt a momentary elation, then looked to his front. The battle still raged around him but Bo could see the Federals were grudgingly giving ground, slowly moving back past the clear area and filtering up among the rocks. Bo started running toward the boulders to help the Confederate troops fighting there. Many of the Yankees were above them outlined starkly against the bright sky. *This ought to be easy*, Bo thought.

He cleared the wheat field, knelt and re-loaded the Enfield. He sighted on one of the men in the rocks above him. Before he could squeeze the trigger, he felt a thud and white-hot streak of pain in his right shoulder that spun him around and knocked the Enfield from his grip. Slowly, as if in a dream, Bo leaned forward supporting himself on one arm, then fell to the ground. Even though the sun was brilliant overhead, it was dark in Bo's world. He felt like he was in a murky shaft, falling, falling…

****

It was night when Bo awoke. He sat up, let out a cry from the pain that shot through his shoulder, and fell back. After a few minutes he tried again. This time he moved more slowly and eased himself up to a sitting position with only a mild discomfort.

Bo looked around him. Other men lay on cots and on the dirt floor in haphazard rows. He heard loud moans and soft cries for water. He looked at the canvas above him and began to realize he was in a hospital tent.

Bo heard two men arguing outside the tent.

Inside the tent the smell of gangrene and death was overwhelming. Bo tried to get up to leave, but the pain, and a severe attack of vertigo stopped him. He groaned and sat back down on the dirt floor.

A strange sight in the corner of the tent caught his eye. At first his mind refused to believe it, but there it was. Amputated arms and legs lay in a careless pile, swarms of flies buzzing around the rotting limbs. Some of the legs still had boots on. Only the pain and dizziness prevented Bo from bolting off the floor and leaving this pestilential place.

Just then the two men who had been arguing came through the tent flap. Bo forgot about the amputated limbs and turned his attention to them.

"—We need the space so you get your nigger friend outta here."

"Listen, you," the other man, with sergeant's chevrons said, "if it wasn't fer that African a whole lotta boys'd be dead now. He's a damn hero, and he—"

The orderly folded his arms akimbo and interrupted. "The surgeon says he goes. I say he goes. So he goes! Now get him on outta here or we'll take no more of y'all's wounded." The orderly turned abruptly and started walking out of the tent.

"Goddamn you, and the doctor," the soldier said to his back.

The sergeant spit a brown stream at the departing figure then turned and walked over to Bo.

Bo smiled, his teeth gleaming against his black skin, and said, "Thanks."

"No, Boy, we should be thankin' you. You were a one man army out there." He shook his head and put his hand on Bo's good shoulder. "If'n you was white they'd a given you the Medal of Honor. You deserve better, but the man says I gotta get you outta here." Under his deep tan the sergeant's face colored red and he looked away, ashamed.

Bo struggled to get off the ground and the sergeant hurried to help him to his feet.

Bo staggered a few steps and the sergeant grabbed him.

"Give me a minute, jes 'til the world stops spinnin'."

"Take yer time, Boy."

Bo tried another step. "I'm all right now. Let's go."

They walked out of the tent, the sergeant holding on to Bo's good arm.

"The boys want you to come to our camp. It's dark now so nobody'll mind."

Holding his arm close to his chest to ease the pain, Bo, with the soldier by his side, walked quietly through the somber camp.

"How come dey is no yellin', or foolin' goin' on like dey usually is?" Bo asked.

"We lost a lotta men today. I guess no one feels like whoopin' it up tonight." The soldier looked thoughtful. "Marse Lee's got his blood up, though, and I bet my sorry britches it's gonna be worse tomorrer."

Bo nodded his head in agreement.

In a few minutes, Bo and the sergeant approached the front of a tent where four men were playing cards by firelight.

"Here we are," the sergeant said.

One man put down his cards. "Is this the boy?" He stuck out his hand. "I never seed such fightin', Boy. Yer a wonder."

Bo reached out with his good hand, a little surprised at the familiarity.

Another pointed to the ground. "Set a spell."

Bo felt uneasy. Strange white men usually worked him or ignored him, but they had never been friendly.

The other two nodded their assent.

The sergeant sat down in the circle cross-legged, while Bo let himself down easy, holding on to his throbbing arm.

After passing a whiskey bottle around, tongues loosened and the night passed quickly. Finally the four men were asleep on the ground and only Bo and the sergeant were still awake. The whiskey had done its job well and Bo felt no pain.

The rest of the camp, except for the brightly lit headquarters tent, was silent. Men were going in and out of the HQ tent hurriedly. Watching the officers come and go, Bo guessed Generals Lee, and Longstreet, were planning the next day's battle.

The sergeant leaned back and stared at the upper half of the Devil's Den where the Yankees were still lodged, and they had done so much hard fighting that day. He could hear the clinking and muffled sounds of the Federal troops digging in. The sergeant gave a long sigh. "This war is tedium punctuated by sheer terror. Tonight it's tedium, but the Bluebellies are diggin' in deep, so tomorrer there'll be some terror when we go up those rocks. The sergeant looked up at the high ground.

"You know, Boy, if they had supported us on the left yestiddy, an' Dick Ewell woulda got off his ass, we coulda driven them Yanks offa that hill and gone all the way to Washington. Some day in the future, some ex-soldier will stand on those boulders, cry for his comrades, and contemplate what might have been."

He shook his head slowly. "We gained a lot of glory today but lost our bravest men."

The sergeant turned and stared at Bo by the firelight. "If is wasn't fer you, we'd a lost even more." His brow furrowed and he cocked his head. "How'd you happen to be here, Boy? This ain't yer fight."

Bo smiled, the firelight making his teeth gleam in the dark. "My massa came to de army and brought me wit him. When he was shot I thought it was mah duty to fight on for him."

"He's daid?"

"Yassuh."

The soldier nodded slowly and leaned forward. "Well then, Boy," he whispered, "don't tell no one I tol' ya so, but yer a free man now."

Bo's eyes narrowed. "Free? Me?"

"Yeah, free! You! If'n I wuz you I'd hightail it outta here and go toward Washington as quick as ah could. Now! Tonight!"

This was heady stuff and Bo felt dizzy again.

The sergeant tapped the ground. "This here place is Pennsylvania soil, a Northern State. They's no paterollers up here. If you bolt now you'll be safe up here. They ain't got no fugitive slave law now, up here. They's no one but usn's be interested in catchin' you, Boy. An' after the kinda fightin' we had all day today, none of the boys in this army be lookin' fer no runaway slave"

Bo was thoughtful.

"If you go across to the Yankee side they's bound ta be a loose wagon or two. They's plenty of horses and mules runnin' loose 'cause their owners got shot daid today. Them Yankees got so much stuff they cain't keep track of it nohow."

The sergeant pointed to the rocks above them without looking. "Hear all that clinkin' an' choppin'? They'll be diggin' in all night, tonight, preparin' fer the battle tomorrer and prob'ly won't notice any such thing as a mule and an ol' wagon be missin'."

Bo pondered what the sergeant said for a few moments. *Freedom! Do I dare take a chance?*

After a minute of intense thought, Bo stood up, smiled, and stuck out his good hand.

The sergeant stood also and took Bo's huge mitt in both of his.

"I admit after watchin' you today, I done changed mah mind 'bout some a you folks. Yer a hell of a man black or white. God speed you, Boy."

Bo grinned and turned toward the Yankee camp.

Three Came Home

It's true that the heroes die first.

Chapter 11

The next morning found Bo and Sam shivering over a fire, waiting for coffee to boil.

A delightful aroma filled the air and Bo smiled at his good fortune. His teeth chattered when he spoke. "Where'd you get de coffee, Boss? Even my po' massa, rich as he was, ain't had none-a-dat for more'n a year now."

"My buddy, Leander, traded some Yankee trooper for the coffee at Durham Station. He said he had to pay dear for a pound of the stuff." Sam took a deep sniff and smiled. "But I say, whatever he paid, it was worth it."

"Yankees, huh. I was wit dem Yankees a while. After I runned away from Get-ees-burg, I got so hongry I jined up with a bunch of dem blue sojers." Bo shrugged his shoulders and stuck out his ample lip. "Dey treated me worser den the Crackers evuh did."

He shook his massive head slowly. "You know Boss, de house niggers on de plantation looked down on de white trash, but I never looked down on no one. How come dem Yankees looked down on me den?"

Bo broke into a wide grin. "Dat man Linkum, he promised all de niggers forty acres and a mule. But all dem Yankees ever showed me was a scrub brush and the bottom of a kettle. After a while I was either cookin' in it, or cleanin' on it."

Sam smiled and poured a steaming stream of coffee into Bo's cup.

Bo sipped the fiery liquid. "An' when it came time to sleep, dey put me in a field with a buncha other niggers. No tent, no cover. My massa woulda had a hissy fit if'n he'd a seen dat. He always tol' me he paid too much for me to let me get sick. 'Boy', he used to say, 'lettin' you git sick is like throwin' a thousand dollahs right down de open seat of a privy.'"

Bo sniffed the coffee and then took another sip. "Forty acres an' a mule? Ha! It was more like we wuz forty mules workin' an acre."

Sam laughed so hard he had trouble pouring the steaming coffee for himself. "You know Bo, I could get to like you. 'Specially if you're really as good a Yankee hater as you say."

"I ain't said I hated dem. How could you hate someone who's gonna give you forty acres an' a mule." He feigned thoughtfulness for a moment. "'Ceptin, dey ain't given me neither one yet." He shook his head knowingly. "I'm gonna give 'em another twenty years. If dey ain't given dem to me by den, I'm gonna hate 'em."

Sam slapped his thigh and laughed again, the sound echoing through the dark, to the puzzlement of the night creatures around them.

"Boy, I'm sure glad I caught up with you."

Bo smiled broadly and gave a self-satisfied nod. "Seems I'se de one whats caught up wit you."

Sam took a long drink of the coffee and smacked his lips. He stared into the fire and was thoughtful, remembering. When he spoke his voice was soft and low. "You know what the worst thing about the war was? Besides the killing I mean."

Bo cocked his head, his attention on Sam. "What's dat, Boss?"

"It was the smell of the battlefield. If only the Confederate Congress could smell that rotten odor once, they would never vote for war. Second to that was hunger! At the beginning the food was plentiful, but the last two years my belly was almost always empty. Except for that time in Pennsylvania, we ate parched corn and green apples for most of the last two years."

He smiled and turned to Bo. "One time my father came to visit me in camp. Well I figgered I can't give him just parched corn so I went to Colonel Fields and asked if we could dine with him that night. To my joy the colonel was very gracious and said 'Of course.' Well you could imagine my anticipation, actually eating regular food with the officers. By the time supper came my mouth was pure watering for a really good meal for once. I dreamed all day of fried chicken and beef and potatoes and all the trimmings. Finally the day ended and Dad and me showed up at the colonel's tent. We sat down, and my mouth began to water again as his Negro cook began to serve us. But when I looked down at my plate there it was, my old friend, parched corn alongside a green apple. Turns out the officers were eating the same damned fare as we were."

It was Bo's turn to laugh, his teeth white against his shiny black face reflecting the flames of the fire.

Sam continued his voice subdued. "You know Bo, at Gettysburg we gained nothing. The generals got lots of glory, but we lost our bravest men." He shook his head slowly and spoke in low, measured tones. "It's true that the heroes die first."

For a while both of them were silent, remembering the heat and the killing.

After a while Sam continued. "When we charged the Yanks on the last day, I got all the way to the stone wall," Sam shook his head. "You know, I think that was the high mark of the Confederacy.

"When I got to the wall, the cannon fire from the Yanks was so hot we couldn't take another step. After an eternity of bullets whizzing around us, and men dropping like flies, the sergeant finally yelled, 'Go back! Save yourselves! Retreat!'"

"So here I go. For the first hundred yards I broke the speed record. But having a horror of being shot in the back, I turned around and for the next hundred yards ran backwards."

For a moment Bo was silent. Then the picture in his mind of Sam running backward was too much for him, and he broke out in peals of laughter.

After a few seconds of puzzlement, Sam joined in.

The Kingdom of Jones

Chapter 12

By dawn Sam and Bo were approaching the town of Folsom.

"There's the sheriff's office, Bo. I bet he'll know how to get to the Forrest place."

Bo nodded wordlessly. His mouth was turned down, his face in a scowl. He'd been in too many of these redneck towns to feel comfortable and he remembered what happened the last time he was in Folsom.

The main avenue was one of those streets that was dusty in the sun and muddy in the rain. A wooden walk with a cover to block the sun for the ladies was built in front of the stores.

Bo and Sam passed the general store, the blacksmith, and the undertaker, and pulled up in front of the Sheriff's office. A small sign, its paint peeling, hung over the door. It said: *Stacey Odom, Sheriff, Jones County, Alabama.*

Across the street, four men were talking in front of a saloon. When Sam got down off the buckboard, the men stopped talking and all of them stared at the newcomers.

Bo was immediately on the alert, his nostrils flaring like a wary animal. "Uh, oh, Boss, looks like we's got a welcomin' committee of po' white trash."

Sam shrugged his shoulders and stepped on the wooden planking just as the sheriff's door opened and a matronly woman strode out.

Sam tipped his forage cap. "Morning, Ma'am."

"Hmmph," she said in a clipped voice as she looked across the street at the four loungers with disgust. "I'm glad someone has some manners in this God-forsaken town."

Sam smiled, watching her bustle swing back and forth as she hurried down the dusty street. He took off his cap and scratched his head. "Guess she's in a hurry."

One of the four men, the one with a full black beard and a crooked smile, yelled to Sam, "That's the Sheriff's wife. She's a doughfaced, copperhead Yankee, and it ain't just you she don't like, she don't like no one." The three others laughed their agreement.

Sam looked directly at the man speaking. He had a hump on his back and his face was disfigured with one eye distinctly lower than the other. He was dressed in a plaid work shirt and overalls. Even as far away as he was, Sam could see his misshapen eyes were ice blue and piercing, with lots of white showing from the eye to the bottom lid. Sam got the feeling the eyes reflected a heart smoldering with hate. The man wore his gun out, like a westerner, just at the level of his hand.

Sam held to the medieval conviction that someone this disfigured had to have evil inside him. He felt a need for caution and his smile faded.

The oldest man, with a white beard and watery blue eyes, left the others and ambled over to Sam. He looked at Sam's uniform with awe. "You done been to the war, young feller?"

Sam turned to him. "Yeah. I seen too much of that elephant."

"Elephant? What do you mean?" the old man said, a puzzled look on his face.

Sam smiled and searched his mind for an explanation. "When the circus came to town, country people had to come see an elephant cause they didn't believe its description. A battle was just like that. You had to be in one to believe what it was like. Seeing too much of it means I've had enough of the war, and I want to forget it."

The other three men walked across the road to the wagon and surrounded it. Bo squirmed uneasily.

The disfigured man nodded his head toward Bo. "If it weren't fer the likes a them, the war never woulda even happened." His two younger companions nodded.

Sam looked them over carefully and didn't like what he saw. Along with the hunchback were two of the meanest looking boys he had ever seen.

One of them blurted out, "The nigger's probably with them Free Staters. He oughter be strung up."

Bo's broad black face turned hard and the cords in his neck bulged. His thick hands balled into fists.

At Bo's movements the two younger men moved slightly and both of them put their gun hands on top of their pistol butts. They were both smiling, but the grins were as cold as ice. Sam could tell they were as full of venom as their deformed companion.

Sam carefully watched their movements as he spoke. "Now wait just a damn minute," he said, his face turning red, "he's my nigger and no one's gonna do anything to him."

The door opened and the Sheriff stepped out. "What's all this caterwallin' about."

The twisted man spoke without turning his head, his uneven eyes still locked on Sam. "Sheriff, this deserter comes here in a Yankee wagon. And he's done brought his nigger with him, and I don't like the looks of either one of them."

"We weren't bothering any one, Sheriff. All I want is directions to the Forrest place and we'll get right on outta here."

The Sheriff looked Sam's uniform over, and turned to the men. "How do you know he's a deserter? Far as I kin tell this here boy's been fightin' fer us. I didn't see any of you volunteerin' to fight fer the Confederacy, or even agin' it. As for the wagon, he might of captured it." He turned to Sam. "Ain't that right, boy."

Sam nodded.

The two younger toughs looked sheepishly at each other, and moved closer to the deformed man.

"We're doin' our share," The twisted man muttered in a low voice, his face sullen, "supplyin' beef."

"Speakin' of supplyin' beef, I'd best be gettin' on back to work," the white haired old man said as he walked up to Sam and held out a grizzled paw. "Sure wish I could have been in the war with you." He shook hands vigorously with Sam and drew him close. "Watch out fer them three," he whispered, "they're bad news, 'specially the one with the humpback. All three of 'em are thieves, but that lumpy one, he's a murderer, and the other two are easy led."

Sam took off his forage cap and scratched his head as he watched the old man amble down the dusty street.

Meanwhile the sheriff was speaking to the toughs. "The least you kin do is respect this boy and his property."

He turned back to Sam. "How's General Lee doin' with that Yankee feller, Grant. Last we heard they was all locked up in Virginny somewhere."

Sam stepped on the hub, grabbed the top of the wheel, swung up on the buckboard seat and sat down hard. Then he turned and faced the Sheriff. "General Lee surrendered to Grant a few days ago, at a place called Appomattox. General Johnston quit a few days later at Durham Station."

"See Sheriff, he's a liar," one of the young toughs said and spat at the wagon. "He's probably a deserter, and lyin' to ya so he can get away. You oughtta arrest him, Sheriff."

The sheriff turned and stared at the tough, a look of disgust on his face. "It's you that's the shirker, Boy. If I had my way I'd throw all three of you bums in jail."

Sam felt the heat rising up his neck. He fought his anger but couldn't push it down. "I know Johnston quit," he said vehemently, "I was with him when he did." He turned to Bo. "Let's get the hell outta here."

Bo backed the buckboard out leaving the three men and the sheriff, on the walk, talking angrily among themselves. As he straightened the wagon to go, the sheriff broke away and came alongside Sam.

"The Forrest place is not but ten or twelve miles straight down this road. But if you go that way you'll have to go through the Kingdom of Jones." He shook his head. "I wouldn't do that if'n I was you."

"Kingdom of Jones? Free Staters? What's goin' on around here, Sheriff?"

The sheriff laughed and slapped his thigh. "Put yer wagon up and come on in the office, Boy. Fer your sake mebbe we better talk."

Sam nodded to Bo and got down. He stepped up on the wooden walk and turned to tell Bo he'd be right back. When he saw the looks on the faces of the toughs, he changed his mind and beckoned Bo to follow him. The Negro tied up the mule and followed Sam and the sheriff into the office.

"Goddamn bombproofs," Sam muttered as he stepped into the office.

The sheriff stopped and turned to Sam. "What's a bombproof?"

Sam laughed. "A bombproof is a man of army age that, by influence or purchase, secures a safe detail or exemption from conscription. In other words, they're skulkers.

"That's them all right," the sheriff said and sat down at his desk putting his feet up. Sam sat opposite him. Bo stood near the door, looking out the window at the three toughs. The sheriff continued. "They're white trash and everyone knows it. They've also got lots of hard money, greenbacks I've been told. They got it sellin' Confederate beef to the Yanks. Nuthin' I kin do about it lessn I catch 'em, an' I ain't catched 'em yet."

The sheriff opened the top drawer of his desk, took out a fat, black cigar and bit off the end. He spat it toward a spittoon and missed. The wet piece landed on a brown spot among a bunch of its predecessors. He lit the cigar, blew the smoke to the ceiling, leaned back in his chair and patted his ample stomach.

"Let me tell you about the Kingdom of Jones. In sixty-one, when the war started, Jones County, named after John Paul Jones, raised seven companies. The County got 'em all new gray uniforms and sent 'em off in high style; brass bands 'n everythin'. But in sixty-two the Confedurit congress passed the Twenty Negro Law. That law said if'n you owned twenty niggers you was exempt from the war. That's when some of the boys started desertin'. When they came 'round here they said they wasn't fightin' fer no rich men who wouldn't even scrap fer their own property." The sheriff stole a glance at Bo.

Bo stayed at his place by the door, his expression blank.

The sheriff turned back to Sam.

"Between one and two hundred of the deserters settled on an island in the Leaf River, jes south of here. They soon was bein' led by a fellow deserter, a bandy legged Irishman named, Newton Knight."

The sheriff shook his head and smiled. "The Rebs in Richmond sent a general down here by the name of, Robert Lowery, to go after the deserters. He spent a couple of years chasin' them, and they had two or three big battles, but the general didn't have much luck. He caught a few, but because of the swamps around the river, the deserters could disappear easy like. 'Sides, they had lots of help from the poor farmers 'round here who thought like they did. And the cotton mouths and an abundant supply of Enfield rifles kept most outsiders outside."

The sheriff exhaled toward the ceiling, which already had a small blanket of blue smoke. "In sixty-three, Newt Knight and his band of cut throats met in a town named Soso, and voted to seceed from Alabama."

"They did what?" Sam said, incredulously.

"Don't laugh!" the sheriff continued. "They said, cause the Confederate Congress passed unjust laws, they was quittin'. Quittin' not only the Union, but the state too. They was already out of the Confederacy." The sheriff shook his head. "And they did it. They upped and seceded from everything, calling their new state, The Kingdom of Jones."

The sheriff looked at Bo again. "When the folks 'round here heard about the free state, lots of the nigras and poor whites went and jined 'em.

Knight married one of the nigra gals by the name of Rachael—"

Bo stiffened.

"—and Knight insisted that all the Africans had to be treated as equals. Now that didn't sit too well with the local gentry 'round here."

The sheriff took a last puff, threw his cigar towards the spittoon and missed. He cussed at it, stood up, picked up the errant cigar and walked to the door. Bo stepped back and Sam got up. The sheriff opened the door, threw the cigar into the street, and indicated the meeting was over.

As Sam was leaving the sheriff touched his shoulder. "My advice to you is to give the Free State a wide berth. It'd be best if you take the first fork left as soon as you leave town and go around the kingdom. It'll be twenty miles longer, but..." he shrugged.

Sam thanked the sheriff and they left. After they got on the wagon, Sam looked up and down the street for the cripple and the toughs. They were gone. He breathed a long sigh of relief.

Bo laid a whip on the mule's back and started down the road.

As soon as they left town the dirt street became a washboard road. The buckboard slid and bounced, jolting the two men until they ached. Finally they came to the fork in the road. Bo guided the mule to the left as the Sheriff suggested, and without warning the road smoothed out.

Sam felt angry and sullen as Bo drove the mule hard down the road.

"I wish those bums woulda been with us in a battle or two. Maybe they'd a been a bit more humble."

"Uh oh, Boss, I was worried about dis."

Sam looked up quickly, concerned at the tone in Bo's voice. Ahead of them he could see two men. *Damn, it's the cripple and one of the hooligans.* They were mounted, their horses blocking the road, their rifles out of their scabbards. Instantly the atmosphere changed.

"How the hell did they get in front of us so soon?" Sam muttered. He turned to Bo, urgency in his voice. "Better turn this wagon and get outta here, Bo. They look like they mean business."

Bo looked back then pulled back on the reins and the mule slowed to a stop. "Too late Boss, they got us cut off."

Sam heard laughter in back of them and pivoted in his seat. There was the other tough, rifle in hand, sitting bareback on a painted horse, a twisted, evil grin on his face. His eyes were two deep ugly weapons that meant other men harm.

Both men in front started toward Bo's wagon in unison, the twisted one's rifle pointing steadily at Sam's chest.

Sam's brain raced, trying to figure a way out. *There are too many of them with the drop on us.*

We can't fight our way out of this. I guess I'll have to reason with them.

Suddenly the tough in front of them began to curse Bo.

Bo stared wide-eyed at the tough while he listened to the vilest condemnation of his parentage and person he had ever heard.

When the cursing was done, the bearded man with the humped back indicated with his rifle for Bo to turn around. Reluctantly Bo turned the wagon back toward town. When they got to the split in the road the twisted man yelled, "Go left.

Bo answered with a sullen, "Yas suh," and started the turn. He glanced up with something in his eyes that Sam couldn't read. Suddenly Bo dropped the reins, bolted from the seat and fairly flew across the ground away from the wagon.

Sam stood up watching Bo run and wished he were with him. "Damn nigger coward!"

The tough on the paint laughed, pulled out his pistol, took careful aim… and missed.

Bo disappeared behind a large tree, reappeared, then dashed into the thick woods.

Sam was disgusted, but couldn't help admiring the surprising foot speed that the large Negro used to escape.

The tough cursed at his miss, snarled and spurred his horse after Bo.

"Damn you," the deformed one spat, "you shoulda used a rifle. Go get him and don't bring him back."

The twisted man turned to Sam. "He'll take care of the nigger while we settle up with you." He pointed to a large oak tree with spreading limbs and nudged his partner. "Get started."

The tough jumped down off his horse and ambled toward the tree.

Sam's eyes narrowed and he sat down. "Listen, I have no quarrel with any of you. Why don't you let me jes go on my way." Sam calculated grabbing the reins and bolting forward. *Nah, I wouldn't make five yards with this mule against those two rifles.*

"We figger yer jes a deserter and a nigger lover," the tough said without turning around.

The twisted man with the black beard leaned forward in his saddle, the whites below his unlevel eyes more prominent than before. He laughed shrilly and said, "He's probably sleepin' with the African.

Sam bristled.

"Yeah," the other man said, "and a liar too! Tellin' us Lee surrendered. Why everyone knows he'd rather die than quit."

Sam looked down and thought hard. He knew he couldn't reason with them but he had to try something.

He looked back up. "Listen, I'm telling you he did surrender. I was with General Johnston when they read us his surrender order."

The bearded man's misshapen eyes glittered with hate. "You liar! Where's your parole? We don't believe any of what you say. Get down off'n that wagon."

Sam jerked involuntarily at the bang of the revolver coming from the trees.

"Well your nigger's gone," the bearded man said, "now it's your turn."

Bo's death hit Sam like a slap across his face. *These people are crazy*, he thought.

"Get down off'n the wagon and walk over there." He pointed to the tree.

The younger man gestured impatiently with his rifle, echoing his companion. "Get down off'n that wagon." He giggled, "We ain't had a lynchin' in weeks."

Thinking as hard as he could for some way to escape, Sam slowly got down. His stomach churned and he could once again taste the fear he knew so well at the start of a hundred battles. *They couldn't be serious. Lynching a nigra is one thing, but me? Nah, they're just trying to scare me.*

"Walk straight ahead," the man pointed, "that way."

What a way to go. After four years of Hell…

Sam followed the man's finger with his eyes to the large oak tree, its branches, some bigger than a man's thigh, stretched across the road.

Sam hesitated and was propelled forward by a push from the tough. "You men can't get away with this—" He flinched as the tough's rifle jabbed into his ribs.

Sam's heart was pounding. His mind raced ahead and went nowhere. "Why are you doing this? I ain't done nothing to you." Sam was getting panic-stricken. He looked wildly right and left for some way to escape.

"Shut up and keep walkin'."

The bearded man reached the tree first. Still on horseback he reached for his lariat.

Sam stared at him in disbelief. *Nah, they're jes tryin' to scare me.... But what if they ain't? Nah, people don't lynch white men.*

The man threw the rope over a limb and tied one end to his saddle horn.

Sam felt strange, as if he were watching what was going on instead of it actually happening to him. "You can't do this," Sam heard himself shout. "The Sheriff'll get—"

Sam saw stars and then he felt the pain. "Oh, my head." Things went black and he sat down hard on the ground.

In a stupor his mind whirled back to Chattanooga, at the last hanging he witnessed. General Bragg had called the whole corps to watch a hanging of two Yankee spies. When Sam saw the provost guard bring out the culprits, he was shocked to find out they were children. The guards were leading two young boys with their hands tied behind their backs. At the sight of the boys being led to slaughter, Sam got physically ill, and sick at heart. The older boy was sixteen, the younger one barely fourteen. The younger one cried and pleaded so pitifully, the hardest soldier had to turn his head. Bragg, on horseback, just stared at the two children.

Bragg was a clown, Sam remembered thinking, *not a circus clown, but a Shakespearian clown, one full of venom and hate who not only destroys himself but all those around him.*

The oldest boy kicked the younger one and said, "Show these Rebels how a Union man can die for his country. Be a man."

Won't somebody protest and stop this? Sam thought. Suddenly he was startled by a voice deep inside him. Why don't you stop it, Sam? He didn't and still felt ashamed

Sam remembered turning away and vomiting when they knocked the Props out from under the two boys. He felt the same sickness in his gut now.

Sam felt his hands being tied behind his back and tried to resist. He was staggered by another blow to the head.

"Goddamn it, you damned deserter, stand still."

"C'mon, c'mon, get those hands tied, and get him up on the back of your horse."

The young tough's eyes sparked crazily and he giggled as he pulled the knot tight. He pushed Sam toward his horse and Sam stumbled against the side of the animal. The tough lifted Sam's leg, put it in the stirrup, and began to lift him up on the horse's back. Sam resisted and the tough thrust the barrel of his Colt into his back. Sam stopped moving.

Again putting Sam's foot in the stirrup, the tough grunted and lifted Sam bodily onto the horse.

Trying to delay anyway he could, Sam slid off the other side. The tough ducked under the horse's neck and grabbed Sam's shirt. He felt the cold steel of the pistol and the ominous click of the hammer. The tough put Sam's foot in the stirrup again and pushed him up, this time holding on to his shirt to prevent him from sliding off.

"Jes sit still nigra lover, and it'll all be over in jes a second or two."

The horse danced a few steps then stopped. Sam stared at the disfigured face of the hump-backed man and said plaintively, "Why are you doing this."

The man's face turned dark. "I'll tell ya why, pretty boy. It's all about you dandies that talk so nice, an' look so good, an' think when ya fart it's sweet. I'll bet you had a momma what tucked you in every night and a daddy what watched over you real good. His face darkened.

"Well, let me tell ya what I had. I was a preacher's son. And let me tell you that weren't no bed of roses. When I was five he spouted the gospel an' used a razor strop on me every day. He said it was to beat the devil an' the willfulness outta me. In between beatings he put cigars out on me. By the time I was ten, I was too big for the strop an' he changed to a two by four, sometimes with nails in it." The man's face got red and began to twitch as he remembered. For a few moments his uneven eyes blazed and he began to shake. When he gained control again he continued.

"The worst was yet to come. When I was twelve I lost a book from school. Well, it was the last time I ever saw the inside of a school. The preacher knew he'd have to pay for the book an' he went crazy. He grabbed me by the hair an' dragged me into the barn. Then he beat me so hard, that even that drunken sot of a mother of mine, roused herself from a stupor an' tried to stop him. All she got for her trouble was a bloody face.

"By the time he finished kicking me with his boots, my face was a mess, my hair was matted with blood an' both my eyes were blacked. I couldn't see my back but I knew from the pain it was black and blue." The man touched his face and glared at Sam. His look was enough to melt iron.

"The bastard made me stay in the barn for three months, and laughed when I asked him to take me to a doctor.

"When I could walk again, my whole face had changed. The first thing I noticed was my eyes weren't on the same level. He had cracked my skull an' nuthin' on my face was even. My back got a hump where he kicked me, an' that gets bigger every year an' hurts worse every day.

"When I got growed, no woman would look at me, an' all the pretty boys with the corn silk hair, an' blue eyes, just like you, snickered behind my back.

"I looked terrible on the outside, but the worst thing was the change inside. The preacher had made himself a killer. Yeah, now there was a whole 'nother person inside of me: a murderer! They said I was a born killer. No! I weren't born that way: He made me an killer." He laughed sardonically. "And guess who I killed first." His eyes glittered with hate. You guessed it, that son-of-a-bitch hisself.

"Then I began to hate all of them what laughs behind my back. An' every time I find one of you pretty boys, I aim to do him harm. And that's what I aim to do to you; you see, I have to get even for what was done to me." He turned to the tough. "Get on with it, Jed."

Sam started to tell him he'd never laugh at him when his voice was stifled by the noose being tightened.

Now in his minds eye he could see himself twisting slowly from the oak tree branch; the Alabama sun filtering through the tree leaves, his body dancing an endless ballet of death. He felt like a damned soul waiting for judgment.

The tough yanked the rope and it pulled Sam up straight. He tried to fight but the tough giggled and pulled the rope tighter. Then the twisted one handed him the end of the rope and he wound and tied it around the horse's pommel.

The tough's cackle ran down Sam's spine like ice water, making him shake uncontrollably.

Desperate, Sam pulled at the bonds tying his wrists. They wouldn't budge. He got dizzy and his body went limp with helplessness.

"In case yer thinkin' the sheriff'll get us fer this, he won't. We'll make him think it was the Free Staters. I'll leave him a note and sign it Newton Knight" He laughed sardonically. "All right, Jed," the bearded man said, "slap that horse's rump and lets get on back to the farm. I need a drink."

The deformed man looked toward the trees. "Hey, wait a minute, where the hell's yer brother?"

Sam struggled again but the ropes were tied securely. He closed his eyes and turned his face skyward. *Oh, my God, they're gonna do it. Father in Heaven, hallowed be thy name—*

"Yeeeehaw," the tough on the ground yelled and swung his hand to hit the horse's rump.

Before his hand could strike the horse, a shot rang out. The tough's hand stopped in mid-air and he stared straight ahead, a look of disbelief on his face. He looked down at the crimson stain spreading on his shirt. Turning slowly he faced his bearded companion who stared back at him, uncompre-hending. Suddenly the tough's eyes rolled back in his head and he crumpled to the ground.

"What the hell!" The bearded man raised his rifle as the horse danced and pulled the rope tight around Sam's neck. Sam pushed his toes into the stirrups in a vain attempt to keep the noose from choking him. He kneed the horse's flanks desperately trying to keep him in place. Sam prayed fervently the horse wouldn't bolt.

At the sound of the gunshot the mule snorted and brayed and began running, pulling Bo's empty wagon clattering down the road.

Sam stared at the bearded one and saw his misshapen eyes go wide.

"What the devil, I thought you was dead—" Another shot rang out. The rifle in the bearded man's hands splintered and he dropped it as if it were hot. His misshapen eyes narrowed and his hand darted to his pistol. He had it half out of its holster when a third shot rang out. He clutched his stomach and stared past Sam into another world. He moved his mouth soundlessly, did a cartwheel off his horse and landed, his humped back striking the hard packed road with a thump.

Spooked by the gunshots the animal pranced nervously, threatening to hang Sam. The animal danced then pawed at the ground threatening to race off. Sam tried to keep the animal still with his heels playing against the horse's ribs. "Thank God, Sheriff," Sam croaked, "you got here just in time. Cut me down, quick."

"It ain't the sheriff, Boss, it's me. You awright, Reb?" Bo urged the paint forward, grabbed the horse's reins and calmed him.

"Bo? You? I thought you ran."

Bo gestured with his head. "So did dey," he said with an ox-like calm. He jerked his head toward the trees. "Dat other white boy done come into de woods lookin' fer me with blood in his eye. He found me and got down off'n his hoss real slow like. Den the son-of-a-bitch started to put on black gloves, gettin' ready to kill me. Dat bastard took his time, enjoyin' my fear. I bet he pulled the wings off'n flies for fun when he was a chile. When he got de second glove on, he reached, slow like, fer his pistol. Dat's when I pulled de gun I had hid, and plugged him. You should'a seen de look on his face."

"Whew, that was close. I owe you one, Bo."

Bo's crooked smile revealed his white teeth lighting up his black face. "You don't owe me nuthin' Reb, we's partners. You'da done the same fer me."

Sam wondered.

Then he thought, *Ah, Mrs. Beecher Stowe, when you drew the picture of the Negro's life, you should have given some of the highlights, not just the shadows. This Bo's is not a shadow he's a highlight.*

Moving carefully, Bo leaned over and loosened the noose around Sam's neck. Sam held his hands back toward Bo and he untied him.

Sam massaged his wrists then took Bo's large black hand and shook it warmly.

Slidding down off the horse, Sam felt exhausted, like a runner who had forced himself through the last lap of a long race. The shock of his near death settled in his legs and they wobbled as he tried to take a step. He reached for the pommel on the saddle to steady himself and his hand shook violently.

He stood quietly for a few minutes to gain his composure. After a while he stopped trembling and got some strength back. He let go of the pommel, walked over to the dead tough and stared down at him. Then he turned away.

Suddenly Sam pivoted back, drew his leg back and kicked the dead tough so hard Bo heard the dead man's ribs crack. Sam spit on the corpse and began to curse both the dead men.

Bo stared at Sam, then threw his head back and began laughing as he heard a string of vile curses that would have made a muleskinner blush. His laugh was cut short when ragged apparitions appeared out of the trees and surrounded them.

A short fat man with a pug face stepped forward. He was dressed in worn out Confederate pants, a mountain man's hat with holes in it, and a calico shirt two sizes too small for him.

The man strolled up to Sam and carefully looked him over as if he were going to buy him at a slave auction.

He had an Enfield rifle in one hand and a plug of tobacco in the other. Putting the butt of the rifle on the ground, he leaned on the muzzle. Eying Sam and Bo, with some amusement, he shoved a new plug of tobacco deep in his cheek. Chewing with obvious pleasure, he stopped suddenly, turned his head and spit.

Turning back at Sam, the portly man grinned a brown stained smile and said to him, in a sleepy Alabama drawl, "You cain't jes shoot folks 'round heah, we got laws. And also, yer trespassin' on the Kingdom of Jones."

Did you shoot Forrest?

Chapter 13

The blindfold around Sam's eyes was tied tightly. The slightest movement of his hands to reach up and ease the pressure was met by a grunt and a rifle in his sore ribs. The wagon rocked on uneven ground, throwing him from side to side adding to his discomfort. After riding for an exasperating twenty-five minutes, Sam blurted out, "Where are you taking us?"

No answer.

Sam flushed with anger and doubled his fists in frustration.

Suddenly the road smoothed out and then Sam heard the clatter of horse's hooves on wood. *Must be a bridge.* He heard bubbling water flowing over rocks, men talking, and a woman's laugh in the distance.

Finally the clattering stopped and they were on soft ground again. Sam heard the voices coming closer. Suddenly the wagon came to an abrupt stop.

He felt the blindfold being rudely yanked off and blinked at the sudden sunlight. He rubbed his eyes with both hands then looked about him.

Fifty to sixty men and women, both black and white, swarmed around them in a semi-circle staring at the two prisoners. Sam looked back and noticed the three horses belonging to the hunchback were tied in a row behind Bo's wagon.

All at once the crowd parted and a short, muscular man with bright red hair strode toward the wagon. Several of the men reached out and patted his shoulder as he passed by. Two steps in back of him trailed a tall, cream-colored woman dressed in a white leather skirt and jacket.

From the corner of his eye, Sam saw Bo start when he saw her. She gave him no sign of recognition.

The red-haired man stopped at the wagon, put his hand on the front wheel and looked up at the two men, his eyes half closed from squinting at the sun above their heads. "What'r you doin' in my kingdom?"

"Your kingdom?" Sam exclaimed.

The man's face crinkled into a big smile and he laughed. He turned and looked at the interested assembly. "Ain't this here state the Kingdom of Jones?"

"Yes," shouted the crowd.

"Ain't my name Newton Knight, and ain't I the governor of this here new state?" Laughter and a buzzing and nodding of heads from the group indicated the affirmative.

The man turned back to Sam. "Any business you got in this here Free State of Jones, you got with me." Knight cocked his head and scrutinized Sam. "What's yer name?"

Sam ignored the question and looked at the man carefully. Knight's muscular frame bulged under his brown and tan buckskin shirt and pants. A full head of red hair hung down almost to his shoulders framing a face covered with freckles. His nose was flat and looked like it had been broken at the bridge. He was a half-foot shorter than Sam and a full foot shorter than the woman who by now was at his side. Knight brushed his fingers through his beard that, aside from a few small patches of gray, matched his hair. Sam eyed an ancient Johnson pistol sticking out of a green sash at his waist. Knight put his hand on the butt of the pistol.

Knight's brows narrowed and he glared at Sam as if he were trying to look inside him. After a few tense moments he turned and touched the tall woman's shoulder. "This here's my woman, Rachael. He turned back to Sam. "What's yer name?"

Sam ignored Knight a second time, his eyes on the woman. Rachael was dark skinned but clearly not fully Negro. She had the high cheekbones of an Indian, soft brown eyes and jet-black hair wound in two tight braids. Her clothes were made of white leather, which contrasted sharply with her copper skin. The tassled white leather jacket had decorative multi-colored beads stitched in Indian fashion. Her leather skirt, also tassled, stretched snugly over her slim body. She gave a tight nod to Sam, and a warm smile to Bo.

Sam noticed her eyes sparkled and stayed on Bo a little longer than was polite.

Knight put his hand on the handle of his pistol, and his voice turned ominous. "I said—what's yer name?"

Sam turned to him. "My name? Yes, I'm sorry. It's Sam, Sam Atkins."

Pointing to Sam's Confederate army pants, Knight said, "You a deserter?"

Sam smiled wondering what reaction he would get this time. "No, but the pants don't matter any more, the war's over. Lee surrendered to Grant at Appomattox in Virginia, and Johnston gave up to Sherman at Durham Station in North Carolina. The officials of the Confederate Government are all probably in jail by now, or hung."

The crowd began to buzz, then spontaneously gave a loud cheer.

Knight held his hand up and the crowd quieted back to a murmur.

"How do I know you're tellin' the truth and that you're not a spy for General Lowery?"

"You don't. I never even heard of General Lowery. I didn't ask to come here. I was brought against my will. And if you don't believe me, well just point my mule outta here and watch me get on my way to the Forrest place."

"You know Cunnel Forrest?"

Sam shook his head. "No, but I got a letter to him from his boy."

Knight looked at Sam sharply. "His boy fit fer the Yanks, didn't he?"

"Yes, he did. He died at the end of the war."

"How'd he get it?"

"Chest wound." Then as an afterthought Sam said, "In the line of duty."

"Too bad. He was a good man."

"I know."

A puzzled look washed across Knight's face. "Wait a minute. How did you know that if you done soldiered with the Rebs?"

Sam managed a small smile. "I was with him after he was shot and became a prisoner. He wrote a note and I agreed to take it to his Pa. That's where I was going when your men changed my itinerary."

"Itine-- what?"

"My plans."

"Oh." Knight walked a few paces stopped and thought a minute. Then he turned back to Sam. "Did you shoot Forrest?"

"No!"

Knight gave one of his men a nod. He leaned over and whispered something in Rachael's ear then addressed Sam again. "We want you to be our guests until we check on a few things. Knight turned back to the woman. "Take these men with you and give them a good meal while we go to the telegraph office."

Knight started to leave again and suddenly pivoted back. He had a scowl on his face. "If'n yer tellin' the truth you'll go in peace. If not—" He shrugged his shoulders and patted the pistol in his belt.

Knight signaled to the man who captured Sam and Bo. The man ambled over. "You and one other man guard this Reb and his man," Knight said. "If'n he gets away, you're gone too."

Grim faced, Sam and Bo went with the woman. The guard picked another man with an impatient gesture and the two of them followed close behind Rachael and the prisoners.

****

Rachael led Bo and Sam to a clearing in the forest. A fire blazed in the center of a ring of stones. Rough logs for seating lay in concentric circles going outward from the fire. Sam guessed correctly that it was a meeting place for the partisans. Two women tending the fire nodded to Rachael as she approached them, then melted into the woods.

Sam watched Rachael set about making a meal. She hummed and sang softly while Bo looked at her with adoring eyes. Sam shook his head wondering to himself. *I wonder if those two knew each other before.*

The two guards leaned against a large tree and talked, but they were alert; their rifles ready, fingers on the triggers.

Bo helped Rachael while Sam laid back on one of the logs and rested as best he could. The events of the day crowded in on Sam, his eyes got heavy and he slept.

In what seemed like just a minute a gentle hand shook Sam.

Rachael's brown eyes, so dark they looked black, peered down at him as he woke with a start.

"I hates to wake you but I guess y'alls be all leavin' soon, and I done taut y'all mought wants to travel on a full stomick."

A grateful Sam said, "Thank you."

Sam got up and joined Bo. "Where's Rachael from, Bo? I'm having a hard time understanding half of what she says.

"She's half injun and half geechee nigra, Boss. She done grew up on de sea islands near Savannah. Dat's where she got all dem good manners."

Looking puzzled Sam shook his head. "I still don't see why I can't understand her."

Bo smiled at him and continued. "You see, Boss, when de slave traders brought de Africans here and deposited dem on de sea island plantations, de black folks was isolated and kept dere African words mixed in wit de trader's white folks words. What comes out is Geechee. You have to be born near Savannah to even understand dem Nigras what speaks Geechee."

Sam shook his head, smiled at Rachael, and with gratitude, looked down at the plate she gave him. Pan fried chicken, corn bread, greens and a bowl of black-eyed peas. He shook his head in wonder that, even these people in the woods could eat this way, while Lee's Army starved.

Sam's teeth were stronger now and he ate his fill.

When he was done, Rachael gave Sam a corncob pipe that he lit while strolling to the edge of the clearing. He turned and observed Bo and Rachael. One of the guards walked with him and stood nearby, watching him closely.

After he was finished smoking, Sam tapped the pipe on a log, knocking the ashes out and walked back to the fire. The guard went back to his companion.

Bo and Rachael sat together, talking in whispers and sometimes laughing quietly. Sam joined them.

The two guards looked at the three of them and appeared uncomfortable, but said nothing.

I guess Rachael swings a lot of weight in the Kingdom of Jones.

Sam swiveled his head toward the sound of horses clattering over the wooden bridge. Overhead gray cumulus clouds swallowed the sun and darkened the day.

It's Knight. Good, now we can get on our way. He laughed to himself. *That is if I can get Bo away from Rachael and vice versa.*

Bo and Rachael stopped talking and looked toward the bridge. Sam stood up, and the two guards came to life. One of the guards scowled and put a finger on the trigger of his weapon. The other put his rifle butt on the ground and stared in the direction of the noise.

In a few moments Knight came striding into the clearing. His fists were clenched making his knuckles white. His clothes were wet and his hair hung down in sodden ringlets. He came right up to Sam's face.

Flustered, Sam took a step back. "Well," Sam said, "can we go?"

Knight bristled. His face was Irish red, and hate flashed in his eyes. "Can you go? Yes. You can go straight to Hell!"

Bo stood up, looking concerned.

The fat man's rifle came up level with Bo's chest.

Sam felt his face get warm. "Why? What happened?"

Knight put his hand on the pistol butt in his belt. "You know damn well what happened." He looked at Rachael standing next to Bo and his eyes flickered a momentary darkness. Then he turned back to Sam.

"Soon as we got to the Leaf River, General Lowery and his sojer boys jumped us. Afore I knowed it, half my boys were dead and the rest of us were racin' our horses through the river like chickens on cookin' day. We were damned lucky to get away." Knight took a step toward Sam and swung his fist at him. Sam ducked the blow. "And you set us up."

"No, I never—"

Knight rubbed his fist as if he had struck Sam, then spun on his heel and faced the two guards. "I want the guards on them doubled. They're both to be shot tomorrer, as soon as the sun clears the trees." He turned to the gathering crowd. "An" I want everyone there."

Bo stiffened, and Rachael's copper face paled.

Knight turned back to Sam. "After your dead we'll cut your privates off and nail your bodies to a tree at the Leaf River so General Lowery can see what happens to his spies."

"But—"

Knight's hand snaked out again but this time he made contact.

Sam fell back, his cheek colored red where Knight's fist had found its mark. He put his left hand to his face and absently rubbed the reddened area. He felt a sticky wetness from his bloody nose. His stomach felt knotted, the same way it did when he was in a battle. His voice was tight when he replied. "We had nothing to do with this attack."

The sun broke through the clouds and Knight's bright red hair caught its rays. It looked to Sam that if his hair were dry it would catch on fire.

Knight pointed to the fat guard. "You! Pick three men. And watch these bastards as if your life depended on it. And it will." He looked at Rachael and beckoned her impatiently with a quick movement of his hand. "C'mon woman, I'm hungry." Knight stopped and for a moment stared at Rachael, "Besides," he said, his voice lowering, "I want a few words with you."

Rachael flashed a look at Bo, then hurried to do Knight's bidding.

Bo stared at Knight as he spun on his heel and left with Rachael.

Sam could swear he saw murder in Bo's eyes.

****

The night passed slowly for Sam. Unable to sleep he paced the clearing under the watchful eyes of the guards. A few hours before daylight, a sleepless Sam watched the four guards put their heads together. After they talked for a while, two of them lay down and were quickly asleep. One of the other two motioned for Sam and Bo to sit near the fire. For a while both guards watched the prisoners every move.

The blaze started to die and one of the guards went over to the fire and kicked the dying wood sending sparks flying. He turned and said to the other guard, "I'm gonna get some more wood. Keep yer eyes open and holler if they try somethin'. I'll be right nearby."

The remaining guard nodded, keeping his eyes glued to Sam and Bo.

A half hour passed and the first man did not return. The lone guard peered into the darkness around him and shifted his feet nervously. He brought his rifle to his chest and put his hand on the trigger. "You two," he said to Bo and Sam, "don't even twitch a muscle. I'm gonna wake the others." He moved sideways toward the two sleeping men, all the while keeping his eyes fixed on Sam and Bo.

Suddenly there was a flash of silver at his back. The guard gasped and tried to say something through the hand clamped around his mouth. Failing that he reached back trying to get at the knife sticking out of his back. He could not. He tried again to say something then fell silently to the ground.

At the sound of the dead man hitting the ground, the two sleepers stirred, turned over and continued snoring.

Sam's mouth dropped open and he stared at the tall stranger who stepped out of the trees into the open.

"What the hell—"

The stranger put his finger to his lips, and Sam choked back the rest of his exclamation.

A female figure moved from in back of the stranger into the light.

Rachael! Sam shook his head and looked at Bo.

The black man gave him a toothy grin.

Damn, Bo knew something was going on all along.

Rachael gestured for them to hurry. "Come to go," she said in a whisper, "you don't have any much time."

The grim faced assassin gave them a nod, wiped his blade on the shirt of the dead man, and disappeared back into the woods.

Sam quickly followed Bo and Rachael into the trees walking on his toes to quiet his steps as they crossed the wooden bridge. When they got to the other side, Sam was glad to see Bo's mule and wagon waiting. The U.S. on the side of the wagon never looked so good.

"Rachael," Sam said taking her hand, "who was the man with the knife?"

"He one of General Looreey's mens. A spy. He's de one dat tol' de General where Noot's men be." She smiled. "He felt bad dat you is takin' de blame. He say he help y'alls all get gone."

"Well tell him thanks for freeing us. But you're taking an awful chance."

She looked at Bo with moist and loving eyes, and took his hand. "Nothin' I wouldn't do for dis ol' man."

Rachael and Bo hugged and he gently kissed her on the forehead.

"Goobye, lover," she said to Bo, then put her arms around him and kissed him on the mouth.

Sam looked on in bewilderment. "Aren't you coming with us?"

She looked at Sam with a great sadness in her eyes and shook her head, "No."

After a final hug, she turned to Sam. "Now you both best get on outta heah." She pointed down the river. "Jes foller dis road 'till you get to de Leaf River and go cross it. Turn right and stay close to de bank fo' 'bout ten mile. When you gets to de hard packed road lined with trees, go on up dat road and you run right into de main house of de Forrest's Plantation."

She turned to Bo, pain etched in her face. "And don't come back here no mo'. Knight'll kill you both on sight."

"What about you… and Bo?"

Rachael saw the puzzlement in Sam's face and smiled sadly. "I can't leave wit choo. I got me chillun heah. Bo'll tell you all about us." She turned to the Negro who was in the driver's seat holding the mule's reins. "Bo, you stays real quiet

’til you gets to de river. Then you kin whoop ’n hollar.”

Bo’s face sagged and his brows furrowed. He took the tall woman’s hand and squeezed it gently. “I won’t never fergit you, Rachael.”

Watching them, Sam thought he could hear the god-awful grinding sound of a heart breaking.

Rachael wiped a glistening eye with the back of one hand and took a step back. The darkness made her white clothing look almost luminescent. For a moment Sam envied Bo.

“Now git, both of y’alls, git!”

She was still standing where they left her, waving goodbye, as they went around a curve out of sight.

Reaching the river, they crossed the bridge, turned along the bank and raced the wagon through a stand of dogwoods along a winding trail.

After several miles they realized they were not being chased and Bo slowed the wagon.

Sam finally felt free to ask a question.

“Bo, what was that all about? Who or what is Rachael to you?”

Bo’s voice was sad and low. “You ’member Boss, when I tol’ you ’bout that woman who pined away fer me in Folsom? Well, it weren’t no story, it were Rachael.”

Sam

As the war went on, the Devil got it perfect.

Chapter 14

By the time Sam and Bo reached the turn-off to the entrance of the Forrest plantation, the sun was up. At the sign that said Forrest, they turned onto a hard packed dirt road lined with stately oaks, their branches joining in arboreal arches over the road. Flocks of rainbow colored wildflowers grew in profusion at the feet of the ancient, sturdy oaks. Behind the trees was a handsome white, three rail fence, decorated with twisted vines of honeysuckle, bordered a rolling pasture of fine blue/green grass. Beyond the fence, splendid looking Arabian stallions, mares, and colts of differing colors, frolicked, kicked and raced each other to the delight of the two men.

An awestruck Bo exclaimed, “I never seed anythin’ so beautiful, Marse Sam.” His face suddenly turned sour. “I bet de slave cabins on this place ain’t so fine.”

Sam ignored the last remark. "This place sure is something, Bo," he said looking around at the splendor. Sam pointed toward a large ante bellum home at the end of the drive. "That must be the main house. I can't believe George would leave this place and go fight with the Yanks. Drive right on up to the house, Bo."

They drove beneath a well carved wooden sign that said, *Fair Oaks Farms*, up on a circular gravel driveway and stopped in front of a two-story plantation house with four Greek colonnades in front. Sam looked at the manicured grounds and thought of the ravaged Virginia countryside. "The war hasn't touched this place," he muttered.

On either side of the great house were cultivated fields and wooded hills. Far in the distance were low gray mountains. He thought of his own home and the swampy, wet, flat land he lived on, and shook his head in envy. The combination of all this beauty made Sam's pulse quicken.

Suddenly two German Shepherd dogs appeared and raced up to them, barking, snarling and baring their teeth. Bo's eyes got as wide as saucers, and he paled, drew back and started shaking.

Sam laughed. "They won't bother you none, Bo. Just stay put."

"I had enough of dogs, Boss. Ran away once and dey set dogs on me. Dem dogs tracked me, caught me, and liked to kilt me."

Sam shook his head. "No one's gonna kill you now, Bo. Besides, your meat's too tough for them. Just stay put and they won't bother you."

The front door opened and a colored man, with an exaggerated dignified air, stepped out and calmly walked down the front stairs. "Quiet, dogs," he said firmly, and the dogs instantly stopped barking and slunk away, whining. He walked up to the buckboard, looked at Bo with disdain, then bowed slightly to Sam. "Can I help you, sir?" he said, a hint of sarcasm in his voice.

The Negro's haughty attitude made Sam bristle. He stared at the black man with narrowed eyes.

The servant had on a frilly white shirt covered by a purple velvet cutaway coat with gold buttons. His black pants were nickered just below the knee above white socks and black patent leather, silver buckled shoes. His clothes were eighteenth century and he had the manners of a boorish French courtier.

Sam recovered his senses. "Is this the home of George Forrest?"

"It is."

"I'd like to see him."

"The Master sees no one without an appointment." He started to turn away. "If it's about employment, you'll have to see the overseer." He pointed to a field. "About a mile that way."

Sam felt the heat creep up from his neck into his face. He jumped off the wagon, grabbed the Negro's arm and spun him around. "Listen Boy," he said, his mouth tight, his words clipped, "I have word— for Mr. Forrest— from his son."

The butler backed away, fear glinting in his downcast eyes. "Yes, suh, yes suh, I will tell the Master immediately." He went quickly up the stairs, and at the top step looked back fearfully. He then opened the ornate front door and disappeared into the house.

Sam looked at Bo and smiled without mirth. "Uppity, ain't he?"

Nodding his head, Bo stayed uncharacteristically silent.

In a few moments the servant was back. This time his tone was more respectful.

"The Master will see you now." The butler looked at Bo and his haughtiness returned. "Please ask your man to stay right here."

Bo glowered at the butler.

Nodding once to Bo, Sam followed the butler inside.

The house was massive and Sam whistled under his breath as they walked down the hallway. Great squares of marble tiles on the floor reflecting the sun streaming through the large windows of cut glass panes. Sam could imagine the amount of effort made by countless slaves on their hands and knees, polishing the tiles. *Greek colonnades that don't hold up the building, tiles from old Italy, slaves from Africa dressed in old French clothing. I Guess the South is bound and determined to cling to the past.*

Imposing curtains hung from the large windows, floor to ceiling. To his right a massive staircase, each stair covered with a long, claret carpet, rose to a second floor.

Sam's ragged shoes scuffed the tile floor. He unconsciously felt ashamed and tried to walk on his toes. *Nothing like this back on the farm,* he thought.

The butler stopped, opened a massive oak door, stepped aside and held it open. "Right in here, suh," he said, "the Master will be with you very soon."

Sam walked in the room and the door closed behind him. He looked around the large room and marveled. Floor to ceiling bookcases, filled with books bound in calfskin and blue morocco, covered two of the opposing walls. Busts of various people filled niches between the books.

Sam walked to the bookcase and stared at the collection. He tilted his head to the left, and started to read the titles on the shelf closest to him. *Les Miserables, St. Elmo, A Tale of Two Cities and Ivanhoe.* Sam nodded his head, impressed. *All leather bound. If my McGuffy reader was correct the owner certainly has good taste.*

Sam left the books and turned to one of the bookless walls. It was dominated by an almost life-size oil portrait of a distinguished man and woman. Sam assumed they were Mr. Forrest, and his wife.

Leaving the painting, Sam roamed restlessly in front of the books picking up one then another, at random, enjoying their beauty. One shelf, devoid of any other book or bust, contained just one leather-bound book lying face down. Sam went to it and picked it up as carefully as he would had it been a sacred relic. He turned it over and stared at the gilt embossed title: *Homer's Odyssey.* Feeling a bit guilty for being too curious, Sam laid the precious book down and turned to investigate the rest of the room.

Two tall windows, going from floor to ceiling, dominated the final wall, presenting the unannounced guest with a perfect view of the Arabians, and letting in great quantities of light. Standing at the window, Sam could see the circular driveway, the fields, and all the playful activities of the horses.

A large ornately carved French Revolution era desk stood at the foot of the windows. Neatly stacked papers and two feather pens in inkwells were at the center of the desk. On one corner of the desk were two picture frames containing photographs. The other corner contained a larger photograph. A riding crop and leather gloves lay carelessly on top of the papers.

Curious about his host's looks, Sam's eyes went back to the portrait. He stared at the stern face and ice blue eyes and thought, *No wonder George said what he did. This man must have been a very strict father.* The woman in the portrait had golden hair and a loving face. *I hope he wasn't as strict with her as he was with George. I would hate to see this handsome woman's spirit broken.*

Sam's eyes moved to another treasure. Under the painting was a rich, red tapestry, depicting a scene of Indian elephants carrying teakwood trees. Sam had never seen anything like it and had a feeling that all the furniture in the room, and probably the entire house, came from exotic places.

Restless, Sam walked around to the back of the French desk, and stared down at the photos. The only pictures Sam had ever seen before were on cartes de visites and daguerreotypes. Sam shook his head in wonder at the photographic portraits. *What will they think of next?*

Three different women in the frames looked back at Sam. On one corner the larger frame showed the lady in the painting. *No doubt Mrs. Forrest.* In the other corner one photo displayed a full body picture of a young woman with a rather large body. She gave the appearance of being almost as wide as she was tall, with ponderous breasts, a double chin and dark hair. *Now that's a healthy woman.*

The other image was a picture of an arresting girl, a younger carbon copy of Mrs. Forrest.

Sam picked up her picture and peered at the image closely. *Gosh, she's the prettiest thing I've ever seen. An angel with looks of elegance and delicacy that must be touched and handled with prudence and courtesy on all occasions. She appears to be at that place between adolescence and womanhood. If only I—*

"That's Lucy. She's the worst."

A startled Sam almost dropped the picture. He quickly put it back on the desk. His fingers fumbled it and the frame fell over, face down. He quickly picked it up with trembling fingers and set it down straight. It fell again.

The newcomer had silently entered the room through the massive oak door. He was tall, with a mane of white hair flowing over strong shoulders. At rest, his mouth was turned down with his long white mustache drooped at the ends emphasizing the downturn. Red cheeks and ice blue piercing eyes reflected authority. He had the posture of a man who had been a soldier in the past. He wore a white cutaway coat, a ruffled white shirt and Confederate gray pants partially covering his shining black boots. In his hand he held an unlit corncob pipe that he stabbed in the air for emphasis.

The man pointed the stem of the pipe toward the pictures of the girls. "They're the bane and the love of my existence, all at once," he said with a hint of resignation. He stopped and looked out the window at the panoramic view of the results of his labors and smiled with satisfaction.

The accent of Gulf Coastal Alabama is thick on his tongue, Sam thought, *but he was not born in these parts. He sounds just like the Alabamians that come to our tobacco auctions at Live Oak.*

Bringing himself back to the business at hand the man sat down at the desk leaned forward and pointed to an overstuffed leather chair opposite him.

"Have a seat, son. I'm Colonel George Forrest. Got my commission in the Mexican war. Who are you?"

"Atkins, sir, Sam Atkins, late of the First Tennessee, Army of the Confederacy."

Forest looked impressed. "I see. Braxton Bragg's outfit." He smiled at the puzzlement on Sam's face. "I have some contacts in Richmond. They keep me abreast of things." He nodded knowingly. "If you were with Bragg, I guess you've seen some action."

Several of the men Sam had killed flashed through his mind and he grimaced. "I've done my share of fighting, sir." He sat down suddenly weary.

There was a long pause as the colonel reached for his pipe and filled it.

"My servant tells me you're here about George. This may come as a surprise to you, but frankly I don't give one damn about him." The colonel waited for a moment for the shocking statement to sink in.

"What's he done? Is he a prisoner? Speak up, boy!" He tamped down the tobacco and lit his pipe, then sat back expansively. "Well?"

Sam eyed the Colonel for a few moments, unable to speak. Shaking his head he fished the note out of his pocket, leaned across the desk and handed the letter to the colonel. "George sent this final note to you."

"Final?" The colonel's face was suddenly tense. He reached over, took the bloody paper, leaned back in his chair and began to read. As he read, Sam could see the blood in the colonel's face drain away. In a few moments he had turned a ghastly white. When he finished, he sat up straight in the chair and crushed the note in his fist. His face now red, he stood up to his full height, walked to the window and stared out at the field, watching the horses cavorting in the grass.

The colonel's voice cracked at first when he finally spoke. "George deserves what he got." His fist opened and the bloody note dropped to the floor. "The goddamned traitor."

The colonel turned back to Sam. "I hope he rots in Hell! I haven't been able to hold my head up anywhere in Alabama since he joined up with them Yankees." He pivoted back to the window. "Another year or two and we'll send all of them bastards scurrying back up north with their tails between their legs, isn't that right, uh, uh—"

"Atkins, sir, Sam Atkins." He shook his head. "No, I'm afraid that won't happen. Lee surrendered at Appomattox in Virginia in April, and Johnston gave up in North Carolina shortly after. I've heard General Kirby Smith is still holding out in the West, but he's not strong enough to do anything but annoy the Yankees. The war's over."

The silence was palpable. At the word, *over*, the colonel's hand stopped in mid-movement and his face turned a deep purple. When he finally found his voice he blurted out incredulously, "Surrendered? Impossible!" Then he blanched. "Is it true? Is it really true?" he whispered. "Will the Yankees be comin' here?"

Sam's voice was subdued. "I'm afraid so, sir. I was right there with Johnston when we surrendered, so I know it's true."

Sam shook his head. *By what I've seen so far my countrymen are not going to take this defeat well.*

The colonel got up slowly, his white hair seeming silver with the sun's rays beaming on it through the window. He gritted his teeth and shook his head. "Then I fear for us, Sam. I fear for the whole South, for our way of life—" He couldn't continue.

After what he had seen, Sam was not surprised at the edge of anger and vindictiveness in the colonel's voice. As he got up to say goodbye he heard a tap on the oak door.

"Who is it?" Colonel Forrest said absently.

"It's me, sir."

The old man turned and looked out the window as the door opened and a Negro of mixed blood stepped into the room.

The mulatto appeared to be six feet tall with a muscular body that moved with the grace of a panther. His young, pleasant face displayed the confidence of a man that knew his place in life and did his job well. His skin was a light dusky brown and he had a shock of wavy black hair, a strong, broad, flat nose, and long fingered, delicate hands that belonged more on the keys of a piano than on a bucking horse. His well-worn work pants were tucked in calf high black boots, and his calico shirt was wet with sweat on the back and under the armpits.

Sam knew him immediately. *This is Forrest's half-breed son, Dakota.* He also noted a palpable tension in the room. Without being asked, Sam sat back down.

"Well, what do you want?" Forrest said, still looking out the window, his pipe bellowing smoke and his hands clasped firmly behind his back.

There was a palpable stress in the room.

To break the tension Sam stood up and held out his hand to Dakota. "I'm Sam Atkins," he said cordially.

Dakota pulled his eyes away from his father, looked at Sam, smiled, and responded. "Dakota Forrest's my name." He took a step toward Sam and they shook hands. The handshake was firm and warm, the smile genuine.

"I came to tell Colonel Forrest about your, uh, family member, George."

"You mean my brother, George?" The colonel's face splotched red in anger, and he turned back to the two men.

Sam explained, in colorful language, meeting George, and then in somber tones about the accident.

When he finished Dakota murmured, "I'm sorry to hear that. I've been anxiously waiting for him to come home."

The old man glowered at the two young men. "Well, what do you want, Boy?" he said again, this time with a raised voice.

Dakota faced Forrest and his smile faded. "The cattle are ready for brandin', sir. It's past time for them." He spoke with forced courtesy.

Colonel Forrest turned back to the window. "Well, what do you want from me? Get on with it."

"Yes, sir, I would 'ceptin' I need a few more hands and there's no one—"

The old man turned, his eyes flashing anger. "You lazy nig—"

Sam stepped in. "I've never branded before, Dakota, but I got a boy who knows his way 'round cattle, and I learn real quick like."

Dakota ignored Sam and stared at his father, his hands balled into fists.

Sam stood up and put his hand on the mulatto's shoulder. He could feel Dakota trembling with rage.

Trying to calm himself Dakota turned to Sam and forced a smile. He appeared glad for the interruption. "A dollar a day for each of you, and all you can eat."

"Done." Sam said, and they shook hands.

Fully under self-control now, Dakota bowed to the colonel with a nod of his head, said, "Sir," politely, and left.

Sam sat down and turned to Forrest. "I hope you don't mind, Colonel Forrest, I could use the money."

The colonel, his back to Sam, shook his head no, and set his white mane swirling.

Sam started to rise. "I guess I better get going."

Forrest turned to Sam and said, "Wait just a moment, I have a few things I want to ask you—about George."

Sam sat back down on the edge of the chair.

Forrest paced behind his desk for a few moments and then eased down in the chair. He leaned across the desk and looked at Sam with glistening eyes.

"How'd my boy die?" Forrest asked softly.

"Gunshot wound, sir." Sam thought quickly. "In the chest, facing the enemy." Sam smiled inside for George.

Forrest nodded his head. He leaned back and folded his hands on his stomach, his head down. For a long while he was silent. Finally he looked up at Sam. "He surprised Sam by asking, "You seen much action?"

"Yessir. Like I told you, I seen action. Too much action. I was with Company Aych, First Florida Volunteers, The Army of the Tennessee, first with Bragg and then Hood. Both of 'em can go to Hell."

The old man shook his head and brushed at his white mane with his hand.

"What battles were you in?"

It was a question Sam had never been asked before. A million memories and images cascaded through his mind. His brow wrinkled and he shook his head slowly. "You sure you want to hear this, sir?"

The white head nodded emphatically.

"I started with Beauregard at Shiloh. That was some battle. We had the Yanks whipped; pushed them back into the river when Beauregard gives the order to halt. We couldn't believe it. Every man in our brigade wanted to keep going but the officers wouldn't let us. We stopped and made camp right there, amongst the dead and wounded." Sam shook his head sadly. "And believe me, there were dead everywhere, theirs and ours. Niether side had learned yet how to deal with the dead soldiers, much less the wounded. The funny thing was, *Shiloh* means a place of peace. Hah! Some peace.

"Why didn't they let us keep going? I guess the officers figured we'd had enough for one day and that we'd finish them off the next morning."

Sam grimaced. "Well, the morrow comes, and with it here comes the Yankee General Buell. And just like Blucher saved Wellington at Waterloo, Buell saves Grant at Shiloh. Then it was us that got chased off the field, not them.

"After that, the battles came thick and heavy, one after another, without letup. Corinth, Murfreesboro, Shelbyville, Chickamauga, Chattanooga— An me shooting at men, live men, men with wives and Ma's and girlfriends…"

The old man's eyes narrowed. He leaned back, tapped his pipe on an ashtray, shook his head and said, "I see."

Sam stood up. "With all due respect, sir, no you don't see. Not only did we have to stand the shock and shell of the battlefield with men suffering all the agonies of life and death, but then to have to spend the night on the same field, cold and wet and hungry, shivering with fright beyond belief, with only the dead men and their demons around you to keep you company. The whole thing was such a nightmare that just to keep my sanity I had to focus my attention on little things that were comprehensible, like rolling a cigarette, or reading a letter from my Ma for the tenth time. Even putting one foot down before the other on the march helped me keep my reason.

"But the fighting was just part of it. Half of the boys died in camp from sickness. All of us were constantly spitting up green stuff. When I first got to camp I was so sick I was afraid I was gonna die, then after a while I was afraid I wasn't."

Sam stood up, remembering. His face contorted, his eyes snapping in anger. "And then we got put with the Army of the Tennessee, led by that infernal General Bragg!

That bastard killed almost as many of us as the Yankees did. He was shooting eight, maybe ten of us boys a day. Why? Because some poor webfoot was getting letters from home saying, 'Come on home, we're starving.' Or, 'I'm sick and there's no one to care for the baby. Come home!' The boy that got a letter like that would get so upset he'd just up and leave for his home.

"And to top it all, every last man in the army was worried about the slaves. Confederate soldiers were loyal men and they mostly stayed by their guns. But how much can you take when the rumors of slave insurrection is everywhere. You see visions of black men killing your women, molesting young girls, burning your home and running off with the silver. Sure the men left to protect their families, wouldn't you?"

The old man sadly nodded his head, a look of worry on his face.

"Sure enough before the poor webfoot would get a mile away from camp, the provost'd catch him. And Bragg'd shoot him. Just like a dog he'd shoot him—" Sam got choked up at his own words and couldn't speak for a moment. He sat down slowly, and shook his head. "No trial, no explanation, just get twelve men and shoot him down like a dog. Just like ol' Rowland. And I helped shoot him..." Sam stared into space remembering. "Just shoot them, like dogs..." his voice faded into nothingness. He sat down and was very still.

Forrest's voice was small. "Is that where the war ended for you, at Chickamauga?"

Sam turned to the colonel with a disbelieving look. "Ended? The fighting just began there. After Chickamauga, we retreated from Missionary Ridge. I'll give the Yanks their due at the Ridge. They came right through the clouds and pushed us back. That was the first time I ever saw our boys run.

"After that disaster, Bragg finally got kicked upstairs to a cushy job in Richmond. He was made military consultant to President Davis; General Lee's old job. Now ain't that a laugh; Bragg for Lee.

"In '63, I got transferred to General Lee just in time to march to Gettysburg. Wasn't I a fortunate soldier.

"There were 50,000 dead men on both sides after that fiasco, and a whole shipload of

Confederate wounded. When we departed the battlefield we left our dead for the Yanks to bury, and we took the wounded home on a long wagon train of misery. On the way back to Richmond, some died, and some wished they would die, and some were unnaturally quiet. Then it started to rain. The heavens opened up and gave us a downpour that no one will forget. I never could figure out if God was crying or just wanted to cleanse the earth of our foolishness.

"Right in the middle of all that misery, at Falling Waters, and Williamsport, here comes Meade's cavalry. Generals Buford, Kilpatrick, and Custer came nipping at our heels, capturing and killing our men and our wounded. If it wasn't for General John Imboden's Confederate cavalry holding them off, they might have got us all.

"While on guard duty I heard General Imboden talking to some officers. He told them that General Lee summoned him to headquarters at 1 a.m. on July fourth. The General was not there yet so he sat down to wait for his return. 'After a while, General Lee came riding in alone at a slow walk,' Imboden said, 'he was wrapped in profound thought. He attempted to dismount and seemed so exhausted I jumped up and stepped forward to assist him. He waved me aside, got down and leaned against Traveller supporting himself with his arm across the saddle. The moon shown on his massive features and revealed an expression of sadness I had never seen before. Finally I broke the awkward silence. "General, this has been a hard day for you." "Yes," he replied, "it has been a sad, sad day for all of us." Then, after the pause of more than a minute, he sighed with infinite regret: 'Too bad. Oh, TOO BAD!'

"After the Gettysburg disaster I got transferred back, and in '64 fought under Johnston. Now there was a real man, that Johnston. He knew how to take care of his army."

Sam smiled. "He personally made sure we were fed, and that we had good rifles and ammunition. He knew how to fight them Yankees, too. When Sherman came to Georgia, we battled them from Dalton to Atlanta. Every time they came at us we bloodied their damned noses. At Kennesaw, we covered the whole mountain blue with Yankee corpses. Johnston sure taught Sherman a few lessons."

Sam stopped and looked at Colonel Forrest. The old man's face was blank, his pale blue eyes heavy-lidded.

"Please go on," the colonel said quietly.

Sam continued, reliving the anguish. "But on the outskirts of Atlanta, Hood took over for Johnston. We couldn't believe Jeff Davis would get rid of Johnston, but he did. I heard Davis and Johnston had bad blood between them. General Hardee was so upset about Johnston's dismissal he asked to be relieved. But ol' Jeff Davis wouldn't let him go. I sure wish he'd a let me go." Sam got up and paced.

"Following that, it was a slaughter. But this time it was us that got the butcher's bill, not the Yanks. Death sure had a high carnival those last few months." Sam sat down again, crossed his legs and tapped his fingers on his knee as if counting the dead.

"After one big battle at Peachtree Creek, none other than our President showed up. Ol' Jeff Davis stood on a platform in front of us boys and tol' us how it was. 'Boys,' he says, 'we will flank Sherman out of Atlanta, tear up his railroads, cut off his supplies, and make Atlanta a perfect Moscow of defeat, just like Napoleon did. Against Sherman and the Federal army, this will be our crowning stroke for independence, and the conclusion of the war.'

"Well, we listened to his brave words and went back into the trenches and died by the thousands. We tried all right, and after trying to fight them in the open, we got beaten so badly we were thrown clean out of Atlanta. I remember marching through civilian gardens, crushed by soldier's boots, just a step ahead of Sherman's minions. If it wasn't for Steven Lee's Cavalry holding the McDonough Road open for us, they'd-a bagged us all.

"After we left, the Serman demanded all civilians leave Atlanta too. I guess they wanted to live in fine houses for a while, then rob and burn them. Well, for weeks and months, wagons with old and decrepit people, delicate women, and little babies filled the roads in South Georgia. General Hood sent army wagons and soldiers to help them. I know; I was one of them." Sam's hands balled into fists. "It was the saddest thing I ever saw. The roads were filled with pregnant women, little children, and old men and grannies trudging south. And, unless they had a relative in Macon, they had no place to go.

"Later, in what the officers called a 'strategic retreat', we fought the Yankees at Jonesboro. Then Sherman left and we went east. We went north and battled the Yanks at Franklin, and finally Nashville." Sam stared into space. "Franklin was the worst—"

After a few moments Sam looked earnestly at Forrest. "After Hood took over for Johnston we got beat in detail in every battle. It's my humble opinion that there were a whole lot of privates that could have led us a lot better'n Hood and his bunch. Our boys fought and died in the battle of Atlanta for nothing."

Getting up and walking to the window, Sam said so softly the colonel had to lean forward to hear him, "A private is an automaton. He loads and shoots and dies. The officers are remembered in song and story but the private is just a number among the slain. For him there is no account." He turned back to Forrest his face grave. "Just like George."

Shaking his head slowly, Sam said in a sad voice, "Except for his wife, or his Ma and Pa, the private soldier is soon forgotten."

Sam looked out the window but wasn't seeing the fields. He was looking past the blue grass and cavorting horses to the last camp in North Carolina. "When I got to the Confederate Army from Florida, the First Tennessee had 3,200 men. When Leander Huckabee and me gave up our guns at the surrender in North Carolina, there was but 65 of us left." Sam shook his head slowly. "That's a whole lot of dying."

There was a long silence in the room. After a while, Forrest got up and went toward the door. In the middle of the room he stopped and turned around. His mouth worked but no sound came out. He dropped his head and tried to compose himself. Finally he said, "My servant'll give you a place to bunk. Work or not, you stay as long as you like." He shook his head and started to leave. At the door he stopped and turned back again. He leaned on the door handle and looked past Sam at the fields. "When you meet my wife, don't tell her about George. I want to be the one to break the news to her."

Sam nodded silently.

Sam

Y'all are all free now.

Chapter 15

It was hot before the sun came up. Sam rolled out of his bunk bed to the sound of Dakota's voice, loud and insistent, rousing everyone.

Bo greeted him at the chuck house door as Sam staggered in, his eyes half closed. Sam, ignoring the Negro, went past him and sat down at a long bench with other white men.

Bo looked at Sam strangely, and quietly sat down at a separate table with two other Negroes.

Sam's face was already wet with perspiration, and sour with the lack of sleep. A fat, surly Negro cook unceremoniously dropped a tin plate filled with cold mutton in front of him along with a steaming cup of boiled coffee.

After eating a few bites of the mutton, Sam's stomach revolted. *After four years of sloosh and green apples I guess I should welcome this mutton, but I can't stomach it.*

Pushing the plate away, he picked up the coffee cup and burned his mouth on the scalding liquid. Blowing a few times on the fire in the mug, Sam drank it in sips and reluctantly went back to the mutton. After a few bites he quit again.

Twenty minutes later, Dakota was at the door. “Okay boys, let’s get started.”

Sam downed the fiery liquid, and stumbled out the door into the pre-dawn.

The sun had barely risen when they rode out to the cattle. The horse Dakota gave Sam was in no mood to work and fought Sam all the way across the fields. When they arrived, he was glad to get off the obstinate paint.

A large bonfire was already burning, adding more heat to the sultry morning. The men milled around in a sullen mood. Dakota nodded for Sam to stay put and moved among the men, instructing everyone on their jobs, including Bo. Sam admired Dakota’s control of the hired hands as he stood in the heat of the morning watching him direct the ordered chaos. George was right, he was a natural.

After a few minutes, the men left and Dakota came back to Sam. They walked to a pit containing white-hot charcoal embers. “Ever been at a brandin’ before?” Dakota asked as other men moved around them doing their various chores.

Sam felt the mutton in his stomach lying like a lump of heavy lead. Sweat broke out on his forehead from the heat of the embers. For a moment the landscape reeled and he thought he would faint. He fought the feeling. "No, never."

Smiling, Dakota reached for a bucket near his feet. "I thought so," he said as he lifted the vessel with a grunt. "This here's a pail of lime paste. When one of the boys makes the Forrest mark with the brandin' iron, you take this here brush and paint the cow's wound with this paste. It takes away the pain and swellin'. Got it?"

Sam nodded glumly. *I shoulda gone home. Sleeping in a tent, even with mosquitoes, on the way to Florida doesn't seem so bad just now.*

Dakota handed him the bucket and Sam almost went to the ground with its weight.

Laughing, the foreman grabbed his horse's double reins, stepped into the open metal stirrup, and with a practiced move, was on his mount in two steps. As Dakota turned the beast, the horse reared and Sam almost dropped the bucket again. He swore at himself.

Shaking his head, his face reflecting doubt, Dakota said, "I'll be back to see how you're doin' around noon." With that, he turned the horse and galloped off.

Not only did Sam paint the wounds, but he was later called upon to help drag a few of the animals to the ground and hold them down. *Why do they call them doggies? Damned fools. Not the calves, the men.*

By the time noon came, Sam was exhausted. The smell of burning hides filled his nostrils and covered his skin. It clung to him like Sunday death. It took a great deal of effort by him not to throw up. The clanging of the triangle, signifying lunch, was a welcome relief.

With the hot sun now directly overhead, Dakota, Bo, and the other men rode in talking and laughing. *Damn, none of them look even a bit tired.* He squared his shoulders and tried to look alert.

The cook, grumbling constantly as he worked, set up a long table, and the men gathered for the noon meal. A tired Sam wanted to rest, but his growling stomach overcame the weariness. He waited impatiently for the food.

When the plate was dropped in front of him he almost gagged. The metal platter was again piled high with mutton. This time it was stewed. Sam muttered a few curse words and, despite his being famished, vowed not to eat it. He took a cup of black coffee from the table, and with a few "scuse me's," went off by himself.

Dakota watched him leave with a wry smile.

Wandering about, looking for some place to sit, Sam found a large apple tree and sat in its shade absently sipping the strong brew wishing he had something lighter than mutton to feed his hunger.

Suddenly Sam heard the faint sound of hoof beats. He looked up and a small figure on a horse caught his eye. The tiny dot eventually resolved itself into a rider on a lathered horse galloping toward him over a field of clover. He cocked his head curiously and watched the horse and rider got closer. Soon he could see the features of a lady. Sam sat up straight. *It's a woman. Probably Mrs. Forrest.* He quickly stood up.

It isn't Mrs. Forrest, it's one of her daughters. I'll bet it's the one that looks like her. When she came close enough to see him, she smiled at him so sweetly it made his heart lurch. He recognized her from the picture on the colonel's desk. It was Lucy.

Her Stetson was pushed back on her forehead and the sun beamed down on her giving her face a soft glow.

Sam took off his hat as she approached and slapped it against his thigh as if that would make it clean again. The dust flew and he fanned it away with the hat. He absently brushed at his soiled shirt.

"Morning, Ma'am," he said as she pulled up in front of him. He wiped the sweat off his brow with the back of his hand, leaving a black smudge.

"Good morning," she answered and looked away so she wouldn't laugh.

It sounded to Sam as if she had sung the greeting. After a morning full of cows, rough men and burning flesh, her voice was like a clear mountain stream.

While she was looking away, he took a careful look at her. She was petite with a waist that Sam thought he could circle with his hands. In contrast to the Southern fashion of using large hats and veils to block the sun, her patrician face was sun darkened to a copper hue that was set off by her dazzeling smile. Her golden hair, except for the part that peeked out, was tucked up neatly under the Stetson.

She had a noble brow above a flawless face, a white cotton shirt that barely hid a full bosom, and brown riding pants that molded to her body like a second skin. Booted to the knee, her black boots, without spurs, were made of the finest calf leather, as was the riding crop that she held in her small hand. The black horse she rode was at least seventeen hands high and a thoroughbred from the end of his tail to the velvet tip of his nose. She looked every inch the future chatelaine of the colonel's plantation.

After a moment she turned back to Sam, her face serious, but her eyes laughing. The color of her eyes reminded Sam of the clear blue Florida sky after a morning rain.

"I came up to give the men some of the bread my mother and I made." She pointed to several loaves of bread in a sack hanging from the pommel of her saddle.

She smiled and Sam reddened. "Would you help me distribute them to the men?"

Moving to the horse, Sam tried unsuccessfully to hide his limp and his soreness.

A flash of concern crossed the girl's face. "Are you hurt?"

Sam felt his face get warm. "No, Ma'am," he said rubbing his hip, "my spirit's willing but my muscles ain't. It's just that I'm new to this kind of work."

She laughed, and Sam heard music again.

"Please call me Lucy. Ma'am sounds so old." She held out both arms to him.

"Yes, Ma'am," Sam said, still flushed. He reached up and put both hands on her waist. He was right. His fingers were just an inch or so from spanning her waist.

Lucy pulled her right leg over the flat English saddle and slid down the side of the horse slowly until both feet touched the ground. Sam held on to her and their eyes locked and stayed there for a moment too long. Her natural perfume, and the sight of her blue eyes, olive face and wine colored lips overcame him and he got lost in her.

Lucy demurely looked down.

Sam could not let go of her waist and stood rooted to the ground, his heart fluttering madly.

After a few more moments she forced herself to move.

Reluctantly, Sam let her go.

She took off her hat, shook her head and her golden tresses came tumbling down to her shoulders. The combination of copper skin framed by the sun colored hair took Sam's breath away.

Remembering why she was here, Lucy took the sack of bread off the horse, handed two loaves to Sam, and went to the men. All eyes were on Lucy as she and Sam cut the loaves and stacked them on metal plates.

In a frenzy of eating and praise, the bread was quickly gone.

Lucy chatted with Dakota for a few minutes and then Sam walked her back to the horse.

"How was the bread?" she asked.

Sam smiled and shook his head. "Never got nary a piece. Those chow hounds would've bit my hand off if I reached for a slice the way they were going at it."

Lucy stopped and put her fist to her mouth in mock surprise. "Omygosh! Well, I'll just have to make another loaf just for you."

"How about tomorrow?" Sam said boldly.

She smiled that smile that made his heart stop. "Yes, I will."

"I would sure appreciate that ma'am."

They reached the horse and Sam cupped his hands. She put her foot in the stirrup he made and leaned on him heavily to mount. He smelled the clean, sweet, natural perfume of her again and it made him shiver.

Lucy let herself down easy on the saddle.

Sam looked lovingly up at Lucy while he patted the horse's neck.

Lucy reached down, touched his hand gently and said, “Thank you.” She kneed the horse and started toward home. After the horse had moved a few yards she pulled on the reins, turned the horse around and trotted back. When she reached Sam she slid down in front of him without help. There was pain in her face. “You’re the man who was with my brother when he died.”

“Yes’m. You can be proud of George. Your brother died bravely.” Sam reached out and touched the horse’s neck again.

Lucy’s eyes glistened and she put a delicate hand on Sam’s. “I would like to know more about what happened when you have some free time.”

Sam felt warmth spreading through his body from her touch. “Yes’m,” he mumbled.

Lucy put her left foot in the stirrup, and mounted expertly. She gave Sam one more warm glance and galloped away.

Sam watched her gracefully riding the horse, as if the two of them were one, until she faded to a small dot and disappeared over the horizon. He turned to go back to work and was surprised by Dakota standing a few feet from him leaning against a tree and chewing on a piece of grass. The half-breed’s mouth corners were down and his face had disapproving lines.

“My sweet tempered sister, Lucy,” Dakota said looking toward where she had disappeared over the rise. “She looks just like an angel.” Dakota stepped away from the tree, half-smiled and shook his head slowly. "But she's really the Devil's child." He turned back to Sam.

"Sam, with all her charm, Lucy's really a wild one. But with all that, she's the Colonel's pride and joy." Dakota shook his head. "I don't know what he'd do if she got hurt. I know one thing, he wouldn't take it kindly if anaythin' bad were to happen to her."

"Ain't nothing bad gonna happen to her, Dakota," Sam growled.

Dakota shook his head again, a hint of a smile ghosting across his lips. "That's right, Sam, nothin' bad's gonna happen to her. Let's get back to work."

****

They worked steadily until the sun went down. In the semi-darkness a tired group of men got on their mounts and headed home.

Sam was easing his horse toward the plantation when Bo caught up with him. With a wave of his hand Sam acknowledged the black man. "Bo, I ain't never before been so glad to see the sun go down."

"You'll make a good field hand yet, Boss," said Bo, laughing.

Sam glowered at him.

As they made their way back, Sam leaned forward on the saddle and tried to stretch his tight muscles. *I thought tobacco farming was difficult. That's the hardest dollar I ever earned.*

When he finally got to the bunkhouse, Sam's leg muscles were so cramped and painful he was afraid to dismount. After a few minutes he slowly and carefully eased off the mount.

Dakota rode by.

Sam held on to the pommel of his saddle to steady himself as he spoke. "I Suwannee, Dakota, this ranch stuff sure looks easy, but I never worked so hard in all my life."

Dakota laughed, leaned down, and slapped him on the shoulder.

Sam winced.

"The first day is the hardest. You'll be just fine after a while." He nodded toward the main house lit up with candles. "Mr. Forrest wants you with the family. Bring your horse to the stable and the groom will rub him down. I'll take your boy to the slave quarters and bed him there." Dakota turned his horse and started to trot away.

"He ain't my boy, and there ain't no more slaves, Dakota. The South done lost the war. Lee surrendered in Virginia, and General Johnston gave up at Durham, North Carolina. Y'all are all free now."

The sound of Sam's voice surprised even himself. It sounded detached, as if the words were coming from someone else. More and more he was realizing the monumental import to the South of the freeing of the slaves.

Dakota stopped his horse and stood facing away for a full minute before turning back to

Sam. There was a strange look on his face, as if he couldn't quite comprehend what Sam had said. After another full minute, he heaved a great sigh, as if a great weight had been lifted from him.

"Sam," Dakota said softly, "go get some rest, it'll be another long day tomorrow." Dakota then turned the horse around, took off his hat, threw it into the air and gave a loud whoop. He caught the hat, then leaned over the horse's neck and urged him on by hitting him on the rump with the battered Stetson. He headed straight for the slave quarters.

Sam shook his head and smiled, watching Dakota spur his horse to a gallop. He stayed there until he saw Dakota dismount, throw open a door and disappear into one of the cabins. He could only imagine what was going on in there.

After he gave his horse to the groom, he slowly and carefully made his way toward the main house. A picture of Lucy appeared in his mind's eye. *What are all these strange thoughts popping up in my head since I met that girl?*

As he reached the steps, the butler greeted him. All his dreams of a hot bath were dashed when the butler led him to a trough-like affair in the barn. He was handed a set of clothes, a rough towel and a bar of home-made soap.

"After you're clean, suh, the Master wants you to come up to the main house for dinner. These clothes are Mister George's. The razor was his too." He shook his head and said, with a small nasty smile playing about his thick lips, "As you know, he won't need them no mo'."

Sam watched the butler leave, shrugged and took off his clothes. He put his toe in the water and shivered. "Oh well," he said resignedly, and got in the trough. "Cold as it is, it's a hell of a lot better than that snake-filled river I took my last bath in."

Sam scrubbed himself clean and dressed. He found a broken mirror he found hanging on a wooden support and uttered a few oaths as he cut himself shaving. George's wrinkled cotton clothes were a little big on him, but it felt good to be out of that hot, tattered uniform. He gingerly walked to the main house, and stepped through the front door.

"This way, *suh.*"

Sam wondered how the butler could appear like that, from nowhere. He followed the Negro staying a few feet behind him.

"Right in heah, *suh.*"

Sam eyed the butler as they stepped into the library. *There's insolence in his voice and his manner. This trouble-making nigger is gonna cause problems when he finds out he's free. I just know it.*

As he entered, Colonel Forrest got up and came around the desk toward Sam and shook his hand.

The Colonel turned back to the desk and lifted a silver decanter. "How was the roundup?"

"Tolerable, sir, tolerable," Sam said, as he grimaced while easing himself with great care into the leather chair.

Forrest watched him, then threw back his head and laughed heartily. He held up two wine glasses. "Have a bit of sherry before dinner? It'll ease the pain." He smiled broadly. "By the way, the guest room is the first room on the left at the top of the stairs. That's where you'll sleep tonight. You can't miss it." He frowned looking apologetic. "I didn't know my boy put you in the bunkhouse last night. Damn inhospitable."

"Yessir, I'm be much obliged, for the wine sir. I'm sure I'll find the room. And, don't fret yourself I'm used to camping out." Sam longed for any kind of bed to ease his aching muscles.

Mr. Forrest poured each of them a drink in the crystal glasses He handed one to Sam. "To the Confederacy."

Rather than argue the dead point, Sam raised his glass in salute and drank to the toast.

All at once there was a flurry of activity in back of him, his head spun around just as a bundle of light and energy burst into the room.

His heart froze. It was Lucy. Despite the pain, he rose hurriedly to his feet.

"Oh Daddy, Dakota won't let me take my horse and I wanted to go riding before supper. He's so fretful today. I can't figure out what's happened to him…"

Lucy stopped suddenly and turned to Sam. "Oh, I didn't know you were busy. Please excuse me. I don't know what's got into me, bargin' in on men-folk like this." She stopped and smiled and batted her eyelashes. "Sometimes I wish girls were able to drink wine, smoke cigars and discuss politics. All *they* want to do is cinch their waists, gorge themselves, then throw up after they eat. And talk, talk, talk about boys, boys, boys! I'm so sick of boys." She fixed her eyes on Sam. "Oh, I don't mean you, sir." She whirled back to her father in another burst of personality. "And Daddy, make Mama—"

She stopped suddenly and spun back on her heel to a bewildered Sam. She held out her hand and smiled sweetly. "I don't believe I've had the pleasure."

Sam went along with her game, remembering what Dakota had said about her being a devil. He graciously took her hand.

She curtsied slightly and Sam bowed his head. When he raised his head, Sam looked into her wide blue eyes that reminded him of a summer sky, and thought she looked even more beautiful than she did at the branding. He was fascinated by the bronzed color of her skin, and the golden hair hanging loose on her shoulders. He'd never before seen a girl who looked quite like Lucy. For a moment he found it hard to breathe.

To him her cheeks looked like rosé wine, spilled on a pale cloth, and her lips the deep purple color of ripe cherries. He lowered his eyes to her white muslin dress sewn with the finest cotton and crowned with a hand crocheted collar.

Without thinking, Sam turned her hand over and gently kissed the back of it. The touch of his lips caused a spark and they were both startled. She jerked her hand back and they laughed together.

"Sam," Colonel Forrest said, eyeing the lad, his head cocked suspiciously, "this is my youngest daughter, Lucy. Lucy, this here is Sam, uh, uh—"

"Atkins, sir," he said to the colonel, without taking his eyes off Lucy. He bowed slightly from the waist. "Pleased to meet you, Miss Lucy."

She looked at him with eyes so wide, and blue, and innocent, it hurt his heart.

Then she curtsied again without her eyes leaving his. "And I'm pleased to meet you, Mr. Atkins."

His heart leaped again at the lively promise in her eyes.

The colonel broke in. "Well, enough of this idle chatter. Let's go in to dinner."

"Would you escort me, Mr. Atkins?"

"Gladly, Miss Lucy."

Sam held out his arm and she easily slipped her arm in his. Looking at each other they walked side by side toward the dining room, a few paces behind Mr. Forrest.

Walking that close to Lucy made Sam dizzy. He stumbled.

Lucy seemed amused at his reaction and feigned concern. “Are you all right, Mr. Atkins?” she whispered.

He whispered back. “As a matter of fact, Miss Lucy, I’m not so sure. Do you think your father put something in my drink?”

She smiled broadly.

“It seems that ever since you came into the room, I have lost my equilibrium and my senses.”

“Are you sure it’s not from that awful work you did today?”

“Quite.”

“Well then,” she said whispering back, “I think there might just be a remedy for your malady.”

Now Sam smiled. “And what might that be.”

She laughed, “Perhaps we’ll discuss it after dinner, in the garden.”

Sam suddenly found it hard to breathe again.

When they reached the table, Lucy’s sister and Mrs. Forrest joined them. Sam noticed Mrs. Forrest’s face was infinitely sad. *Colonel Forrest must have told her about George. I’ll have to talk to her after dinner.*

After the proper introductions, the grace was given by Colonel Forrest to bowed heads. As they had been taught, all the Negro house servants came into the room by the doors and stood with the family, all heads bowed. Although they believed not one whit in the words exalting the White God, the soothing words of the grace by

Colonel Forrest seemed to meet some deep need inside them.

Two Negro women in their mid-twenties stood silently at the head of the table behind Colonel Forrest. They were dressed as twins in plain, pale blue cotton dresses with white kerchiefs tied around their heads. Both of them were barefoot. When the grace was done, they sprang to life. Returning from the kitchen, they were carried silver trays loaded with food.

Turkey, ham, and so many other dishes were laid out in front of him, that Sam lost count. The dinner was far beyond anything he had ever experienced. The dinner at the plantation, where George was killed, paled before this sumptuous meal. *I wonder if they eat like this at every meal?* After four years of hardtack and sloosh, it was unthinkable. For a moment, it angered him again that civilians in the South ate like this while he and the Southern Army starved. He thought about the slave quarters and wondered what Dakota and Bo were having for dinner.

Carefully eating every bite, Sam stuck to the softer foods. In the time since he surrendered, his teeth had tightened, but, since he would see Lucy later, he thought it best to be cautious.

After dinner, Mrs. Forrest bid the men goodnight and she and her daughters left. Sam was sorry to see Lucy go without even a goodbye. He noticed Mrs. Forrest had her arm protectively around Lucy's shoulders.

The Negro women cleared the table, and Sam and the colonel retired to the library once more. Soon after the butler brought an after dinner wine and two glasses.

Without ceremony Colonel Forrest poured the wine and drank to the Confederacy, Sam's health, his own family, and to another year of good business. The two men chatted for a while, the colonel drinking several more glasses, while Sam nursed the one.

Hearing the grandfather clock strike ten, the colonel put his wine glass upside down. "Well, I've had four glasses of this sherry and I think I am ready for bed." He stood up unsteadily.

A surprised Sam stood up after him.

"Boy," Forrest shouted. Before the echo of his voice died, the butler was there, took his arm, and walked the colonel to the stairs. Sam stood in the doorway watching.

At the staircase, Forrest stopped and turned back to his guest. "Now Sam, I want you to make yourself at home. I like you, and if you fought with Gen'ral Lee," he slurred, "you're always welcome here." He hiccupped and turned to the butler. "What are you waitin' for, Boy, get me to bed."

Forrest took the first step on the carpeted stair then stopped and turned back to Sam again. There was a sly smile on his face. "You know, Atkins, at the beginning of the war, our delegation tried to get Alabama to secede from the Confederacy. As modest as I am, I stood up and tol' 'em the following: "Gentlemen," he slurred, "I figger Alabama is too small for a country and too large for an insane asylum." He belly laughed and slapped his thigh. Then he turned to his silent butler. "Ain't that so, Boy?"

The butler pasted a fake smile on his face and said, "Yassuh."

When the Negro spoke, Sam thought he detected a flash of anger and a good deal of resentment in his eyes.

Sam shrugged it off, and laughed to himself as he watched the two of them, leaning on each other like two old crones, stagger up the stairs.

As soon as they were out of sight, Sam rushed to the garden.

Stepping out of the French doors, he anxiously looked for Lucy, his heart thudding so hard he could feel his pulse. He looked right and left and saw no one. He walked around bushes and trees and found nothing. Gradually his excitement turned to disappointment when he realized she was not there.

Wait, someone came out the door and sat down on the bench... Sam moved quickly toward the shadowy form.

As he approached he heard two blue jays quarreling in the tree. Just as he got there they postponed their argument and flew off.

"Oh! Mrs. Forrest, good evening."

"Mr. Atkins, I'm so glad you're here. I've been wanting to speak to you alone." She looked down as if she were ashamed. Then she looked up at Sam, her eyes haunted and full of tears. "Colonel Forrest is really a wonderful man. It's just that he's so— so— rigid. Once he gets his mind made up he—"

For a few moments neither of them spoke. Then she continued. " I wonder if you would tell me about my son's last minutes. The colonel wants to know what happened too, but he's so full of hate it's blinded him to his own son."

"I'll be glad to tell you as much as I know, Mrs. Forrest."

Sam sat down on the bench and related the entire story. When he finished by telling her of his prayer, she was crying softly into her handkerchief. She sobbed for a few minutes more, then dried her eyes.

Mrs. Forrest looked at Sam in a way that made him ache for his own mother.

"You know, Mr. Atkins," she said so softly he had to lean forward to hear her, "when I didn't hear from George for a while, every day I would die a thousand deaths. And when a telegram would come, I would leave it in my lap, knowing I was pale with fright because I could hear my heart thump and feel my stomach churn. I dreaded even touching the message, it might as well have been a rattlesnake."

She shook her head slowly. "When I would finally open it and find it wasn't about George, I would sink to my knees and thank God."

A new tear escaped her eye and rolled down her cheek. "Now that my worst fears have been realized, I want you to know, I am grateful that someone as Christian, and considerate as yourself brought the dreaded news."

Mrs. Forrest stood up and Sam followed suit. She took his hand. "I want to thank you for your kindness. I shall always be indebted to you. At least now I know how he died and where he is. One day soon I shall go there." She leaned over and kissed Sam's cheek. "God bless you."

"I wish I could have brought him back for you—" Suddenly Sam remembered the letter. "Mrs. Forrest, George did write a letter to y'all. Colonel Forrest read it and then dropped it on the floor in back of his desk. It may still be there."

Her eyes went wide and she took his hand and squeezed it. "Thank you, Sam. Thank you. I'll always be indebted to you." She hurried into the house.

Sam watched her leave. Out of the corner of his eye, he saw someone move in the shadows. It looked like Lucy, or was he dreaming. Before he could call out, the silhouette vanished. Sam ran to where the vision was, but when he got there it was gone.

Resigned to his fate, Sam slowly walked into the house and up the stairs to his room. The room was like the rest of the house, formal and stately. For a moment Sam thought it would be best to leave and sleep outside just like he had for the past four years. *I guess they would be insulted if I did that.*

He took off George's clothes and laid them neatly on the dresser. He washed his face and hands with the pitcher and bowl on the dresser, tested his teeth and rinsed his mouth. After first bouncing on the down-filled mattress, he pulled back the cover and got into the four-poster bed. The mattress was soft, much too soft for him.

For a while he tossed and turned, while pictures of Lucy filled his head.

He opened his eyes, but the image of her was still there. Finally even the thought of that beautiful face could not keep him awake. Cobwebs filled his head and he started to drift off to sleep.

Sam was just at that place where oblivion comes when he was startled by a sound from his door. He forced himself awake and peered into the darkness. Before he could place the disturbance, his door squeaked open and there was a dark shadow beside the bed. He smelled a familiar perfume, and suddenly he knew. It was Lucy.

No, sir, I'm a tobacco man!

Chapter 16

Sam woke early the next morning more refreshed than he had been in four years. At first he thought he dreamt about Lucy, but when he smelled the perfume of her hair on the pillow, he knew she had really been there. He had lost his virginity and wanted to shout it to the world.

He washed his face, dressed, and bounded down the stairs two at a time, sailed out the front door and onto the carriageway. Turning around slowly, Sam marveled at the beauty of the house and the primeval oaks and vast carpets of blue green grass that surrounded the plantation. Somehow it all looked more beautiful this morning.

He stopped and listened to the deathly quiet around him. But his heart was full, and waves of energy coursed through him. He simply had to move. He ran down the gravel carriageway, hopped over the fence and into the fields, all the while thinking of his beloved.

Dawn brought the first golden rays of the sun peeking through the fleecy clouds on the horizon, though it was still dark enough to lend the land a spectral quality.

In the half-light, Sam could make out the outlines of newly born foals frolicking in the grass. Nearby, keeping a watchful eye on the colts, were the mares that gave them life. His eyes went to the top of a rise. There, on the hill overlooking his harem, Sam saw the pure white sire of the brood. Off to the side was another, younger black stallion, anxious and willing, but not yet strong enough to take his place.

Sam sighed. *What a beautiful plantation. I have half a mind to ask the Colonel if I can stay here and work for him. I sure would like to be near Lucy for a while. If I didn't have to help my Dad on the farm, I would.*

After an hour of walking the fields, Sam came back to get ready for work. As he neared the front door, he heard two, no, three voices shouting. It sounded as if the uproar were coming from the library. Sam felt apprehensive, and a bit guilty. He reluctantly went inside and stopped at the foot of the stairs. He listened for a moment but could not make out what they were saying. He did catch words like *betray* and *fool,* being batted back and forth like a tennis match.

Shrugging Sam went into the kitchen. As he opened the door he saw the butler. "Ah, there you are. Where are my work clothes?"

The butler's mouth twisted cruelly, showing two large rows of yellowed teeth. "I don't think you'll be needin' them Marse Sam," he said sarcastically. With that cryptic message, the butler left the kitchen, his laughter echoing down the hall.

An angry Sam started after him, but stopped, deciding he'd better see Dakota first. He went out of the kitchen past the library door cringing at the still loud voices emanating from there. He tip-toed past the loud voices and started toward the front door. Just as he got there, the library door flew open and Lucy, her face tear streaked, burst out of the room. Her bottom lip was tucked under her top teeth, her brow was furrowed and her eyes were dark with pain. She stopped, gave him the oddest look of love and hate all mixed in, then raced up the stairs.

Forrest appeared at the door. "Oh, there you are, you young bastard," he shouted, his eyes two pinpoints of anger, "we've been looking for you. Get in here!" he commanded, then turned and stormed back into the library.

Sam's heart sank. *They knew.*

Deciding not to run, Sam reluctantly walked into the library where Colonel Forrest confronted him. The colonel's hands were two white knuckled fists, and his face a bright red, like an over ripe tomato about to burst. He glared at Sam, his whole body trembling with rage. Smoke from the cigar clamped in the corner of his mouth formed an unholy halo over his head.

Mrs. Forrest sat in the chair by the desk, head down, crying softly. Lucy's sister stood in back of her mother, a Cheshire cat grin on her face.

Colonel Forrest's mouth worked for a few moments, without making a sound. Then he took the cigar from his mouth, shook a fist at Sam and pent up words came tumbling out, full of gall and fury. "My oldest daughter told us Lucy spent the night in your room," he thundered. "Do you think we're running a harlot house here? Is seducing my daughter the way you return my hospitality?"

Her head snapping up, Mrs. Forrest gave Sam a look that accused him of perfidy. It hurt far more than all the shouting the colonel did.

"Oh, my poor daughter," she said softly, "what will become of her, of us? Oh, the shame, the shame."

"Oh shut up, Mother!" Forrest whirled back to Sam, his eyes slits of venom and his hands still shaking. "Well!"

Sam thought about lying but thought better of it, and replied in a small voice. "No, sir."

Lucy's sister, a twisted smirk still on her face, quietly stole from the room. Sam wished fervently he could go with her.

Colonel Forrest started pacing, his face fuming, both hands clasped tightly behind his back, his cigar clamped firmly in his teeth. Small amounts of spittle appeared at both corners of his mouth.

Later, Sam would swear Forrest's moustache was twitching and that steam was coming out of his ears, but at that moment, Sam felt alone and frightened. *This is worse than the war. I wish Lucy would come back. Maybe she would tell them it was her idea.* He immediately felt ashamed at the thought of blaming it all on her.

Taking the cigar from his mouth, Colonel Forrest stopped pacing and faced Sam, his pale blue eyes as cold as winter ice boring through Sam. His voice became low and threatening. "We don't know anything about you, but even then, there's only one thing for it." He smacked his right fist into his left palm, his cigar ashes spilling on the rug. "You'll have to marry Lucy."

Mrs. Forrest instantly stopped crying and looked at Sam expectantly.

Sam shook his head slowly, trying to comprehend what the colonel said, Then, fully understanding, he swallowed hard. "Yyyes, sssir." He stuttered.

Mrs. Forrest almost swooned.

"And after you're married, you'll stay here and help me run the ranch. The old man looked away and gritted his teeth. "Since George is gone, someday it'll all be Lucy's," his voice lowered and he looked away in disgust, "and I suppose, yours too."

Sam swallowed hard again. "Nnno, ssir." He leaned forward as if tilting against a hard wind in a storm. His jaw was set, his shoulders squared for the tempest he knew was coming.

"Whaaaat?" Forrest thundered as his eyes locked back on Sam.

Mrs. Forrest stood up and started crying again. "Oh my God!" she said, shaking her head. "Calumny! *Calumny!* What will happen to my little girl, to her reputation? To *our* reputation?"

Sam braced himself and repeated his answer. "No, sir! I'll marry her, sir, 'cause I love her— I think. But I ain't coming here to run no ranch. Dakota can do that fer you a darn sight better'n me." He shook his head firmly. "No, sir," Sam said firmly, "I'm a tobacco man, and I'm going back to my farm. And I mean to grow the best tobacco in the state of Florida."

"And I'm going with you." Lucy appeared at the door and ran to his side. She slipped her arm in his and defiantly stared her parents down.

Mr. Forrest nodded once emphatically, admiring the pluck of the two youngsters, Mrs. Forrest sat down heavily in the chair and fainted dead away.

She's a spirited filly, Boy.

Chapter 17

The wedding was a subdued affair. Only a few bewildered friends of the Forrest's attended. Dakota sat in a straight back chair in the back of the room, a bewildered look on his face. Just in back of him was the butler barely disguising a large smirk. The two Negro serving girls, their faces masks of indifference, stood at the dining table dressed in their usual calico blue, ready to serve the guests. Bo was outside on the porch, looking in through the large window, a huge smile stretched across his black face.

Sitting at the piano, Lucy's sister, her eyes moist, and her brow furrowed, struggled through a Mozart piece while the couple prepared to say their vows.

When Sam, with a trembling hand, put the borrowed ring on Lucy's finger and said, "I do," there was a mild smattering of applause. When

Lucy said her vows there was silence, except for Mrs. Forrest's crying which got progressively louder.

The Episcopal preacher said a few more words in Latin, that Sam didn't understand, and it was over.

Lucy's sister stopped playing and abruptly left the room.

There was a reception, but it was uncomfortable and people didn't stay very long. There were also a few gifts left by people trying to curry favor with Colonel Forrest.

That evening the family gathered together in the parlor looked at three dimensional slides and played *Whist.* At promptly ten o'clock, the Forrest family went to bed and left the newlyweds to their own devices.

Sam and Lucy sat on the couch and looked into each other's eyes. Same spoke first. "Lucy, I know that we only just met, but I want you to know I love you dearly and I will do all I can to make you happy."

Lucy smiled that magical smile. "Sam, I appreciate that, but I'm *already* the happiest girl in the world."

****

The next morning, just after daybreak, found Sam, Bo, and the butler packing the two-wheel hooded carriage Mr. Forrest had given the bride and groom. Dakota put his strongest horse in the traces, the black stallion Lucy had ridden when she metSam. He was a bull of a horse as strong as an ox, standing seventeen hands high.

Sam had nothing but his bedroll to put in the buggy, but Lucy's trunks, full of her clothes, some of them purchased as far away as Paris last year, filled the luggage space.

While Lucy had packed her clothing this morning, Sam had looked on in wonder. *I don't think I can keep her like she's used to.* He mentally compared her multiple suitcases to his simple bedroll and shook his head.

Colonel Forrest walked up to Sam as the butler put in the last of her belongings in the chaise. His face was cordial.

"I want to give you this as a wedding present, Sam. Something to get you both started." He handed Sam a small black metal box.

It's more jewelry for his daughter no doubt. "Thanks Mr. Forrest." Surprised at its weight, Sam reached into the carriage and put it under the seat. He hesitated for a moment, then turned back to the colonel. "I want you to know I love Lucy, and I'll do all I can to make her happy."

The colonel nodded slowly. "She's a spirited filly, boy. You'd do best to give her some slack and not keep the reins too tight." He thought a moment then threw back his head and laughed. "If you were one of Lee's Miserables I know you're tough enough to do the job." His brow wrinkled and he stepped back and looked at Sam critically.

"You know, Sam, I think you may be just the man to finally tame my filly."

Just then Mrs. Forrest, with her eldest daughter trailing, rushed out of the house and ran to Lucy. They hugged her fiercely, all three of them talking of twenty things at the same time until they had no breath left for conversation.

Sam got up on the carriage seat, released the brake, and stared straight ahead into the unknown; a few wrinkles formed on his formerly smooth brow. Thoughts of the whirlwind affair and marriage caught up with him and every muscle in his body tightened and twitched with the longing to bolt from Lucy and the buggy and run. After a few moments of thought, his muscles sagged and he reluctantly accepted his fate.

Dakota sidled up alongside on his horse. He leaned toward Sam and offered his hand.

"You alright, Sam?"

Sam gave him a wan smile and nodded.

He gripped Sam's hand tightly. "I want to wish you the best, Sam." He looked past Sam at Bo sitting on his wagon and casually waved his hand. "You too, Bo."

A great grin lit up Bo's face. "Don't need no luck, Boss. I got me forty acres and a mule jes awaitin' fer me."

Sam laughed.

Dakota smiled, shook his head slowly and turned to leave. He got a few yards away when Sam called out to him.

"Dakota!"

Stopping the horse abruptly, Dakota turned the beast's head and trotted back to Sam.

Sam patted the horse's mane and tipped his head toward Colonel Forrest. "He knows you love this place. You just stick it out, he'll come around."

For a long moment, Dakota was thoughtful. Then a ghost of a smile appeared briefly across his dusky face. He waved goodbye, turned his mount, and trotted off. As he passed the family, Colonel Forrest called out to him. Dakota guided the horse to his father and leaned over to him. Forrest whispered something quietly into his ear. When he sat up again there was a wide grin on Dakota's face. The mulatto turned in his saddle and nodded knowingly to Sam.

In a few moments, Lucy left her sister and mother, and climbed up beside Sam. She slipped her arm in his, felt his strength and competence, and was secure. She smiled lovingly at her family.

Sam felt odd, suddenly unsure of himself with Lucy. He pushed the thought away, pulled his arm out of hers, and smacked the horse's rump with his whip. The animal at first protested against the heavy load, then found his strength and moved smoothly down the driveway. The family dog followed, barking furiously and trying to nip the horse's legs. The stallion bent his neck, gave the dog a baleful look then lifted his head ignoring the cur.

Lucy's sister broke away from her mother, and waddled after the chaise for a few steps, then stopped and waved furiously, the flaccid muscles of her arm flapping, her double chin bobbing like a dewlap, and her eyes filled with tears of longing. Mrs. Forrest, her fist to her mouth, her eyes also brimming, quietly mumbled, "Goodbye, Lucy," and turned away. Lucy waved back excitedly, while Colonel Forrest and Dakota, still on his horse, watched quietly as the buggy followed by Bo's wagon, rolled down the road.

Lucy half turned in her seat and blew kisses until they turned onto the main road toward town.

Sam leaned outside the buggy and turned his head to look at Bo driving his own wagon not twenty feet in back of Sam's rig.

"I'm follerin' you right smart, Boss." Bo then gave Sam the oddest smile, his teeth gleaming in the morning sun, laughing inwardly at a joke he wouldn't share. Suddenly, they both burst out laughing as if conspiring, then Sam turned back to the front.

"What's so funny?"

"Nothing, Lucy. Nothing and everything."

Lucy shrugged her shoulders. In a few minutes, she snuggled up to Sam, took his arm in hers, and kissed his ear. "Will there be gay parties and long visits by relatives in Florida, Sam?"

Sam thought about his lean, tough father, plump, bossy mother, the backbreaking work in the tobacco fields and smiled to himself. "Sure, Lucy, your relatives can stay as long as they like."

She giggled and squeezed his arm. "Oh, Sam, I can hardly wait."

The only incident t mar the lovely morning was passing by the hanging tree. As Sam moved under by the stout oak limb that had held the noose, he fingered his throat and wondered, *If Bo had been a few seconds later...*

****

Two exhausting days later, they passed the Florida border. On the third night they reached the outskirts of Tallahassee. After four more hard days they got to a fork in the road. A pole stood by the side of the road with a sign facing east that said, *Jacksonville*. On another sign just below it, with an arrow pointing south, were the words, Lake City.

It was dark when they camped. Bo made a fire and Lucy handed out some of the cold food from a large basket her servants had fixed for them.

The air was warm and moist and mosquitoes buzzed around them. To ward off the pests, Bo got as close as he could to the fire and smoke. After eating, Lucy retired to the buggy and covered herself as much as the heat would allow.

Used to the heat and pests, Sam wasn't bothered much by them. After making sure Lucy was as comfortable as possible, he strolled down the rutted dirt road, drinking in the hot, moist Florida evening.

The moon was full, and moss hung from the trees giving the night a dreamy quality. Sam stopped and took a deep breath. The war seemed so far off. Almost as if none of it ever happened. *It's good to be near home. It's even better to just be alive!*

Something teased the edge of his mind when he thought of still being alive. For a moment he couldn't grasp it, then the realization came full upon him. "Leander!" he said aloud, "I wonder what's happened to him? I hope he's all right. Maybe he's already home."

Home. I never really thought I would get home. Sam's mind mused back to the men in Johnston's army of Tennessee. Camping and fighting together, and seeing wounded friends gasp their last breath made a bond of brotherhood that few men outside of an army ever have. *Company Aych, First Tennessee. Will there ever be another like it? 3,000 strong when we started, me and Leander and 63 others left at the end.* Sam's eyes got moist.

When he got back to the fire, Lucy was fast asleep. Bo was in the back of his wagon, curled around packages, snoring heavily. Sam smiled at his bride as he got up on the seat of the buggy.

Despite the heat, she moved close to him and laid her head on his shoulder. Sam felt the warmth of Lucy's body and tried to sleep. A mosquito bit him. "Damn Galinipper!" He exclaimed as he slapped at the pest too late. Lucy stirred, got closer to Sam, and then went back to sleep. The heat from his wife, and the biting mosquitoes were almost too much for Sam, but he stayed where he was and had a fitful night.

At dawn, still unable to sleep, Sam slid away from Lucy and got off the buggy. As the first rays of the sun approached the horizon, Sam thought about the metal box Colonel Forrest had given him. With a few grunts he lifted the metal box, put it on the floor of the chaise and opened it. At the floor of the box was a cloth sack. Puzzled, Sam pulled apart the drawstrings and peered inside. The first light of day reflected dully off the pieces of silver and gold inside the sack. He had never seen so much money all at once. With wide eyes he reached in and took out a handful. With a sudden apprehension without cause, Sam looked around him for anyone who might be interested in sharing his new fortune. Realizing they were alone, and feeling foolish, he replaced the coins in the sack and again stored the box under the seat.

After the sun was up, the sleepy travelers had a breakfast of hot coffee. When they were finished, Bo came up to Sam. "Well, Mister Sam, dis is it."

“What do you mean, Bo. Ain’t you coming with me, er, us? I sure could use you on the farm.”

“Naw suh, I thinks I’ll go on up nawth. I got a passle a family up dere in New Yawk. Lots of free issue niggers up dere, like me, and I thinks I’ll jes go up dere and jine ’em.” He laughed. “You know, I’ll be passin’ through Washington city if’n ah goes dat way. If’n ah does, I’ll put mah hat in mah hands and go see de president. For sure den ah knows I’ll git me my forty acres and a mule from de Yankee gov’ment.”

They both laughed.

“I sure wish you’d come with me, Bo.”

Bo shook his head. “You know, Boss, ordinarily I would. But I had a dream last night,” he said with a wistful smile. “De Debil came dare to me, an’ he say, ‘Bo, you come go wid me.’” Bo shook his head firmly. “De Debil say we’d be headin’ south. Well, Boss, if de Debil is headin’ south, den Hell must be south. I think I’d best be goin’ nawth, and so dat’s where I’se goin’.”

Sam laughed, got down and went to the wagon. Bo handed Sam a few packages from the back of the Federal wagon and he stored them in the hooded chaise.

When they were done, Sam took the black man’s hand and shook it warmly. “You be careful, Bo, it’s a long way up there and there are lots of people on the way who won’t like you walking ’round free.”

"I know it Massa Sam, an' I'll be durn careful, you betcha." He patted his pistol.

"And, if you're ever down this way again…"

Bo smiled at Sam's hospitality, knowing it might not suit his family, and saluted his friend.

Bo stepped up on a wheel spoke and slid onto the buckboard seat. He clicked his tongue, slapped the beast's rump with the reins, and the mule bolted forward. Just before Bo disappeared at a bend in the road, he turned and waved goodbye.

After he was out of sight, Sam watched for a few moments, his eyes glistening. Then he hung his head, feeling a bit depressed.

"Well I never—" Lucy said indignantly, her hands on her hips, her face splotched red with anger. "Consortin' with niggers, just like they were home folks."

Sam turned his head and looked at her with surprise, that turned to revulsion, and then anger. *Just look at her. If she had a cigar in her mouth she would look just like her father.* "Lucy," he said with disgust, "shut your damned trap!"

Lucy's face instantly turned as red as a Christmas dress.

Sam was immediately sorry he cursed at her. He could see the pulses on her temples beating a rapid tattoo.

It took a long time for normal color to return to Lucy's face.

It took an even longer stretch for the knot in Sam's stomach to unravel. Finally the anger and shame inside Sam subsided enough for him to speak. He turned his head and stared at the sun coming up. "Lucy, he may be a soulless nigger to you, but he's been a good friend to me. And remember this, he saved my life."

He turned and stole a glance at Lucy. She was silent, her face set in stone. *I can see we're sure cut from different cloth. This is a heck of a way to start a marriage.*

For a while they were both still much too angry to speak reasonably, and they turned away from each other.

After a while Sam turned back and tried again, this time in a softer voice. "You know Lucy, President Thomas Jefferson once said, 'Slavery is like holding a wolf by the ears. You simply don't dare let go.' Well, the Yankees made us let go. And after a while the South will realize it may not be such a bad thing.

"We fought long and hard for our rights, but those rights put people of another culture, another continent, in bondage. Along with that, our soft Southern life was gone with the first shot at Fort Sumpter. Just think of it, Lucy, a million of our boys, coming into the army as innocent as new fallen snow. But now, they've all seen too much blood, too much death to ever be innocent again. The South now has a half million widows and God only knows how many orphans. All in all, I think it best we let the Africans go."

Lucy didn't speak; she met his narrative with snapping eyes and a toss of her head. Sam stole another glance at her. Her face was still pinched and her cheeks splotched with red.

Sam gave up, broke camp, and got the horse headed south toward home. For a long while the newlyweds didn't speak, then Sam thought he would try to reason with Lucy once more.

"I heard while the men were away fighting, the women had a hard time controlling the slaves. Personally, whenever I was around the niggers the rich soldiers brought with them, I could see in the set of their shoulders and in their eyes, that rage, that hunger that says; 'When I get free, I will pay you back.'"

Lucy turned to Sam with a furrowed brow.

Encouraged, he continued. "Even your own butler and those pickaninny servants that waited on y'all hand and foot, had that attitude. Do you think they love you? Lots of times when they didn't know I was listening, I heard them whispering the name, 'Linkum.' You can bet the nigras had their own telegraph system. I realize now that they knew all along what the war was about."

He shook his head again. "And don't think for a moment we were fighting for slavery. There wasn't a man below lieutenant in my company who even owned a slave. I didn't. Most of the officers owned slaves though, and if we fought for slavery, well don't you think *they* should have done all the fighting? No, the real argument, and all the killing was about, whether the Yanks could or couldn't tell us what to do. And, did the Constitution of the United States say we could go our own way when things got intolerable? That's what I believe in, and what I fought for, States Rights. But the abolitionists were bent on freeing the slaves and now they have. Whether we like it or not, they're all free. Like Dakota."

Dakota's name had some magic, and the anger and venom left Lucy's eyes, gradually being replaced by a puzzled look. Sam realized, like him, she had always accepted the putting of Africans in bondage and never thought about the consequences of slavery.

He was about to speak again when suddenly Sam realized there was something wrong with the world. A black darkness descended upon him as he looked up and saw the frightening picture of the sky swallowing the sun. Sam stared at the murky, roiling, sullen anvil, the leading edge of pregnant black clouds gathering on the horizon. Long rolls of thunder reached his ears and a hot wind began to whip his hair, first one way then the other. What started out as a small dark blot in the distance was now working into an angry storm.

Sam looked around him. The trees were bending, and loose debris began sailing on the air. He felt the swirling wind rocking the chaise, and realized what was brewing— a *hurricane*!

Sam forgot his petty arguments and grabbed Lucy's arm. "I don't like the way the sky looks. I think we're in for a nasty squall. We'd best get going. We'll have to race ahead of the storm to get clear of it." Sam let Lucy's arm go and laid the whip on the stallion's back. The horse bolted ahead.

"Surely we can outrun a little storm, can't we, Sam?" There was a questioning, fearful look in Lucy's eyes.

"Sure we can, Lucy," Sam said with little conviction. He urged the horse on to a faster pace.

Suddenly a bolt of lightening struck the ground in front of them making the horse stop and rear with fright. The buggy started to tip and forced Sam to battle the stallion to hold him in place. The following clap of thunder just above them was like a gunshot in a closed room. It deafened Sam and made his eardrums ache. For a moment he was disoriented, then sound came rushing back in a confusing stream.

The horse started to bolt at the crash of thunder and Sam had to stand up to hold him. The twelve hundred pound horse and Sam battled each other. Sam's arm muscles bulged and ached as he fought to hold the horse from running off. Sweat poured off his face, down his neck, and his arms trembled with effort. Finally the horse stopped pulling against the bit, and danced in place, wild eyed and snorting.

Sitting back down, Sam reached out to touch Lucy's arm to comfort her. She was staring straight ahead, rigid with fright.

Darkness engulfed the buggy and the wind roiled around them, blowing first one way then another. The rain, at first just large cold drops, now came down in unrelenting sheets, limiting their visibility. As Sam started the horse moving again he looked up ahead, through the curtain of rain, and saw a sickening sight. The sky was as black in front of them as it was behind. There was no chance of getting away from this storm.

In frustration he gave the horse the whip and the animal lunged forward. Another lightening bolt and the following crash of thunder made the horse rear once more. The wind swirled around them making the buggy rock one way then the other. Great gusts of wind threatened to turn them over. The horse whinnied in fright and turned his head toward Sam. He could see the terror in the beast's eyes. And he knew he had to act.

He turned to Lucy, but before he could speak to her she leaned over the side and threw up. When she sat back up she stared straight ahead, face ashen, body trembling, saying nothing.

Clouds, that in the distance moved slowly, now began to boil past them. Sam realized they were in serious trouble, in the middle of a maelstrom, with no chance of fleeing the storm. He quickly wrapped the reins around the brake, and leapt over the side of the buggy. He leaned against the wind and moved to Lucy's side and gently touched her hand.

"Lucy, we have to secure the buggy, dig in and ride out the storm." The curtain of rain washed Sam's face, and the wind drowned his words, but Lucy somehow got the message. She shook from cold and fear but nodded her head stiffly.

Sam got to work, conscious of the branches of the surrounding trees dancing and swaying in the fierce wind, making anything loose become dangerous missiles.

Lucy looked up at the black sky, and dropped her head in her hands.

Conscious of a new rumbling, Sam stopped, looked up and saw the storm clouds moving west to east, toward other ominous looking clouds coming quickly the other way.

A tingle of fear went down Sam's spine just at it did before battle. To him it appeared as if the two warring storms were hurtling toward each other and would collide right over the buggy.

A sudden reflection of lightening splashed across Sam's face and his skin prickled with an electrical discharge.

The following boom of thunder made Lucy jump, and made the stallion begin to neigh and buck again, pulling hard against the brake. To Sam's relief, the brake held and the horse stayed.

The wind began to blow even harder and bent the towering slash pine trees, making them look like leafy men bowing before a sovereign. One of the pine trees broke with a great snap and fell across the road barely missing the buggy. The fierce rain had now turned into a boiling, rolling curtain, soaking everything in its path.

The last bolt of lightening and resultant thunder galvanized Sam into action. He moved the chaise next to a large old twisted oak tree, and then quickly let the horse out of his traces. The horse neighed and shied, terribly afraid of the more frequent lightening and following thunder. Sam pulled the reluctant stallion across the muddy road and tied him to a picket pin, leaving a thirty-foot length of rope for the animal to move about.

Sam heard Lucy scream and he spun around. The wind was pounding the buggy against the tree. Sam stared across the road at a petrified Lucy. His heart constricted when he saw her face was a mask of fear. The rain had soaked her hair and made it fall in strings over her forehead, like a mass of golden seaweed. She looked to Sam very much like a small, frightened animal.

The wind howled, and the rain became a raging torrent. Sam had to lean forward on the wind as he tried to move across the road to the buggy. The road was now muddy and every step made his shoes sink in a few inches. The muck threatened to suck the brogans off his feet. He wished now he had taken George's boots.

Sam fought the wind and slowly made his way across the road, his jacket catching the draft and billowing out, his pants flapping against his legs.

He felt a small jolt of anxiety, as he saw the hood of the four-wheeler catch the wind and leave the ground. Lucy held on as if she were in a small boat in a wild sea. To Sam, the small craft looked so puny against the elements. His skin prickled again, simultaneous to another lightening strike close by.

Sam struggled through the wind and mud toward the buggy, cupping his hands and yelling, "Lucy! Pull the rubber tarp out from under the seat while I secure this damned chaise." *Why couldn't the Colonel have given us something more substantial.*

As he approached he saw Lucy's mouth corners turn up, a grimmace without mirth. Her brow, usually smooth, was creased with worry.

A sudden gust of wind hit the buggy broadside, raised it up, and smacked it against the tree. Lucy screamed with fright and pain as the movement threw her into the side of the buggy and then to the floor of the craft.

A bolt of fear went through Sam when he saw the buggy tilt the other way. *God, it's going to turn over.* He cupped his hands again and shouted into the wind, "Lucy! Get the knife and make a hole in the roof."

Lucy was on all fours. She looked at Sam, her face wrinkled up in puzzlement. "Get what? I can't hear you," she shouted back, her voice thin, like a reed in a tempest.

Sam compressed his mouth into a thin line as he finally reached the buggy. *Oh, God, it's going over.* With a last desperate effort, Sam lunged and caught the buggy as the wind started to throw it to the ground. Ordinarily no match for the weight of the craft, a flood of adreneline hit Sam's blood stream and helped him stop the fall.

Now the full weight of the craft, the luggage and Lucy were all on Sam's body. The sweat popped out on his brow and his arm pits and back turned wet. Taking a deep breath, Sam pushed with all his might. Slowing the buggy began to move. When he got it almost upright, another gust of wind caught the craft and Sam almost wend down under it. He struggled mightily to keep it from toppling over, every muscle in his body trembling with the effort.

Suddenly he felt as if something was helping him lift. It wasn't much but it was enough. He looked to his lift and saw a wondrous sight. It was Lucy pushing with all her might to help Sam right the buggy. Without him knowing it, Lucy had somehow jumped out of the chaise, struggled around the craft and hoined him. Gaining new strength from her, Sam gave a mighty shove and the buggy flopped back over on its four wheels but still being lifted by the ferocious wind.

Shaking and spent, Sam helped Lucy back onto the seat of the buggy. He leaned in, opened the storage compartment, and pulled out a Bowie knife.

He raised it and Lucy shrank back.

Reaching over her, Sam cut a hole in the roof and instantly the vehicle settled to the ground. The loose ends of the cut in the roof flapped about, making a staccato sound.

Lucy nodded and breathed a sigh of relief. Now she had to help Sam secure the buggy. She tried to hand Sam the tarp, with difficulty, as it caught the wind and tried to sail from her hand. Sam saw the problem and grabbed the tarp. Now they both held on to it as he reached under the seat, this time to pull out a coil of rope.

Lucy slid back onto the seat and held onto one corner of the tarp with both hands, watching helplessly as Sam fought the shifting wind to tie down the corners of the billowing tarp.

Putting the ends of the flapping tarp under his feet, Sam cut four pieces of rope from the coil with the Bowie and was able to secure the ends of the tarp to three of the wheels. Then he began to bind the buggy to the tree. He wound the rope through the wheels several times then around the chassis and over the roof as many times as the length of rope would allow.

The rain slanted into the buggy and drenched Lucy's face. She wiped it absently with the back of her hand. Her white dress was soaked through and clung to her body.

Climbing through the ropes Sam got back in the buggy, secured the last untied corner of the tarp to the brake and both he and Lucy slid under the makeshift cover.

Sam tried to relax, but couldn't stop shaking from fear and the cold. It was pitch black now and only bolts of lightning lit up their surroundings, making flashes of a desolate and macabre landscape. Each splash of light showed the muck-filled road, and the wagon wheel ruts becoming a gushing waterway.

Lucy reached down, lifted her skirt, tore a large swath of her cotton slip and balled it up. "Take off that shirt," she commanded.

Sam meekly complied. As she reached toward him he looked lovingly at her and saw her cheeks were rain speckled. Or was she crying? He was unable to tell where the raindrops stopped and the tears began. His heart opened to her and right then he knew he loved her dearly.

"If it wasn't for you, Lucy, I might be dead now."

"Hush now, Sam. I wouldn't want to go on without you."

Lucy reached over and dried him gently with the piece of her slip.

Sam forgot the storm and moved toward her, glorying in her touch.

Lucy blushed, but did not move away.

Sam saw the pain in her eyes surrounded by the tears and rain on her face, and took her in his arms.

He kissed her long and hard. “Lucy, forgive me— I love you—” He was interrupted by a frightening close bolt of lightening, followed by an enormous clap of thunder, that drove them closer together. They found warmth and refuge in each other’s arms. Soon the four-wheeler rocked from the tempest, outside and in.

Meanwhile, the storm raged around the buggy, and the sky turned a sickening green, as if the end of the world was approaching.

With a fury neither of them had ever seen

Chapter 18

Sam rode out the storm fully awake and not a little frightened. The small vehicle seemed such little protection from the ferocious tropical storm.

When Lucy awakened, the storm was still battering the buggy. The lovers held on to each other, and both of them breathed a sigh of relief when the wind finally died down.

Sam shook his head, his face grave. "This may only be the eye of the storm, Lucy, I'm afraid there's more to come."

"The eye? I don't understand."

Sam gave her a wan smile. "Just wait, you'll see."

Sam was right and the storm struck again, this time with a fury neither of them had ever seen before. Sheets of rain drowned the small craft and even with the hole in the roof, the wind lifted the buggy with ease. Sam made a few more holes and prayed that the ropes would hold. For a while he feared for their lives and held on to Lucy, his arms encircled tightly around her.

The small craft creaked and shifted with the wind. The tarp flapped and the hood leaked through the knife holes, but Sam's supplications to God, the buggy's solid construction, and the rope circling the tree held the tiny vehicle together through the worst. Finally, the tempest abated and gradually the storm moved east.

When peace came, Sam slowly lifted the tarp and looked about him. There was a break in the clouds and a blistering sun beat down on the destruction around them. The snapped pine tree lay next to the road at the right of the buggy. Other uprooted trees and branches lay across the road in deep puddles of muddy water. Once tall grass, low palmetto trees and large bushes leaned east as if a giant broom had swept them that way.

Lucy stirred. She smiled wanly and sat up. "Will there be another eye?" she said half joking.

Sam laughed. "No, we're safe until the next storm."

"Next storm?" Lucy said incredulously.

"Yes, Lucy," Sam said, laughing, "we have lots of storms this time of the year."

Lucy didn't think it was funny. She shook her head and the water flew in every direction.

Sam thought she looked a lot like a wet dog but he thought better of saying anything at her expense. He slid out from under the tarp and stepped out onto the wet road.

At the first step, he sunk into the mud to his ankles and cursed. Sam heard a neigh, looked up, and sighed with relief. The black horse came splashing down the road dragging the picket pin and the rope. The horse stopped a few yards from Sam and nickered.

Sam sloshed to the stallion, ran his hand over the horse's neck, along his back and down his forelegs. *He looks sound enough.* Sam whistled gratefully reached into his pocket and gave the horse a piece of apple he kept for a reward.

Tying the loose rope around a slash pine, Sam walked around the buggy looking over the damage. A bolt of fright struck him when he saw the large tear on the side of the roof, and the branch that made it lying in the road. It was at least six inches around and jagged at the broken end. *If that had come down on top of Lucy…* Sam could not finish the thought.

He continued walking around the vehicle until satisfied that the rest of the buggy was all right.

The horse whinnied, came up to him and nuzzled his back. Sam smiled and gave him the rest of the apple. The stallion thanked him with an additional push of his velvet nose.

Sam busied himself getting the chaise untied. He looked up at the blue sky and the orange sun overhead, making its way toward the flat horizon. He pushed his toe down into the mud on the road and shook his head. "No sense in trying to travel in this mud, Lucy. Let's bed down here again tonight and get a good start tomorrow morning."

Lucy's smile faded, but she nodded her head. "This is some welcome to Florida," she muttered, "I hope it's not a portent of the future."

Sam stopped and leaned on the wheel of the buggy. He looked over the bent grass and the battered trees tipping their leafy heads in the slight breeze. "It's not always like this, Lucy. Sometimes at night, when the calm of evening is on the world, a soft southern wind comes over the banks of violets and lilacs and roses my ma grows. It rustles the magnolia trees and stirs the orange blossoms and bathes you with their fragrance."

"Humph," Lucy said as she jumped down, I'd like to smell some of that perfume right now, but first we'd best find us some wood dry enough to start a fire. I'm starved."

Sam got busy helping and soon, though the wood was damp, they had enough fire to cook their food and start to dry out. The rest of the day was spent exploring.

As they walked down the shoulder of the muddy road, Sam explained to Lucy the folly of going into the palmetto brush, where rattlers and wild boar lived. He also showed her the beauty of the lush green swamp and the explosion of color and life on the nearby Suwannee River. Lucy marveled at the logs that turned out to have teeth and long snouts.

Just past noon, and after a hurried lunch, the mosquitoes swarmed and Sam and Lucy retreated to the cover of the buggy.

"Damned galinippers!" Sam spat.

"Galinipper? What's that?" Lucy asked.

"A galinipper is soldier talk for a mosquito," Sam answered.

"Oh," Lucy said, "I can speak English, and French. I guess now I have to learn how to speak soldier." They both laughed at that.

Later they decided to get out of the mid-day sun and stayed in the buggy for the rest of the day. When evening came, the air cooled somewhat, and they got out of the crowded chaise to stretch their legs. When they got back to the buggy, Lucy dug into the rapidly diminishing food basket and they ate cold leftovers. When they finished, they talked into the night, as lovers do, until sleep took them both.

Duty, honor, or a broken promise.

Chapter 19

Lucy arose the next morning before dawn, lit a smoky fire using the still damp wood, and boiled coffee. After drinking two cups of the steaming brew, Sam tested the road. Although there were still some puddles, the ground seemed firm enough and they were soon on their way.

Late in the afternoon, Sam urged the tired horse into the cool darkness of the north Florida woods. The air was warm and moist and a gray mist rose from the cold ground.

"It's getting late Sam, and I'm tired. Can we stay here—

Lucy stopped abruptly when she saw Sam's face. His eyes were narrowed and his nostrils wide as if he were sniffing danger.

Sam sensed something ahead in the mist. There was no way of knowing who or what, but four years of living with death gave him a sixth sense for risk. He knew if there were deserters in the woods they might not have an officer to control them. And they would surely have guns. But maybe, just maybe, even if there were deserters, they were still Southerners, and there might be some honor left among them. But still…

Sam turned to his wife and whispered, "Lucy, take the contents of the box your father gave us and hide it, quickly."

Lucy gave him a puzzled look, then a frightened one. She reached into the box, pulled out the pouch of gold, and then to Sam's horror, put it under her dress and secured it at her waist.

Before he could protest, gray phantoms stepped out from behind the trees surrounding the buggy. They were dark, ragged figures, inching closer, sifting through the mist like spirits, their guns glinting dully in the fading light.

Sam heard Lucy gasp, and felt his pulse thumping. He reached for Leander's LeMat then put it down on the seat and doubled his fists in frustration. *I could get two, maybe three before they got me. Damn, there's too many of them. DAMN!*

Massive trees blocked the light and someone lit a lantern. The yellow light eased the darkness. A soldier stepped forward.

Sam's heart slowed a bit when he saw the gray uniform. At least he was a Southern trooper.

The soldier had the stripes of a sergeant, and the wary eyes of a veteran. His gray regulation uniform was splashed with mud and his black slouch hat, which had long ago lost its shape, was pulled down close to his eyes.

He leaned his long Enfield rifle against a wheel, put one hand on the side of the buggy, and stroked his full black beard with the other. He spoke in a liquid, languorous, Mississippi voice. "Who air you, Boy, and where y'all goin'?" The soldier took a moment to doff his cap and nod to Lucy. Sam's stomach relaxed.

Putting his elbow on his thigh, Sam leaned forward. "I been with the First Tennessee for four years. Just got back from the Johnston's surrender in the Carolinas. I live not far from here and my bride n' me are going home."Again Sam wished he had waited for his parole to show this non-com.

Suddenly another voice; imperious, demanding. "Sergeant, what's going on here?"

From the darkness of the wood, a man in civilian clothes stepped into the clearing. The phantoms deferentially made a path for him and he stepped into the light of the lantern.

"Sorry, Gen'ral, this here ex-soldier came upon us sudden like. We're just checkin' him out. Thought we might confiscate his buggy. It'd be jes right fer the Pres—

The civilian's face turned hard. "You'll not do that under any circumstance, Sergeant. We haven't been reduced to banditry yet."

The newcomer approached Sam.

He had a large intelligent forehead, thinning black hair and a long, luxurious mustache that extended beyond his cheeks.

He nodded politely to Lucy then turned back to Sam.

"Mister," he said to Sam in a firm, steady voice, "my name is General Breckinridge and we've got ourselves a serious problem."

Sam leaned forward, listening intently to the general.

"Up the road a ways I have President Davis, his wife, Varina, and their children. As you probably know, the war is pretty much over, and the Union Army will be looking for the President to try him for treason. The President wants to get to General Nathan Bedford Forrest and with his cavalry, cross the Mississippi and join General Kirby Smith in the west to continue the war. Personally I think that's a waste of time. With Lee and Johnston surrendered, well…." Breckinridge shrugged his shoulders.

"I know it's over for me. On the train leaving Richmond," Breckinridge said, "I read a week-old *New York Times*, that said a Washington D.C. grand jury had returned an indictment against President Davis for high treason, along with Judah Benjamin, and General Breckenridge.

They are the ringleaders and should die by the most disgraceful death known to our civilization, death on the gallows.'" The general absently fingered his throat.

"My son was captured by General Williamson during the Battle Above The Clouds, and I want to stay alive long enough to be reunited with him. So, I intend to save the President, his family, and myself. There's a boat waiting for us on the Indian River, east of here, to get us to Bermuda. Unfortunately, during the hurricane— The general stopped and looked dolefully at the chaise. "Were you in this buggy during the storm?"

"Yessir, General," Sam said proudly.

Breckinridge shook his head. "Incredulous! Anyway, our horses bolted and ran off the road. On the rough ground the axle on our wagon broke down and we are, at the moment, helpless. Can you let us buy your chaise, or perhaps use it for a while? At least until we get to a place to purchase another wagon?"

Sam turned his head and looked at Lucy. She was smiling broadly and her eyes danced with excitement. She gave Sam a quick affirmative nod.

Sam marveled at her. *Maybe it was true that it was the women that kept the war going so long.* Sam swiveled back and gave the general a brisk salute. "Private Sam Atkins, Company Aych,

First Florida, Army of the Tennessee, reporting for duty, sir. Our vehicle is yours, General."

Breckinridge saluted back and turned to Lucy. "Madam, the heart of a volunteer, fighting for his home and his rights, makes the best and most reliable soldier on earth. You should be proud of your husband."

She hugged Sam's arm. "Thank you, General," Lucy said, "I *am* proud of him."

The phantoms melted into the trees and the sergeant, smiling broadly, took the lantern from a private and led Sam down the trail.

When they got to the clearing, there were fewer trees and a great deal more light. The sergeant extinguished the lantern.

Sam saw the distressed wagon leaning to one side, one set of its wheels stuck in mud to its hubs, the others on solid ground. The axle between the back wheels was splintered.

A man was bending down, looking at the damaged axel as Sam's party approached.

Breckinridge went to him and said, "Mr. President."

The man stood up to his full height and acknowledged the General's salute with a wave of his hand.

Sam could see the president clearly. He was tall and spare, with a strong, patrician face, an aquiline nose and dark piercing eyes that, to Sam, seemed incapable of admitting error or accepting defeat. He wore a long Prince Albert waistcoat, and gray pants tucked, like a cavalryman, into black riding boots. When he moved, he moved stiffly, as if his spine was not capable of bending.

Davis and Breckinridge spoke for a moment, and then the President walked the few steps to the buggy. He nodded to Lucy and held out his hand to Sam. When their hands touched, Lucy gave a small squeal of delight.

Davis smiled at her, and shook hands firmly with Sam.

Davis' voice was soft but authoritative. "General Breckinridge says you have offered to help us. My family and I are indebted to you, sir."

"All I have is at your service, Mr. President."

"You will be well paid."

"That's not necessary, sir. I am a soldier who will do his duty."

Davis smiled. "Then you shall have to wait until we reach General Kirby Smith, finish this war and establish our independence, for your reward."

A shocked Sam wondered, *Is it possible he doesn't know Lee surrendered?*

"But, Mr. President—

It was then, out of the corner of his eye, that Sam saw General Breckinridge frantically signaling with his finger on his lips, imploring him not to say anything further.

He nodded and turned back to Davis. "Again, sir, I am at your service."

Suddenly, the sergeant came running into the clearing. “Gen’ral Breckinridge! Yankees, comin’… this way… fast.”

Breckinridge swung into action. “Sergeant, get your men into a skirmish line, quickly, and have the rest of your men come with me.” He turned to Sam. “And you, driver, if you want to help, you come with me too.”

Sam jumped down off the buggy and looked back up at Lucy. “Darling you stay with the President and wait for me. I’ll be back as quickly as I can.”

“Sam, Don’t—

Sam didn’t hear the rest as he sprinted down the road.

Splitting the men up with hand signals, the sergeant quickly got several of his men into a skirmish line and moved them forward. As he passed by, the sergeant threw Sam an Enfield rifle and a pouch of ammunition and caps, whispered orders to the others, and led the way double time down the road.

As he ran, Sam tore a powder cartridge with his teeth and fed it into the barrel, loading the Enfield expertly, as he had done a thousand times before.

After he set his skirmish line the sergeant came running back and signaled General Breckinridge to move forward. When they reached a clearing, the sergeant ordered the men to spread out across the road and into a firing line. Sam dropped to one knee and brought the rifle to his shoulder. He then heard the familiar pop, pop, pop of rifles, and in a few moments the Confederate skirmishers came running, moving back in good order. The Union troops ran up fast behind them.

The veteran sergeant stood just in back of his makeshift line with General Breckinridge at his rear. The sergeant spoke softly but firmly. "Now boys, hold your fire 'til you kin read the U. S. on their buttons."

Sam fit a percussion cap on its nipple, and looked over his sight at the onrushing Yanks. In the dying light, Sam saw his target. Just like Sam was, the Yankee Trooper was kneeling, his rifle to his shoulder, blue kepi pushed back on his head so he could look down the sight of his Springfield rifle.

With dismay and a sinking heart, Sam realized the boy was young, very young. *Probably put a slip of paper with the number eighteen in his shoe so he wouldn't have to lie when he said to the recruiter, 'I'm over eighteen.'*

"Ready now, Boys, wait for my signal."

Sam started to squeeze his trigger in anticipation, his sight trained on the boy's forehead.

"Fire," the sergeant yelled.

Suddenly the Yank's head was bandaged and his face was that of George. Sam tried to pull his trigger but couldn't. It was as if his hand was paralyzed. Sweat poured down his face as he fought with himself. His mind flashed back to his promise. *I'll never kill another living thing.* Sam wiped his forehead with the back of his hand. *Duty, honor, or a broken promise, what's it going to be, Sam?*

Gunfire went off all around him and Sam decided. He pulled his gun up and aimed his rifle over the boy's head and pulled the trigger. His bullet went harmlessly over the boy's head. *I've had enough of killing.*

At the first volley the Yankee troops jumped up and ran wildly back to the safety of the dark wood.

Sam and the men stood up and the sergeant gave a Rebel whoop. "Did you see 'em skedaddle, Gen'ral?"

"Sure did, Sergeant." He patted the sergeant on his shoulder. "Tell your boys they did a good job. Leave a guard on the road and let's get our people to safety."

The sergeant hesitated, his brow wrinkled in indecision. "Uh, Gen'ral, I meant to speak to you before about this, but… well…"

"Speak up, Sergeant."

"Well, sir, my boys have all been paroled by the Yanks and were jes waitin' to be exchanged. They really shouldn't even be fightin'. We all talked it over, sir, and, well, the boys all think they've had enough. They want to go home. This caravan is goin' so slow it makes 'em nervous.

'Sides it'd be a shame to be killed now, when the war's much over."

Breckinridge stroked his mustache. "I understand completely, Sergeant."

"Now, sir, that doesn't include me. A couple of the boys and me, well, we'll stay with you 'til you're on the boat, sir."

"I appreciate that Sergeant. Tell the boys who want to leave to line up. The confederate treasury will give each man twenty-six dollars in gold, his mustering out pay."

"Right away, sir." The sergeant started to leave. He stopped abruptly and turned back. "This'll do wonders for their morale, sir."

****

The next morning, Sam was wakened by a shake of his shoulder. It was General Breckinridge.

Sam sat up quickly and rubbed his eyes. "Is there trouble again, General?"

"No, Sam, we're leaving soon, and I just wanted you to get your final soldier's pay."

Sam cocked his head quizzically. "Pay?"

Breckinridge handed Sam a handful gold coins. "We have enough in the Confederate treasury to give each soldier twenty six dollars. It'll help you boys in the lean years that are sure to come. This is your mustering out pay, Sam, with a bit extra for your help. I wish it could be more but we don't know what expenses we're going to face in our escape."

Sam looked at the coins in his hand glinting dully in the morning light. He counted twenty six dollars and put it into his pocket. The rest of the coins he held out to the general. "Twenty six dollars is enough, General. I don't want any special consideration."

Breckinridge shook Sam's hand. "With men like you, Sam, I know the South will survive." He swiveled his head and watched an osprey fly overhead. "We're close to the Indian River. The sergeant went on ahead to meet our contact. In a few minutes I'm going to the river and get the boat ready. I know you want to get on home, but there are still Yankees around and I would count it as a personal favor if you would stay with the presidential guard until we come back to get Mr. Davis and his family, and get them safely aboard."

"Consider it done, sir."

A half hour after Breckinridge left, the rest of the camp awoke.

Helen, the mulatto nurse to the President's children, was making a fire and muttering to herself about being rudely wakened when her head snapped up. Suddenly there was the explosive sound of carbine fire.

Sam had parked the buggy some way away from the camp for privacy. He grabbed his rifle, took Lucy's hand, eased her to the ground and leaped off the buggy. Sam quickly made his way toward the campsite and ducked behind a large oak tree. To his surprise, Lucy was right beside him, the LeMat in her hand. Sam shook his head. *This is quite a woman I married.* He quickly kissed her on the cheek and loaded his rifle.

Sam watched as President Davis, Varina, and Helen emerged from the tent. In a gesture of endearment Varina threw her shawl over the President's shoulders for warmth then quietly told Helen to walk with Mr. Davis to the stream and disappear in the woods. The reluctant president nodded to his wife and started to leave.

A Yankee corporal appeared suddenly on horseback and yelled for the two retreating figures to stop.

Varina ran to the corporal. "That's my Mother and her servant," she said. They're just going to the latrine.

The corporal laughed. "What's your mother doing with cavalry boots on." He lifted the carbine out of its saddle holster and aimed it at the pair. "Halt, or I'll fire!"

Ignoring his vow Sam lifted the Enfield to his shoulder and aimed it at the corporal's head. Just before he squeezed the trigger, Varina lost her self-control and screamed in fear for her husband's life.

It was too much for Davis. He stopped and ran back to protect his family. When he got to her, Varina put her arms around his neck, got her body between the corporal and her husband and yelled, "Don't shoot."

Several Yankee troopers then rode into the clearing just as President Davis was being arrested by the corporal.

There are too many of them. Sam shook his head sadly and slowly lowered the Enfield. With a silent signal to Lucy to back away, they eased their way back to their vehicle. As quietly as he could, Sam put the horse in his traces and moved away from the camp, Lucy walking beside him.

The camp site was now full of activity with Yankee Soldiers and surrendering Confederates. No shots were fired.

"Nothing we can do now, Lucy," Sam whispered.

Lucy nodded silently and got up in the buggy.

Sam stepped up next to her, sat down and quietly moved the horse away from the Union soldiers.

After a half hour of tense driving away from the camp, Sam began to breathe easier. He stopped the buggy and listened. They heard only silence. Sam said quietly, "I hope General Breckenridge got away."

Sam started the buggy down the road, turned to Lucy and said, "I guess it's really over now. President Davis is arrested, and the Confederacy is dead."

Lucy was surprised to see tears in Sam's eyes.

It's like I never went away.

Chapter 20

They drove all that day, and that night camped on the Suwannee River.

The next day they were up early. Lucy divided the last of the food they had left. After they finished the coffee, Sam hitched the stallion to the buggy and they began to make their way down the forest road.

An exhausted Lucy asked, "How much longer, Sam?"

Sam didn't answer right away. After a few moments he shook his head slowly. "I don't rightly know. Everything looks so different."

Lucy turned away and looked at the storm battered, primeval forest around her. The morning sun was hot and beads of perspiration appeared on her brow. She looked depressed.

After another mile, Sam sat up straight on his seat, his eyes narrowed and his brow knitted. Then he smiled broadly.

"Hey. I know where I am now. This is Ginny Springs." He laughed. "It won't be long now." He mused for a moment. "We'll have to come here and swim in the spring. This water gets so cold it'll shrivel up your— Never mind."

Lucy blushed and they both laughed.

By noon the sun was at its highest point and Lucy was fanning herself and sweating profusely. "Does it always get so hot here?"

Sam smiled. "No," he said hesitating for effect, "sometimes it really gets warm."

Sam stole a glance at Lucy. She stared straight ahead, a look of disgust on her face.

I guess she doesn't appreciate my jokes.

Suddenly Lucy narrowed her eyes, furrowed her brow and cocked her ear as if she were hearing a strange sound. In the distance, like wind through the trees, there came a melodious blend of voices. As they got closer they heard a deep bass voice sing a refrain, followed by a chorus of alto voices answering him in harmony.

"What is that, Sam?" Lucy asked. Then her eyes lit up. "I know, an outdoor church."

Sam smiled broadly. "No, Lucy, the sounds you hear are Negro workers in a field tending a crop. By the way they're singing, it's most likely cotton they're picking."

Just then they cleared the trees and Lucy and Sam both leaned forward to hear better, their heads close together like two faces on an old Roman coin.

As Sam predicted, when the singers came into view, the couple looked upon a large field filled with cotton plants as far as the eye could see. The bolls had mostly burst, revealing their snow-white contents. Negro men and women, with large croker sacks trailing behind them, were bent over, singing while they plucked at the white fruit of the plants, and filled the bulging sacks. Small black children darted to and fro among the adults, carrying water, removing grass and weeds from the sacks, and doing other less strenuous tasks.

In the short time Sam had been on the Alabama plantation, he had gained a great respect for the thousand ministrations that had to be given to the black workers. Births, deaths, marriages, and sickness all had to be dealt with and recorded. And, as Sam had learned from Lucy's father on the handling of his own bastard son, plantation owners demanded strict obedience.

Giving the slaves the creature comforts, and attending all their needs should make them happy, shouldn't it? But they weren't happy, were they? Bo surely wasn't, and Dakota? I know he isn't. Maybe if a man were free he would develop his own comforts, his own ministrations, and tend to his own welfare. Sam nodded his head emphatically. *I sure see things differently now.*

Lucy and Sam watched in silence as they drove past the field. None of the Negroes looked up at them or stopped their work, but the white overseer waved at them, as did many of the children. *I wonder what will happen to these farms when the Africans learn they are free?* Sam smiled and nodded his head. *There'll be a big change in the economics around here, for sure.*

Lucy waved back keeping her eyes fixed on the field, turning her head slowly until her vision was blocked by the slash pines that flourished on both sides of the road. When she could no longer see the Negroes she looked at Sam thoughtfully as the singing faded in the distance.

She cleared her throat. "I know about cotton," she said almost in a whisper, "we have lots of it in Alabama. But I don't know anything about tobacco farming. Tell me how you go about planting tobacco. Will I be expected to work in the fields like those nigger—" Lucy stopped, mindful her husband's sensitivity. —I mean Negroes?"

Sam turned and looked at his wife in disbelief. "None of the womenfolk in my family do heavy labor. You'll be expected to clean the house, get the meals and take care of your family. That is, if God grants us children."

Lucy reddened at the thought of bearing a child. She had had a lot of reality thrust upon her in the past few days. Now inside her there was a change going on, from a flighty girl to a common sense woman.

Sam smiled and shook his head. "Tobacco farming is rough work, Lucy. It's not for the weak or faint of heart, let me tell you. No, Ma'am, it's all about hard work."

Sam watched the back of the black stallion moving easily along the hard packed road, his shoulder muscles bulging with each step. He measured his words as he thought about what he had done all his life before the war. He had never put these thoughts into words, and speaking them was like slowly dispensing newly minted coins.

"First you have to spread the tobacco seeds in freshly dug nursery plots. Then you water them and watch them grow. When bugs get on them you pick them off and squash the bugs with two fingers."

"Ugh!" Lucy exclaimed.

Sam laughed. "After a while, when the plants get out of the baby stage, you have to carefully pull them up and plant them in a special tobacco growing soil in plowed furrows made by the most cantankerous mule in Florida. Then you wait and hope for rain and sun. When the leaves are mature, they're put in the tobacco barns, and cured with a heated fire." Sam laughed. "If you're spooning with a girl, you gotta get outta the barn quick-like 'cause it gets real hot in there. Sam laughed again. Lucy didn't.

After the tobacco leaf turns from green, to yellow, to brown, and they're fully cured, you tie 'em by their stems into bundles and take 'em to auction."

"Whew," Lucy said wiping the back of her hand across her moist brow, "it does sound like a whole lot of work."

"It is, Lucy, it is. But when the price is right, the rewards are great."

Sam turned the horse onto a gravel road with elm trees forming an arch over them thick enough to block the sun. A symbol of civilization in the form of a three rail white fence lined both sides of the road. Moss hung from the trees and in some places almost reached the ground. An old brown and white cow, her head sticking through the fence so she could reach the new grass, chewed her cud and eyed them both.

Lucy spied a small stream running a little way back of the fence. "I'm dying of thirst. Do you think we can stop so I can get a drink, Sam?"

"You can drink right outta my pa's well, Lucy, we're home."

Lucy stared where Sam pointed and saw nothing but the same palmetto brush and more of the thick forest of pine trees.

Sam spanked the horse with the reins and the black stallion quickened his pace.

Soon parts of a white house peeked through the trees. As they got closer, the parts turned into a large rambling structure with a porch that circled the entire house. The foundation was set on flat round stones that Lucy was to learn later, prevented termites from crawling to the wood above.

The farmhouse looked gleaming white in the afternoon light, and its numerous windows reflected the western sun, making them look like they were on fire. On the porch two old rockers and a hard-back chair flanked the front door.

Sam glanced over at Lucy. Her mouth corners were pulled down in dismay.

Gosh, I know it's not a plantation, and I guess Lucy's used to a lot better. Well, she just better get damn well used to this farm. There are no fine carpets and satin curtains here. But there is love, and there is work. Anyway, it's all I got.

As they got closer, Sam's heart began to beat faster. He felt Lucy move closer to him and wrap her arms around his as if she needed his protection from the unknown.

Sam pulled into the yard and an old yellow Labrador struggled to his feet and began barking furiously. Sam wound the reins around the brake, jumped off the battered buggy and kneeled down to the dog. "Hey, dog, don't you remember me?"

The dog began to whine and licked Sam's hand.

Sam ruffled the dog's fur and patted his head. The cur's eyes stayed sad, but his tail wagged happily.

The front door flew open and a stout woman came bustling out. Her gray hair was pulled back severely and tied in a bun. Smudges of white powder on her round face matched the flour she had on her hands. She brushed her hands and the white powder went flying. An old cotton dress fit loosely on her ample frame, was covered by a stained apron. She patted the beads of sweat on her brow with the hem of her apron.

In a flash of insight, Sam realized that this pioneer woman was the glue that held his family together.

"Bad dog! What's all this fuss—" She stopped in mid sentence and narrowed her eyes. Then her eyes flew open as wide as saucers. "Sam," she shouted, "is that you?"

She bounded down the stairs, not knowing whether to laugh or cry. Sam met her half way and they embraced. Tears ran down her face as she hugged him. After a few moments she held him at arms length, and looked into his eyes. Her face took on a puzzled look. This was not the handsome young boy that left her four years ago. This was the lined countenance of a mature man, with darkened eyes that had seen way too much. She drew him back to her, embracing him tightly.

"Oh, Sam, we didn't know what happened to you. All of the boys are home, 'ceptin' you an' Leander, and not one of them knew anything about you—" It was then that she became aware of Lucy.

Sam's mother colored with embarrassment, backed quickly away from Sam, dusted her apron with her hands and patted her hair, tucking in a few errant strands.

Sam laughed and held his hand out to Lucy. "Ma, this here's my bride, Lucy Forrest— I mean Atkins— I mean Lucy Atkins. Anyway, she's my wife, Ma."

"Wife? er, oh yes, your wife." Mrs. Atkin's puzzled face recovered quickly and she went to Lucy.

Lucy stepped down off the buggy and they hugged guardedly.

Sam breathed a sigh of relief as he heard his mother say hesitantly, "Welcome to your new home, Lucy."

"I'm glad to be here, Mrs. Atkins. I've been feeling sick every morning, since we've been traveling."

Mrs. Atkins nodded and gave Sam a knowing smile. She took Lucy's arm and patted her slim hip as they began to walk to the house. "You come on into the kitchen with me and we'll fatten you right up. You'll soon feel fit as a Georgia fiddle."

Lucy stopped and sniffed the air. "Gosh, Mrs. Atkins, what's that awful smell?"

Mrs. Atkins laughed. "That's the tobacco. Around these parts you'll smell it everywhere you go. But don't worry dear, you'll get used to it."

Feeling left out, but happy and secure, Sam yelled to his Mother, "Ma, where's Pa?"

Mrs. Atkins tossed back over her shoulder without looking, “Where else? Out in the tobacco field with your little brother.” The two women stepped up the three steps to the porch, and disappeared inside the house. Sam heard the familiar squeak of the screen door and for the first time really felt at home.

He stretched and then patted the black horse’s soft nose. The horse nickered and tossed his head. “Good boy. Let me say hello to Pa and I’ll come back, let you off this contraption, and give you a feedbag and a good rubdown. You’ve done a heck of a job getting us home, and I won’t forget it.”

Sam walked around the house with the old dog wagging his tail and staying dutifully at Sam’s heel. The dog barked at him then scooted underneath as Sam hopped the fence.

Sam surveyed the farmhouse and the fields of tobacco that stretched in front of him as far as the eye could see. He breathed in the smell of the tobacco and sighed. Being home at last, after four years of daily mayhem, gave him a feeling too complex to be put into words.

He started walking and soon the drying barn loomed in front of him. He opened the door to the barn, stepped in and stared at the yellowing tobacco, air cured, and drying in the heat. He took in a deep breath savoring the distinctive odor, trying to recapture his youth. He took a step closer to get a good look at the rows of wrinkled leaves. He reached down to the lower leaves, called lugs, and fingered them. He snapped off two middle leaves, called smokers, and sniffed them. He smiled contentedly. *Great looking crop this year. They're almost ready to put into hands(bundles) and send off to auction.*

Looking for something he knew would be there, Sam's eyes fell upon a rusted hammer and nails, kept in a corner of the barn for various chores. He picked up the hammer and two rusted nails and went to one of the barn doors. Slowly and carefully he unbuttoned his shirt and took out the regimental flag he had been carrying since Durham Station. He reached up and put one corner of it against the warm wood of the door and nailed it up. Then he stretched the flag out and nailed the other corner to the door. After being nailed up the regimental flag hung proudly in the humid air.

Sam stepped back, looked it over, and a thousand emotions almost overcame him. His eyes got moist remembering. After a few moments his heels came together and he braced, making his spine ramrod straight. Slowly and carefully his four fingers came up over is right brow, thumb tucked underneath, and he saluted all the comrades he remembered, living and dead.

God bless them all, in the vault of heaven, and at the right hand of God, where all good and true men go.

Sam went back outside, closed the door, and started walking toward the fields again. He came to a rise and could see over the tobacco leafs. In the distance he saw two small figures working among the large, green tobacco plants. Sam started down the small hill and into the fields again. When he got to the top of a second hill, the two workers stopped and stared at him. He waved. After a few moments they conferred, then shrugged and went back to work.

Sam began to trot toward them, pushing his way steadily through the green leaves until he was less than fifty yards away.

Sam's fifteen year old brother stopped hoeing and stared at the figure moving toward them. His father stopped too, smiled and leaned on his scythe.

Suddenly Sam's brother dropped his hoe and started running toward Sam, yelling, "Sam, is that you? Is it really you? Are you home for good? Where's your uniform?" When the boy reached Sam he grasped him in a bear hug then stepped back, grabbed his hand and shook it furiously. "Boy, am I glad to see you. When did you get back home? Are you alright? Where's your uniform?" He stepped back and looked Sam over. "You look like you're in one piece. We heard some terrible things—"

Sam patted the boy's shoulder. I'm all right little brother, I'm just a mite weary. My uniform's gone— burned— I hope I never see the likes of it again." Sam looked his brother over. "I declare if you're not all grown up."

The boy blushed and looked admiringly at his brother. "I'm going over to the Huckaby's and tell them you're home. They bet me a sarsaparilla, Leander would get back before you."

Sam started to say something about Leander, and thought better of it. He would speak to Leander's folks himself.

The boy's voice softened. "Me n' pa looked at the casualty lists every week at the Lake City court house. Damn, them lists were long, and when you didn't come back after all these months— we thought—" He shook his head. "Ma's done only three things since you n' Dave have been gone. She stayed to herself, went to the hospital to tend the injured, and every day studied the bulletins of the dead and wounded. Me and Pa studied the bulletins too, but—"

"I know, Boy, I know. But I'm okay and Dave's okay."

"Okay?" the boy asked, a puzzled look on his face.

"That's just a saying. It's army talk. It means alright."

He shrugged his shoulders. "Oh." Then he smiled. "Okay."

They both laughed.

"Why don't you go on over to the Huckaby's while I talk to Pa. Tell them I'll be over right soon."

With a quick grin and a nod the lad ran off with the Labrador following him, nipping at his heels and barking. When the boy got to the fence, he vaulted it in a single bound and kept running until he disappeared among the tobacco leaves. The old dog stopped and stared at the top rail, judged his chances, then squirmed under the bottom rail and raced furiously to catch up with the boy.

Sam smiled as he watched his brother run with abandon. *At least he's not running from a bomb.* When the lad was completely out of sight, Sam turned around and faced his father. The old man had gone back to work and was hacking at dead tobacco leaves when Sam walked over to him.

Mr. Atkins stopped cutting, picked up the hoe his youngest son had dropped, and without a word, handed it to Sam.

Sam took the tool, nodded once to his father, and began to turn the soil.

The old man nodded back, a satisfied look on his face, and went back to his own work. After a few moments Sam's father stopped, took a step toward Sam and touched his shoulder.

Sam looked at him and saw that his eyes were moist. The older man swallowed hard and squeezed Sam's shoulder. He shook his head and went back to hoeing.

For a few minutes they both worked steadily, turning the soil, picking out the weeds, and smoothing it out.

Sam stopped, stood up, put his hands on top of the hoe and rested his chin on his hands just like he had done so many times at parade rest.

Four years with Bragg, Johnston, Lee and Hood. Shiloh, Shelbyville, Chattanooga, Chickamauga, Missionary Ridge. Gettysburg, Kennesaw, Franklin, and finally, Durham.

He thought of George Forrest, Leander Huckaby, and the soldiers of the First Florida, Tennessee Brigade. He shook his head. *All those men. All that pain. All that death. There were so many killed and then replaced, that I was many times a stranger in my own company.*

There were sixty-five soldiers alive at the end, out of three thousand that started, in the Florida regiment of the First Tennessee, under General Lane. He shook his head in disbelief, and went back to hoeing.

Suddenly Sam stopped again and looked around him at the green tobacco, the white farm house with its windows on fire, and a sky so blue it hurt your eyes.

He looked at the hoe in his hands. *This is what I was doing the day I left. It's like I never went away. Did it really happen? Did I really fight, and kill, and watch friends die around me? Or was that just a nightmare and I've just awakened?*

He shook his head, smiled at his foolishness, stirred up some black dirt and dropped a tobacco seed into the fertile soil.

In the house Lucy cried, “Ouch,” as she felt a quickening pain in her stomach.

The end

Epilogue

In 1938 there was a reunion of the Grand Army of the Republic, and the Rebel soldiers of the late Confederate states, at Gettysburg.

The now old soldiers, with canes, long beards, and watery eyes, came together for three days in Confederate and Union camps on the old battlefield.

During the eventful day there were cookouts, speeches, martial music, and arguments over tactics and slavery, as the aged veterans, with creaking knees and shaking hands, spent the time trying to recapture their youth.

But deep in their hearts, they knew that the Civil War they honored was not about morality, but was really a calamitous struggle over two very different ways of life that came down to a bitter hand to hand, person to person conflict, of life and death.

The fact that the Northern and Southern soldiers were affable in each other's company on those three days in no way said that all their wounds were healed. No doubt men on both sides, on their way home, rubbed the painful stumps of lost arms and legs, and tried to salve the gruesome mental and physical wounds that kept them from sleep each night. Surely those men cursed the other side.

When it was time to leave the ex-Confederates lined up to board their train. The Union Army band, with a large Confederate battle flag waving briskly in back of them, struck up *Dixie*.

While they played the spirited rendition, one old soldier, remembering dead comrades, stared at the Union band members, and then at the fluttering flag of stars and bars.

For a while he watched the flag and listened to the music, his eyes narrowed, and his gray eyebrows almost knitted together in concentration.

Suddenly he leaned over to a long bearded comrade and said thoughtfully, "*Yankees playing Dixie!* I wonder what the ghosts of a half million of our Confederate dead would make of that?"

General John C. Breckinridge

General Robert E. Lee

Dr. Edward Aronoff is the author of several books including the award winning *Betrayal At Gettysburg*, as well as:

Last Chance
The Pagliacci Affair
Three Came Home Volume 1 – Lorena
Three Came Home Volume 2 – Sam
Three Came Home Volume 3 – Rutherford

and his most recent work on diet and nutrition,

Toxic Food / Healthy Food – Your Survival Guide to Healthy Eating and Better Nutrition

Dr. Aronoff was educated in New York, Iowa and Florida, and began a medical practice in the Tampa Bay area. Moving on to a literary career, he has been writing ever since. He has four children, nine grandchildren, and lives with his wife in Florida, and the mountains of North Carolina.

Made in the USA
San Bernardino, CA
18 December 2015